# A PATTERN
# FOR MONSTERS

By
RANDALL GARRETT

I0541444

ARMCHAIR FICTION
PO Box 4369, Medford, Oregon 97504

# WAS IT REALLY A TWO-HEADED MONSTER?

It didn't make sense to reporter Brad Stevens. The Larchmont nursing home fire had been a big one—the biggest blaze in years. So why wasn't he allowed past the fire lines like reporters usually were? Then after the fire when he called the nearby hospital he was told that—strangely enough—there hadn't been a single admission from the Larchmont fire. Then it turned out there were no records of the ambulance service whose vehicles had taken the victims away. It was a perplexing mystery that Stevens and his photographer pal Parker couldn't figure out. The police denied every ugly rumor and called their iron censorship a routine matter, explaining that the fire was nothing out of the ordinary. But the telephoto lens told a different story. And when Stevens saw Parker's photo of a fire victim with two heads, they both realized it had been far more than a routine fire and rescue operation…

FOR A COMPLETE SECOND NOVEL, TURN TO PAGE 79

# CAST OF CHARACTERS

## BRAD STEVENS
*This high profile newsman had the scoop of his life fall right into his lap—too bad he couldn't figure out what it was all about!*

## NORA DOUGLAS
*Who was this dame really? One minute she seemed like a seasoned professional, the next minute an elusive con artist.*

## PARKER
*This news photographer always brought back a great set of pictures—even if he had to climb on your roof to do it!*

## DR. EDWARD FITZHUGH
*He was the Director of the Atomic Research Commision and a brilliant scientist—but a scientist with something to hide.*

## LEW BRONSON
*A crafty lawyer who knew all the tricks of the trade, including how to get you out of a murder rap.*

## AL COSTELLO
*He was a close pal of Brad Stevens and a good cop—a good cop who knew how to keep his mouth shut when told to.*

# CHAPTER ONE

BRADLEY STEVENS scowled at the smoke pouring from the upper floors of the Larchmont Nursing home. He was a reporter and his press card was supposed to get him past fire lines, the rank of police officers that kept the crowd from getting too close to a blaze.

But not this time. The cops had taken one look at Stevens' press card and given him a flat *No.*

And that was the sort of thing Brad Stevens didn't like. He'd climbed out of bed at two in the morning to cover the blaze, and now it looked as though he wasn't going to get any kind of story at all.

Parker, the photographer for American Press, approached through the crowd of onlookers.

"Brad," he growled, "the cops won't let me take pictures. They won't even allow the TV boys to set up their cameras."

Parker was a thin, wiry man with thinning, graying hair. He was a top-flight operator with a camera—any kind, and he had a nose for news that always led him to the right place for a good shot.

Brad Stevens thought a minute. "There's something damned funny going on here. Why no cameras? Why no reporters, no TV?"

Parker shrugged. "Beats me. It's just a nursing home, not an atomics plant."

THE Larchmont Nursing Home was surrounded by a high storm fence and topped with barbed wire twenty feet up.

The building itself stood in the middle of about an acre of ground, and was surrounded by grass and shrubbery.

"Biggest blaze I've seen in ten years," Brad said.

Parker nodded. "Yeah. Ever since they brought out those new automatic fire robots in—when was it…'61?—there hasn't been much chance of a blaze like this getting started."

Brad Stevens turned his back to the blazing building. The nursing home was surrounded by a middle-class residential neighborhood on Long Island, just a few miles from Queens.

"Parker!" Brad said suddenly, turning to the photographer. "I've got an idea. Have you got a telephoto lens for that camera of yours?"

"A couple of 'em," said Parker. "A 152 mm and a 300 mm. Why?"

Brad pointed. "See that house up on that little hill there? If we could get that guy to let us use his second floor window, we might be able to get some shots after all."

Parker grinned his ugly, good-natured grin. "I think you've got something there. I'll try it. You want to come along?"

Brad shook his head. "Nope; I'll stick closer to the fire just in case something comes up."

"Right." Parker took off in an easy lope toward the house Brad had indicated.

Brad Stevens made his way through the crowd to the police lines again.

The area was a sea of sound. There were the excited conversations of the onlookers, which acted as a background against the roar of pumping machines and the hellish crackle of the flames.

The barrel-chested sergeant of police who had stopped Stevens before was again blocking his path.

"I told you, Stevens; you can't go in."

"I know. But I can watch from here." He paused, then asked, "Look—why can't the press get in? What's going on in there?"

The cop shrugged. "Stevens, I honestly don't know. All I know is that I've got orders to keep everybody out, and that includes everybody."

"Whose orders?"

"The captain's, naturally. And don't ask me who gave *him* the orders because I don't know."

There was another wail of sirens as two ambulances went through the fire lines and up to the open gate of the storm fence surrounding the Larchmont Home.

Brad toyed with the idea of getting in by hiding in an ambulance, but discarded it when he saw a cop at the gate stop the machines and search the inside for unauthorized passengers.

*What in the hell is going on?* he thought. There was no logical reason why such precautions should be taken. At least he couldn't think of any. But there must be a reason, and it was going to be up to Brad Stevens to find out what it was.

He could see the ambulances were taking several people out of the building, but in the flickering light from the flame, he couldn't make out any details.

He shrugged. There wasn't much he could do but keep his eyes open and perhaps do a little snooping on his own.

WITHIN half an hour, the fire was out. There was smoke and steam still drifting from the windows, but the danger of fire was over. And still Brad had found out nothing.

The police sergeant was keeping his eye on everyone, especially the reporters. Brad had talked a little to the man from United Press and a team from *Life,* but no one knew any more than Brad did.

When the smoke from the burned building had become mere wisps of gray, the sergeant suddenly called out, "Hey! Stevens! The rest of you guys! The captain says it's all right for you to go in there now—but don't go inside the building!"

They went in, but they didn't find out much. The firemen weren't talking, and the Fire Captain just said that the blaze had apparently begun on the top floor. The automatic fire robots were presumably out of order.

"Nothing much, really," the Fire Captain said. "Not mysterious. There's nobody dead, and only a few seriously injured. They'll be all right at the hospital."

And that was that. To most questions, the Fire Captain "didn't know." His ignorance was appalling.

"Why'd you keep out the press?" he was asked.

"Orders. Didn't want anyone hurt."

That sounded fishy, and the United Press man said so. The Fire Captain shrugged.

Brad looked the building over. It looked perfectly ordinary—a brick building of four stories, the top two of which were gutted black by the fire. The first two floors were wet and smoke-filled, but as far as Brad could see through the windows, they were otherwise unharmed. The basement was about half full of water from the firemen's hoses.

Parker came up, carrying his camera. Brad noticed that there were no telescopic lenses in sight. Parker motioned Brad away from the others.

"I got some shots," he whispered. "Can't tell yet how good they'll be, but I shot up plenty of film."

Brad nodded. "You'd better take a few pictures from here, too. Then let's scram. We're not getting anything out of the Fire Captain, so there's no point in wasting our time."

"Good enough," said Parker as he unlimbered his camera. "I'm ready to go home."

The AmPress helicopter was parked in a lot a few blocks from the fire. A police copter had made them land well away from the burning building.

"Where are we headed?" Parker asked as the whirling blades lifted the vehicle from the ground.

"I'm going to drop you off at the AmPress Building; I want you to get those pics developed. I'm going to find out what hospital the people in that nursing home were taken to. If I can interview them, I might be able to get a break. If anyone knows anything, they should."

The copter rose to two thousand feet and headed toward Manhattan.

There were a few other helicopters in the air, but not many. The Air Transportation Act of 1963 had forbidden private helicopters over cities; only official vehicles and press copters were allowed freedom of the air. The average man-in-the-street was just that—in the street. And there he stayed. Too many aircraft over the city simply wasn't safe for anyone; an aerial traffic-jam could kill thousands.

Brad settled the copter on the roof of the AmPress Building on West Sixtieth Street. The two men climbed out and took the elevator down to the offices of American Press.

Parker went into the developing lab and slid his negatives into the auto-printer while Brad Stevens went to his desk. The night editor called across the room, "Did you cover that fire okay, Brad? What's the story?"

"I'm not finished with it yet. It may be something or nothing—I don't know."

The night editor nodded and went back to his own work. He knew Brad Stevens, and he knew the big, dark-haired man could be trusted to follow up his stories and judge them for himself.

Brad sat down in his chair, which protested somewhat at being forced to support a two-hundred pound body that was built like that of a heavyweight boxer. Brad did some checking with a map and a phone book and dialed a number.

When the TV plate on the phone cleared, a middle-aged woman wearing a white nurse's cap smiled out at him.

"St. James' Hospital, sir," she said in a pleasant voice. "What can I do for you?"

# CHAPTER TWO

Brad identified himself and then asked, "I'd like to know how the patients from the Larchmont Nursing Home are getting along."

She looked puzzled, but she said, "One moment, sir; I'll look."

She glanced away from the screen, obviously looking at the file of patients. She went through it carefully and then shook her head. "We have no transfers here from Larchmont."

"I'm not talking about transfers," Brad told her. "The Larchmont burned about an hour ago; these would be emergency patients."

Her face cleared and she shook her head. "No, sir. We haven't had but two emergencies all night, and they were automobile cases. It must be some other hospital that they were taken to."

"Are you sure?"

"Positive, sir; I've been on duty since midnight." Her voice sounded a trifle offended, as though she wasn't used to having her word doubted. "You might try Gardenview or St. Mary-of-Lourdes."

Brad nodded. "I will. Thank you very much, Miss." He hung up, and the woman's face vanished from the screen. He sat for a moment his face puzzled.

*Now that's peculiar,* he thought. St. James' was the closest hospital; surely the victims of the fire would be taken there, and not somewhere farther away. He began dialing again.

Fifteen minutes later, he was genuinely puzzled. No hospital in the area knew anything about the Larchmont victims. Well, there was one other way. The ambulances that had made the pickups were all from the same firm, the Steadmann Emergency Service. It had been painted on the sides of the ambulances. He reached for the City Directory.

There was no such company listed.

Knowing that a big news story was about to break usually made Brad Stevens tingle with excitement; it was like electrical currents running through his nerves. But not this time. For some reason, all he could feel was a chill in the small of his back. An uncomfortable feeling.

He used the phone twice more, once to call Information to find out if Steadmann Emergency Service was listed…it wasn't…and once to the Centre Street Station where he asked for an old friend of his, Inspector Costello.

Costello was a lean-faced man with sun-browned skin and startlingly blue eyes. He had an easy grin, but his eyes always seemed to be probing, digging for information to send to the calculating brain behind them. He liked to remark occasionally that his father was an Irish *Cost*ello and his mother was an Italian Cost*ello,* and he'd inherited the best traits of both of them. Brad agreed with him.

"What'll it be, Brad?" he asked when his face came on the screen.

"Have you got anything on that Larchmont Nursing Home fire this morning?"

Al Costello lifted his brows. "No. Where is the place?"

Brad told him. The inspector frowned a little. "Yeah. That's out where the Long Island Power Station is. Why? What's the matter?"

"They wouldn't let newsmen anywhere near it," Brad said. "But the funny part is this: the people who were hurt in the fire were carted away by ambulances from the Steadmann

Emergency Service. Now, there's no such service listed anywhere in Greater New York. Not only that, but those patients have not turned up in any hospital in the area."

"What? Are you sure?"

"Check it yourself," Brad told him.

"Now, wait a minute," the inspector said, holding up a hand, "that's out of my jurisdiction. Why don't you talk to the cops out there? Maybe they'll help you."

"They wouldn't give me any information. I tried. The men on the fire line wouldn't give me the time of day, and I doubt that their superiors would. They don't know me; you do."

Costello thought a moment. "Well, I might take a look," he said at last. "Won't do any harm to try."

"Thanks a lot, Al," Brad said. "Call me later, huh?"

AFTER he had cut off, Brad leaned back in his chair, stuck a cigarette in his mouth, and lit it. Nothing made any sense. There was a pattern here, he was sure, but none of it seemed to fit together. The important piece, the keystone of the whole puzzle, was missing.

"Hey, Brad! Come here a minute!" It was Parker, calling from the developing lab.

Brad exhaled a cloud of blue-gray smoke, lifted his muscular bulk from the chair and walked to the lab.

"I got some good shots," Parker said laconically, waving a hand toward the table. At least fifty photographs were spread over it, freshly warm from the auto-printer.

"Some of 'em are pretty good," Parker went on. "This one—remember when that window blew? Caught it. And this—and this—" He tapped several of the prints. "I think we've got enough to make a good spectacular."

"Yeah. But we don't have enough copy to make a good story," Brad said bitterly.

"Yeah. Say, here's a funny one." Parker picked up one of the photographs. "This is when they were loading the patients into the ambulances. Most of 'em were covered with sheets, but this guy was delirious from pain, I guess. He's pushed the sheet back. And look at this…" He held it out for Brad's inspection. "I must've got two people in at a funny camera angle—but don't it look as though that guy had two heads?"

Brad was staring at the photo. "Yeah," he said very slowly, "it does. It looks *exactly* like he had two heads."

IT WAS after five in the morning when Brad finally got back to bed. He was so weary that, in spite of the queer problem running around in his head, he dropped off in a very few minutes after climbing into bed.

And at five forty-five, the telephone rang.

Groggily, Brad reached over and switched on the instrument.

It was Inspector Costello. "Brad, about this Larchmont thing. It's out of my jurisdiction, as I said. I've got other things to do." Costello's voice sounded strained, almost jerky, as though he were saying something he didn't want to say—but had to.

"Well," Brad said evenly. "It's not out of my jurisdiction. A newsman doesn't have any. I just thought that you could help."

"Brad…" There was a pause as though Costello were trying to frame his words exactly. "Brad, take my advice. Forget it."

"I can't forget it—you know that."

"*I* can," Costello said. "I hope you will."

And he hung up.

This time, Brad Stevens didn't get back to sleep so easily.

# CHAPTER THREE

When Brad returned to his desk that afternoon after five fitful hours of sleep, there were two photo facsimiles from Peoria, Illinois on his desk. The one on top said:

*"Peoria, Ill. 12 July (AmPress) In an unusual accident here today, a failure in the electronic control system of the Chicago-Mexico City Throughway threw an ambulance off the edge of the highway, killing the driver. The witnesses reported that a man in the rear of the ambulance ran away from the scene of the accident. No other information is available yet."*

The second one said:

*"Peoria, Ill. 12 July (AmPress) Police report on ambulance accident. The driver's name was William Corby, 26, of Chicago. Ambulance belonged to Steadmann Emergency Service, Chicago.*

*"Earlier report on someone seen leaving ambulance is false. Delete from story."*

Brad grabbed the phone and put through a fast call to the American Press office in Peoria.

"Sam," he said to the editor who answered, "who covered that story on the ambulance accident?"

"Fritz Norse, why?"

"Let me talk to him, will you?"

"Sure."

There was a pause, and a young man's face appeared on the screen.

"Hi, Brad; how's the Great Metropolis?"

"I'm beginning to think it's gone nuts," Brad said. "Look, did you check on the ownership of that ambulance?"

"Sure. It's in the police files. I called up Steadmann's to check on whether there was anyone else in the car. They said the driver left Chicago with an empty wagon."

"What about this passenger who was supposed to have run away?"

Fritz Norse laughed. "That was funny. It turns out that a couple of scared kids saw the wreck. People on the Throughway couldn't stop, of course.

"So, anyway, these two kids claimed that it was a giant, fourteen feet high that got out of the ambulance and ran into the woods." He laughed again. "Nobody else saw any such thing, of course. The kids were either scared by the accident or were telling a tall one to get their names in the papers."

"Maybe they were just exaggerating," Brad said.

"Huh?"

"Maybe he was only twelve feet tall."

After he had finished his call to Peoria. Brad lit a cigarette and stared at his desktop for a long time.

Whatever was going on, it didn't smell right. The Steadmann Company was registered in Chicago. What was it doing in a small Long Island town? If there's a fire in Long Island, you don't call Chicago for ambulances—not if you expect them on time. But the funny thing was that they *had* been there—and on time, too.

And where were the mysterious patients? If they were badly hurt, they'd have to be taken to a hospital, wouldn't they? Maybe not. But if not, then where *would* they be taken?

And what kind of patients were they? First a blurry picture of a two-headed man, and then confused reports of a fourteen-foot giant.

They all fit together, somehow. But how?

One thing Brad knew; he'd have to find out. He couldn't let something like this go without doing anything. His news sense wouldn't let him.

He decided to take the copter back out to Long Island.

As he flew, he wondered about Inspector Costello. What could have made him back out so fast? And the other police—the ones on Long Island—why had they been so reticent?

If it was such a big secret, how could it be let out to so many? The firemen surely must know. If he could get one of them alone, maybe he could induce the guy to talk.

He settled the machine in the copter lot near the police station of the little town and headed for the fire station.

There was a big hook-and-ladder rig parked outside, and a uniformed fireman was sitting on its running board, just waiting for something to happen and lazily soaking in the warmth of the July sun. He looked as though he were in his late forties, or early fifties.

"Quite a fire last night," Brad said as he neared the man.

The fireman looked up and grinned. "So I hear. Must've been a real beaut. I'm glad I wasn't there, frankly."

"Off duty, eh?" Brad tried to keep the conversation easy and friendly. He didn't want the fireman to think he was prying; the guy might clam up fast.

"Oh, no," said the fireman. "I was asleep upstairs. But we never even got the alarm."

Brad tried to keep the surprise out of his voice. "You didn't? Then who put out the fire?"

"That was the Power Station's special squad. The man who runs the Larchmont must've called them by mistake. They went anyway, because they're closer. It's all right by me; I get my salary anyway."

"Is that usual around here?" Brad asked. "I mean does that squad normally put out public fires?"

The fireman shook his head. "Matter of fact, it's never happened before. Wouldn't have happened this time, except that the guy at the nursing home called the wrong number, he was so excited. That'll happen. I guess. Usually, the Power Station squad just puts out fires around the station."

"I see." Brad exchanged a little more light conversation with the fireman and then strolled off. There was nothing more to be learned there.

He went to an automatic news vendor on a nearby corner and fed it coins. It hummed for a second, then began feeding out a freshly printed photofac. Brad looked through it for references to last night's fire.

It was there, a tiny squib that merely stated that the nursing home had burned, that no one was killed, and only a few injured—none seriously.

Funny—the Fire Captain had said that only a few were hurt seriously, the newspaper said none. Brad began to wonder if perhaps someone had died in the blaze and it was being successfully covered up.

He wadded up the paper and dropped it into a corner disposal chute. For a moment, he stood there indecisively; then he hailed a passing cab.

"Long Island Power Station," he said.

The huge Atomic Power Reactor that serviced all of Long Island and Greater New York didn't look very impressive from the main gate of the steel fence that surrounded it. There were several brick buildings, many of them windowless, which were scattered in a seemingly haphazard manner around the square mile of area. The central building itself was a low, blocky affair with broad, high windows.

THE guard at the gate looked at Brad's identification and said, "I'll have to check." He made calls on the phone and finally reached the Assistant Director. He explained that there was a newsman here to write about the plant.

The guard listened for a moment, then said, "Yes, sir. Yes, he's right here. Okay." He handed the phone to Brad. "The Assistant Director wants to talk to you."

Brad took the instrument—an old-fashioned job without a viewscreen. "Hello, this is Bradley Stevens of American Press."

"Hello, Mr. Stevens. This is George Merriwell; I'm the Assistant Director. What can I do for you?"

"I'm writing up a little series of articles," Brad said half-truthfully. "You know the sort of thing—what is being done here, what a great job everyone is doing—that sort of thing."

"I see. I think that's excellent, Mr. Stevens. Could I meet you, say, for dinner?"

"Fine," said Brad. "I'd like to take a look around the plant, too—you know, see how the thing works and all."

"I'm afraid that would be impossible at the moment, Mr. Stevens," said Merriwell. "There has been some trouble in Section Seven; one of the insulation fields has become a little leaky, and we don't want to endanger anyone's life or health. We expect to have it repaired by the end of the week, however, if you'd care to come by then."

Brad hesitated. What could he say? "Very well, then, Mr. Merriwell; I'll come back when it's more convenient. Thanks."

He handed the phone back to the guard.

Brad flew back to the city with the sense of having been beating his head against a stone wall—and then having the stone wall turn out to be murky fog that yielded before him and still showed nothing. And the more he thought about it, the less he knew. What should he do next?

He reached out and grabbed the copter's phone, at the same time heeling the machine over to change direction. He dialed.

"General Editor, American Press," said a voice.

"Boss, this is Stevens. I've got a hot lead on a story. Check with Parker. I'm taking a plane to Chicago. You want to have someone wire me a check? Yeah."

He gave the General Editor all the details, then hung up as the copter headed for LaGuardia Airfield.

# CHAPTER FOUR

The Steadmann Emergency Service was one link in the chain that could still be looked over. Brad arrived in Chicago after most businesses had closed, but having eaten on the plane he decided to look up Steadmann's.

He found the address in the phone book. It wasn't actually in Chicago, but up in the little suburb of Evanston. Brad got in a robotaxi, dialed the taxi port nearest to the address, and leaned back to wait while the electronic brain that controlled the cab sped him through the streets of Chicago.

He decided he'd walk from the taxi port to the Steadmann establishment. He wanted to do a little scouting before he just walked in and started asking questions.

Chicago and environs was hot and damp, even though the sun was hovering near the horizon. It had probably been blistering earlier in the afternoon. A faint breeze seemed to be springing up from the lake, but it was too weak to do much to dissipate the heat.

Brad found the address. It was a smallish building that looked like a garage. There was no way of identifying it because there was no sign in front. It looked deserted, which was odd for an ambulance service.

The newsman walked on by the place, circled the block and took a look down the alley. There didn't seem to be any activity in the rear. He walked down the alley toward the rear entrance. It was closed, but inside he could hear sounds of hammering. There was a short passageway between the Steadmann garage and the business next door. Brad walked down it, toward the fire escape that went up the side of the next building.

The fire escape was one of those old-fashioned jobs with a counterweighted lower ladder that swings down if someone steps on it, but swings up out of the way when not being used so that, theoretically, at least, no one could climb up it from the alley.

The trouble is that the things are remarkably easy to gimmick if a man knows how. One way is with a long piece of rope. Unfortunately, Brad wasn't carrying any rope, and there didn't seem to be any conveniently laying around. There did, however, happen to be a few heavy bricks piled up in one corner of the passageway. Brad decided to use method number two. It was a little noisier, but he'd have to take that chance.

He pulled off his light coat and put in a few of the bricks. They weren't the cleanest bricks Brad had ever seen, but the synthetic fiber of the coat would brush clean afterwards, and the tough fabric would stand plenty of abuse.

Tying the bricks into the coat by knotting the sleeves was the work of a moment. Then, judging the distance carefully, Brad swung the bundle with the practiced ease of an expert hammer-thrower. It arced into the air, just barely cleared the horizontal section of the ladder, and landed on the end step with a faint clunk.

It was just enough weight to barely tip the balance. Slowly, the end of the ladder swung downward. It stopped about nine feet off the ground. Brad jumped up, grabbed it, and brought it down the rest of the way.

He was grateful that the thing didn't squeak. Some of the really ancient iron fire escapes became so rusty with disuse that they sounded like a banshee with a stomach ache if someone tried to use them. But these aluminum alloy ladders were quiet and smooth.

He picked up his brick-and-coat bundle and ran quickly to the top of the stairway. There he undid the bundle, put the bricks on the roof, dusted off his coat, shook the wrinkles out, and put it on, all the while surveying the roof of the building next door.

The passageway was only four feet wide. The jump could be made easily. But would a jump alarm those in the building? Not necessarily. Not if he landed right on the brick edge of the roof, where the wall would be rigid enough not to give aloud thump. It would take tricky timing, though.

He stepped back from the edge of the roof, took three quick steps and launched himself into space. He landed easily on the edge of the next roof.

He stepped carefully on the roof and walked quietly over to the door that led down into the building. It came open softly when he turned the knob.

Everything was dark below; the sun had set, and the faint afterglow wasn't enough to penetrate the darkness within.

From downstairs, he could hear the faint rumble of voices and the echoing din of hammers and other tools being used.

Walking cautiously, Brad started down the stairs.

Something crashed thunderously against the back of his skull, and the darkness increased ten thousand fold.

WHEN he came to, he wasn't quite sure where he was for a minute. His head felt properly crushed, but probing with his fingers told him there was nothing but a bump. The rest of his body had bruises here and there; he'd probably fallen down the stairs after being slugged.

He was lying on the floor of an empty room. Through a window came the faint glow of a street light.

Brad picked himself up, wincing as the movement shot pain through his head.

There wasn't a sound to be heard.

A glance through the window oriented him; he was in a room somewhere in the front of the Steadmann Emergency Service garage.

Cautiously, he pushed open the door. The door opened into a huge room that had grease and oil spots on its floor. It had quite obviously been used as a garage; there was room for several automobiles.

But now it was as empty as a church on Monday.

He decided to investigate, half-hoping he would find somebody to punch in the face for slugging him.

There was no one in the building. All three floors were empty. There was no furniture, no equipment of any kind, not even a phone; the building showed no sign of having been occupied for months.

And yet he knew there had been several men in the place; there must have been to make all that noise.

And then a faint noise broke the silence. Someone was opening the front door!

Running on his toes, his soft shoes making hardly any sound on the concrete floor, he went to the door and stationed himself behind it.

It opened slowly, and a shadowy figure entered the room.

With the fluid motion of a panther, Brad launched himself at the figure's back and brought the edge of his right hand down on his opponent's neck with a hard rabbit punch. He pulled the punch just a little; he wanted a knockout not a broken neck.

The shadowy figure said, *"Uhh!"* and dropped to the floor.

The door swung open a little farther, and the street lamp's fluorescent glow streamed over the figure.

"I'll be doubly damned," Brad said softly.

The figure was that of a girl.

Bradley Stevens had never clobbered a girl before in his life and he hadn't intended to start now, but he wasn't going to cry about it after it was over.

He knelt down and examined the girl. She was breathing evenly. A neck punch shocks nerves, but it doesn't do much permanent damage unless a vertebra is fractured.

Brad pushed the door shut and lit his cigarette lighter. He set it on the floor and opened the purse the young woman was carrying.

The first thing he came across was a gun—a small but very deadly .300 Magnum. He dropped it into his coat pocket and opened the wallet the girl was carrying.

According to the badge and identification card inside, she worked for a California detective agency—the Consolidated Investigation Corporation of Los Angeles. A private cop!

THE girl moaned a little, shook her head groggily, opened her eyes, and closed them again. When she opened them once more, she said, "What the devil did you hit me with?"

"This," he said, holding up his hand.

She moved her neck around, trying to get the stiffness out. "Well," she said after a moment. "I suppose you'll want to get me on a burglary charge. Frankly, I doubt if you could make it stick."

Brad grinned. "I doubt it, too, since I could probably be grabbed on the same charge myself."

She sat up. "Who are you?"

"Maybe I should ask you the same question," he returned.

"Maybe. But you're no fool. I can see that. You've already gone through my purse." She glanced at his coat. "You've probably got my gun in your pocket."

"Suppose you tell me who you are, anyway," Brad said evenly.

She sighed. "Lenora Douglas, investigator for the Consolidated Agency of Los Angeles. Now, who are you?"

"Bradley Stevens, of the American Press."

"Stevens?" Her eyes opened wider. "I've read your stuff. You're a good newsman. I used to watch you on TV. Sure— I thought the face was familiar."

"It's too damned familiar," Brad said. "There are times when I wish nobody had ever heard of me."

"You must be on something hot," she said. "I wonder if we're looking for the same thing."

"Might be. Let's go get some coffee and talk it over. There's nothing here."

He showed her through the building to convince her that they had come up against a dead end for a while at least.

Then they headed down the street to the taxi port.

Over the coffee cups, Brad outlined part of what he'd found. He didn't tell her anything about the photograph Parker had taken, and he didn't mention the Peoria kid's story about the giant.

After he was through, the girl nodded. "It tallies. My client—I can't tell you who it is, of course, or reveal anything confidential, but I'm free to tell a little. Anyway, my client had an aunt in his house; he was taking care of her, and she became suddenly worse. He called an ambulance. It picked her up, and she was never seen again.

"We were asked to investigate, and I've traced the outfit to here."

Brad nodded. "That fits," he said.

"How?"

"The same way all the other stuff fits," he said. "Because it's senseless; it doesn't mean anything."

"I see what you mean." She thought about it for a moment, then said, "Look here; suppose someone is picking up sick people—kidnapping them for—well—experimental purposes. Wouldn't that account for it?"

Brad mulled the hypothesis over in his mind. "It might," he said after a few moments, "but it'd have to be a big operation. There's an awful lot of cover-up, and it's spread all over. One case in New York, one here in Chicago.

"I didn't say my client was from L. A.," she reminded him. "I'm not at liberty to—"

"—disclose that information," Brad finished for her. "Yeah, I know. But look here; why didn't he go to the police and say she'd been kidnapped?"

"He did. They investigated. This guy couldn't even prove he had an aunt. The police found no evidence of any crime. They dropped the case."

"Oh, *brother!*" Brad moaned. "As Alice said, 'Curiouser and curiouser.' The more information we get, the less we have to hold on to. About all we can do is find out what we can about the Steadmann Emergency Service. Right now, that's the only lead we've got."

She nodded her agreement. "I'll tell you what. You're working on a news story. I'll tell you anything I find out that pertains to that story. But we'll leave my client out of it—okay?"

"Fair enough," said Brad. "Nora—Lenora—which do they call you?"

"Nora," she said.

"Nora, has anyone ever told you you're beautiful?"

"Many times," she said, "I'm almost convinced. And while we're on the subject, let's get one thing straight: I like men in general and I might learn to like you in particular. I like dancing and parties, and I'm not averse to a little smooching—but when there's business at hand, I like to keep my mind on business. Clear?"

"Quite clear," Brad told her. "That was a test question. You can find out an awful lot about a girl by the way she answers that old standby: 'Has anyone ever told you you're beautiful?'"

She thought that one over for a minute, then grinned. "Yes, I suppose you can. What does it tell you about me?"

"I refuse to answer on the grounds that it might give you a swelled head. Now let's figure out where we go from here."

Nothing much could be done that evening, they agreed; the best thing to do was get a little sleep and make a stab at tracing down the mysterious Steadmann the first thing in the morning. They checked into separate rooms in the Hilton. Brad took a couple of aspirins for his throbbing head and a couple of sleeping tablets. He felt as though he hadn't slept for a week."

# CHAPTER FIVE

At eight the next morning, Nora called on the phone. Her face looked clear and bright on the visiscreen, but she smiled when she saw him.

"You look as though you'd had a fight with an eggbeater."

"I feel like it."

"How's the head?"

"A little tender in back but otherwise okay. Look, I'll meet you in the coffee shop in ten minutes. That all right?"

She smiled. "Fine. And comb your hair." Then she cut the circuit.

Brad shaved, bathed, and dressed quickly. As he picked up his coat, it felt strangely heavy. He reached in the pocket, and pulled out the little blue-steel .300 he had taken from Nora's purse. He grinned to himself. The girl had known he had it, she'd said so. And then she'd completely forgotten to ask for it back. He shoved it back in the pocket and went down to the coffee shop.

She was waiting for him at a table across the room, sitting by the broad window that faced the street.

"You look better," she said, smiling. "Now what?"

"Breakfast first, then conversation," he told her. "I long to gaze into the glistening yellow eyes of a pair of eggs—sunnyside up."

They ate through a quiet stream of small-talk, then when the coffee came he said, "All right, let's see what we've got."

"From where do we start?"

He grinned. "First, you hold hands with me under the table."

She frowned. "I thought I told you—"

"This is business," he interrupted. "I took something from your purse last night—remember?"

"Oh!" she looked startled for an instant, then smiled. "I'd forgotten."

She put her hand under the table. He handed her the gun, and she slipped it deftly into her handbag.

"Now we'll take a look at the position we're in. What information do we have?

"One: there's a mysterious fire in a Long Island nursing home. Ambulances run by Steadmann took the patients away, and they're never seen again.

"Two: A Steadmann ambulance somehow has an accident on one of the most foolproof highways in America.

"Three: Steadmann runs out of his headquarters, leaving no trace."

"Four: Your client, whoever he is, has an aunt who is kidnapped by a Steadmann ambulance and is never seen again.

"Five: In every case, the authorities have tried to keep the thing under wraps."

"Except in this last one—we don't know yet," she pointed out.

"That's right; and that's one thing we'll know today."

"How do you figure we ought to tackle it?" she asked.

Brad lit himself a cigarette, belatedly offering one to Nora. She shook her head no and waited for him to go on.

"Steadmann had a business here," he told her. "He's registered in the phone book. Or, at least, the name is registered. We actually don't know if there is a Steadmann, but we'll have to call him that until we know better.

"The first thing we'll do is look up the old phone directories and see how long he's been here. We'll check with whoever owns that building and find out how long it's been rented. We'll check his reputation with the Better Business Bureau.

"Now, he hasn't been gone but a few hours. The news won't be around for a few hours more, if we're lucky. We may be able to run our checks before that happens.

"Here's what we do; you check with the police. That badge of yours will get you farther than my press card. You can also check the telephone company.

"I'll check the building owner and the Better Business Bureau. Okay?"

She nodded. "It sounds fair enough to me."

"Good. We'd better get started; we don't want to waste any time."

She rose from the table. "Let's get moving."

"One more thing," he told her. "When we get our information, we'll come back here. And we'll phone in and check with the hotel every hour. Okay?"

"Okay."

TWO hours later, Bradley Stevens sat in the lobby of the Hilton, smoking a cigarette quietly and mulling over what he had found. At first, it had seemed even more senseless, but now a dim ray of light seemed to be trying to seep through the fog of confusion.

The Better Business Bureau hadn't had much information on the ex-proprietor of the little building in Evanston. But they had it listed as the Steadmann Emergency *Auto Repair* Service.

On the other hand, the owners of the building, the Chapman Realties Corporation, had rented the building to the Steadmann Emergency *TV Repair* Service.

And in the phone book, it was simply listed as the Steadmann Emergency Service.

Why? Well, it made a kind of wild sense. If someone called for an ambulance, all they had to be told was that they had made a mistake—that this was a TV or an auto repair place.

"Yes, that's right, madam. The phone company didn't get the full name in the book. I'm sorry, madam."

Brad could almost hear the words in his ears.

But if that was the case—*why put the number in the book at all?* They could have had an unlisted number, which could be given out to special people, if they didn't want to give it out to the public.

Damn! Just as he'd think he was approaching an answer, he'd strike a perfect *non sequitur.*

He glanced at his watch. It was almost time for Nora's call. He lit another cigarette from the stub of the first and went on with his thinking.

HALF an hour had passed before he realized, with a start, that the girl's call was long overdue. He got up from the comfortable pneumochair and walked across the lobby to the main desk.

"Have there been any calls for Bradley Stevens?" he asked the clerk.

"Just a moment, sir." The suavely polite young man went to the autotally and punched buttons. He noted the answer that came up on the screen.

"There have been no phone calls, sir," he said, "but I notice that a letter has been sent to your room."

"If any calls come," Brad told him, "have them transferred to my room."

He took the elevator up to the ninth floor and walked down the hall to his room. There was an envelope in the letter receptacle.

*Dear Brad:*

*I'm sorry to take a run-out on you this way, but my superiors have recalled me to Los Angeles. As far as I've been able to find out, the police have no record of any Steadmann, and the telephone company knows nothing except that they installed an instrument there.*

*Again, sorry, Nora*

Brad frowned at the note. It sounded all right, but it seemed odd that the whole thing should be typed—including the signature.

He picked up the telephone and called the desk. "Has Miss Lenora Douglas checked out?" he asked.

The polite young man consulted his register. "No, sir, she hasn't."

"Connect me with her room."

After a full minute of ringing, it was obvious that there was going to be no answer.

Three minutes later, he was knocking at her door. There was no answer to that, either.

Ten minutes after that, he had the assistant manager unlocking the door. He had explained who he was, and told him that he was afraid the girl was in trouble. The hotel man seemed to be more worried about the girl skipping out on her bill.

The door swung open under the assistant manager's hand, and the two men stepped inside. The room was neat; the bed had been made. Brad opened a closet door. Nothing. No one in the bathroom.

Her luggage—a single brown leatherette suitcase—stood by the dresser.

The assistant manager knelt down beside it and opened it. The suitcase was full of flatly-folded, tightly packed newspapers.

The hotel man stood up with a sigh. "It happens every so often. As long as people have luggage, we don't ask for rent in advance. So, every once in a while, someone comes in with a cheap suitcase full of trash and just leaves it when they're ready to go."

Brad frowned and shook his head slowly. "That suitcase is pretty new; it's worth more than a single night's rent."

The assistant manager looked at the piece of luggage thoughtfully. "You're right. Probably stolen."

"Even so," Brad reasoned, "she could pawn it for a night's rent in a cheaper hotel. She wouldn't pull a trick like this unless she intended to stay here several days."

The hotel man thought that one over. "By George, you may be right! I'll tell you what I'm going to do; I'm not going to rent this room unless I absolutely have to. She may show up later in the day."

Brad didn't agree, but he kept his mouth shut. He pulled open a bureau drawer. Empty. He opened another.

And blinked.

The only thing in the drawer was a blue-steel .300 Magnum pistol.

The assistant manager was kneeling down, closing the suitcase; his eyes were below the level of the drawer. Brad pocketed the weapon with one smooth motion of his hand.

Casually, he closed the drawer and opened the next one.

"Anything in there?" the hotel man asked as he rose to his feet.

"Nothing in there now," Brad said truthfully.

"Well, there doesn't seem to be anything missing, at least. Funny what some people will do, isn't it? Do you know that people with plenty of money will steal things they don't need just because they can get away with it? Why, you know those Bibles..." He pointed at the black-bound book on the night table. "Those Bibles are put in hotel rooms by the Gideon

Society, for nothing. And people will steal them; people who wouldn't ever read..." The hotel man continued with his lecture as they walked out into the hall. He was obviously a little angry at being taken for a night's rent, even though it was no great loss to the hotel as a whole.

*It ain't the money...* Brad thought sourly.

But Brad's attention was no longer on the man's words; he was thinking of Nora's disappearance. For a moment, he thought of offering to take care of the girl's room rent, but he realized that the hotel was a powerful ally; hotels stick together, for their own protection in such cases as these, and they keep their eyes open for skippers. They had long ago discovered that skippers, like other kinds of petty criminals, usually repeat themselves.

A photograph of Nora had automatically been taken when she registered, and she had had to give her thumbprint. The news would go out to other hotels that she was a skipper, and they'd have their eyes open.

If she registered at another hotel, they'd have her.

But Brad suspected it was something worse than just a skip-out. If so, her name would be redeemed, eventually.

He felt as though his whole life had suddenly come tumbling down about his ears. It wasn't the girl, exactly; he hadn't known her long enough for that. But his whole concept of life had been that there are reasons for things; he believed that events were orderly and meaningful. And now they no longer had any sense to them; they seemed to be isolated events; occurrences almost totally insulated, only vaguely connected.

So many mysteries with only the wispiest of relationship to each other.

"...had you known the girl?" asked the assistant manager.

Brad jerked his mind back out of its reverie. He had only been half aware that the man was talking.

"How long had I known her?" Brad repeated. "Only since last night; she was a casual acquaintance."

"I see," said the hotel man dryly.

Brad knew what the man was thinking, and he also knew it would be useless to deny it, but he had a faint impulse to smash his fist into the smug face. He suppressed the impulse and felt childishly noble because he had.

"Thank you for bringing this to my attention, Mr. Stevens," the assistant manager said. "We appreciate it."

"Don't mention it. And now, if you'll excuse me, I have to make a phone call." He headed for his own room.

THE call was to the Consolidated Investigation Corporation of Los Angeles, and it took only a few minutes.

The head of the agency himself informed Brad that no such person as a Miss Lenora Douglas was, or ever had been, working for them.

"Look," Brad said, "I saw the girl's badge and identification card."

"Thank you for telling us," said the detective. "They're forgeries, of course. We'll have it investigated. But, you see, we're only licensed to operate in the State of California. We'd never send an operative to Chicago."

"I see," said Brad dully. "Thanks."

"Glad to have been of service. And thank you again."

Brad cut the connection.

Well, what did that mean? Was the girl lying, or was there a cover-up going on here, too? Which? But the big question in his mind was not so much which, but—

*Why? In the name of Heaven why?*

The phone rang. Brad flipped it on and watched the pleasantly homely face of Parker fade into view.

"Hi, Brad. Find anything in Chicago?

Brad shook his head wearily. "Nothing. Absolutely nothing. Except, maybe negative leads. Whoever or whatever is behind this has thrown stone walls in front of me at every turn. And I can't seem to break any of them down. They lead nowhere.

"I've been conked on the head and I can't even prove assault. I think a girl's been kidnapped, but I have so little evidence that I couldn't take it to the police. I'm not even sure, myself."

Parker said, "Well, maybe I've got a new lead. It looks just screwy enough to be connected."

"Give."

Parker looked down and read from a piece of paper:

"A woman's been arrested for malicious mischief. She called the police and told them that she'd been attacked by a four-armed monster. She said she'd shot and killed it and that it was in her back yard, dead.

"When the cop's got there, there was nothing to be seen. And—get this—she claimed the police had *already* been there to pick up the body!

"They've got her in a psychiatric hospital now, for observation."

Brad slammed his palm down on the table so hard that it made Parker jump. "It fits! My gawd how it fits!" There was excitement in his eyes. "We may have a better lead here than we've ever had! Where did it happen? There in New York?"

"Los Angeles, California," said Parker. "But why do you say it's a better lead than the others?"

"Because this time we've got an eyewitness that actually saw something, up close—actually shot it!"

"Maybe." Parker looked doubtful. "So far now, all you've really got to go on is a telephoto shot that might be an accident, the eyewitness account of two kids who were a long ways away, and the word of a woman who's in the twitch-bin. Doesn't sound promising to me."

"Maybe not, but that Los Angeles dateline, it means some—"

Parker spread his hands. "Okay; it's your story." He grinned lopsidedly. "Good luck."

"Thanks. So long."

He cut off and started repacking his suitcase. The last thing he put in it was the girl's .300 Magnum.

# CHAPTER SIX

As he was checking out and asking the clerk about strato-plane reservations for Los Angeles, the assistant manager walked deferentially over to him.

"Oh, Mr. Stevens; I thought you'd like to know that Miss Douglas isn't a skipper at all. We're much relieved, of course; we hate to find ourselves suspecting our guests.

"The bill was paid by telefac money order, with a request that we ship the suitcase. It seems the newspapers were for reference purposes, and—"

"Just a minute," Brad cut him off. "You say the money was wired in by Miss Douglas? From where?"

"Why, from Los Angeles. But not by Miss Douglas; by her employer, the Consolidated Investigation Corporation."

Brad took a full thirty seconds to digest that. He forced himself to keep his voice calm. "I see. I suppose her employer will give her her suitcase."

"Oh, no; that was sent directly to her home." He gave an address on Laurel Canyon.

"Did she leave anything else here?"

The hotel man shrugged. "That's all she asked for." Then his brows drew down and his face became stern. "But, see here, why are you asking so many questions? You admitted that you hardly knew the girl. I told you about the payment because you were ever so kind enough to tell us of her leaving, but—"

"I was just worried that maybe something had happened to her," Brad said engagingly. "I'm happy to hear that she's all right."

The assistant manager's smile returned. "Yes, of course. Well, I hope you enjoyed your stay here, Mr. Stevens. Have a good trip, and do come back!"

Brad said something appropriately banal and beat a hasty path toward the door.

The weather in Los Angeles was its usual beautiful. It was sunshiny, pleasant, and refreshing, like all the other days that march through Southern California with monotonously fine weather.

Brad Stevens stood at the airport after the two-hour ride from Chicago and wondered why anyone ever lived in the vicious weather of New York and Chicago.

*It's either too hot or too cold...* The words of the newly popular revival sang in his head. *Not in Los Angeles.*

Two hours of relaxation in the smoothly cruising strato-plane had begun to give some pattern to his thoughts. So hectic had this chase been that it was hard to realize that it was only a little more than thirty-six hours since it began. It might make a news story yet, if he could crack it before the Larchmont Nursing Home story got cold.

He half smiled as he thought to himself that the nursing home itself probably wasn't too cold yet.

As he walked through the milling crowds at the airport, he kept trying to sort the various elements of the puzzle in his mind. They began, at times, to make a dim sort of sense, then he'd find another angle that made the whole thing look crazy.

He went over theory after theory, discarding them one after another.

A two-headed man, a giant, and a four-armed monster.

How did they fit in?

He stepped out to the robotaxi line and started to climb in when a voice said, "Are you Bradley Stevens?"

Brad turned to face a pair of ordinary-looking, well-dressed men.

"Yeah, I'm Stevens. Why?"

One of the men held out a card. "Police officers. We'd like to talk to you."

Brad hesitated. If they were real cops; he didn't mind talking to them at all, but he was getting a little cagey about peculiar credentials.

"Mind driving down to the station with us?" the other cop asked.

"I'll take your suitcase," said the first. Any choice the one cop gave him was negated by the other.

Brad realized there was nothing he could do. They both carried guns near their fingertips, while his only armament was the .300 in the suitcase. He had three choices: run, fight, or follow orders.

He handed the cop his suitcase. "Let's go," he said.

They flanked him and the three of them took the escalator to the roof, where a police helicopter waited.

No one said anything as the machine lifted. Brad knew he'd find out soon enough, and he wanted time to think and figure out his strategy—if any was going to be needed.

Several minutes later, he was glad he had not decided to fight or run. The copter settled gently to the roof of the great, new Los Angeles Municipal Building.

"Let's go downstairs," said one of the cops.

Resignedly, Brad did as he was asked.


BRAD sat in a chair, holding his head in his hands. "I don't know what the hell you're talking about!" he said, for what seemed the fifty thousandth time in the last two hours.

"Well, we'll try it again," said the First Cop. (Brad had never been told their names; he had long ago simply tagged them as First Cop, Second Cop, and Third Cop.)

"Now, tell us again where you got that gun we found in your suitcase." First Cop went on.

"I told you," Brad said with weary patience, "I got it out of the girl's hotel room."

"Stole it," said Second Cop laconically.

"Drop dead," said Brad.

"I like that," said Third Cop. "That's very witty and very clever and very original. 'Drop dead.' Isn't that witty?"

Brad looked up at him and forced a smile. "I'm glad I'm appreciated by a man whose wit is obviously on a par with my own."

Third Cop flushed. "Look, wiseacre—"

"Now *you* look," Brad said, pointing a finger, "I am flatly not going to answer any more of the same old questions. I've tried to help you guys, and I'm still willing. If you come up with any new ones, ask 'em, but let's knock off the monotony."

"Now, look, Mr. Stevens," said First Cop soothingly. "You're newsman, a well-known newsman. We're just police officers that nobody ever heard of.

"Now, when you have a job to do, you do it—right? Well, that's all we're trying to do—our job. All we ask is that you answer a few questions. Now, if you had a news story to get, why we'd cooperate to help you. Why don't you help us?"

Brad recognized the old "buddy-buddy" treatment; was Standard Operating Procedure with cops.

So far, he had been given almost no information. Lenora Douglas was dead, and the bullet that had killed her had come from the .300 Magnum he had been carrying. She had been found somewhere in Chicago at sometime in the morning. Suspicion had been aroused in the hotel assistant manager's mind, and the call had gone out for Bradley Stevens.

"I have nothing more to say," Brad said flatly.

First Cop sighed. "Okay, lock him up for awhile." He stood up. "We'll talk to him later."

ONE thing Brad Stevens could say for the hospitality of the Los Angeles police, the jail cells were comfortable. He leaned back on the bunk and went over his story again.

He'd told them when he'd arrived in Chicago. He had told them about his trip to Evanston to see Steadmann "on a news story." He had told them that he'd met Miss Douglas there, without mentioning the fact that they'd both been inside the building.

He'd told them about checking into the hotel, and how they had had breakfast together. And he'd told them that that was the last he'd seen of her.

And they'd kept saying: "Look, Stevens, you're lying. We know it; you know it. Now, come on and tell the truth."

Police officials cooperated with each other a lot more than they had in the old days. They had to. A man could get from one state to another too easily.

Years ago, if a killing happened in Chicago and the suspect was in California, the Chicago police would have to extradite the suspect before they could question him.

He still had to be extradited for trial, of course, but the local police were given all the facts by telefacsimile, and they could question the subject and relay the information back to Chicago. Sometimes, suspects were questioned by television, but a TV screen doesn't have the psychological effect of a ring of living policemen.

Brad closed his eyes, suddenly feeling about ninety-nine years old. It was another gimmick that didn't make sense. The Gang—whoever they were—could kidnap a whole burning hospital full of patients and they'd never be seen again. But they couldn't get rid of one girl's body. Why?

Did they want to frame Bradley Stevens?

Brad sat up straight and opened his eyes. That must be it... He was getting too close—or at least they thought he was. So they had decided to frame him and... Brad let himself slump back.

No, that couldn't be it. If they wanted him out of the way that bad, they'd have killed him in the garage. No fuss, no muss, no bother.

Suppose there was more than one group involved? It was possible, of course; there might be two or three or even more groups involved.

He shook his head. In a deal like this it was best to use Occam's Razor; dig for the simplest solution. He'd have to go on the assumption that there was only one group, with the possibility of a second group in the background.

But why all the cover-up? Something like this would have to be really big in order to get so many people to clam up about it.

And what were they up to, anyway? Kidnapping on a grand scale, obviously. And murder. But what was the motive? How about profits? A big organization like that wouldn't be working for peanuts.

THE door to the cellblock clanged, and the guard brought in a fat, seedy-looking man wearing a blue textron suit. His head was thinly covered with meager strands of gray hair, and his brown eyes glittered with extra brightness caused by contact lenses.

Brad jumped to his feet. "Lew! Thank heaven you got here!"

Lew Bronson was one of the finest criminal lawyers in the State of California. He didn't say a word until he had been locked in Brad's cell and the guard had left.

The first thing he said when he sat down was, "Brad Stevens, you know better than to lie to your lawyer. Now, did you kill that woman, or not?"

"I didn't kill her, Lew."

"All right, then; what happened?"

Brad went over the story again—right from the start. This time, he didn't leave out a single detail. He included the photo of the two-headed man, the giant, and the story of the four-armed man. He included the little *tete-a-tete* in the Steadmann garage. He missed nothing.

Brad was no fool. When you talk to a lawyer, it is as stupid to lie or omit facts as it is to lie about your symptoms to your doctor.

Lew Bronson listened in silence while he lovingly filled a briar pipe with expensive tobacco and carefully puffed it alight. His head was entirely enveloped in smoke by the time Brad finished.

He puffed in silence for a few more minutes, then said, "If we ever have to tell that story to a jury, they'll think we're pleading insanity—both of us. Now, look, I haven't been able to get all the dope on the Chicago situation, but it looks something like this:

"The girl was found just a few hours ago, in a room in one of the less expensive hotels. She'd been shot three times with a .300 Magnum pistol, and the markings on the bullet check with the gun you were carrying.

"She'd been robbed and stripped of identification, but since all private detectives are registered with the Federal Bureau of Investigation, they soon had her identified.

"The desk clerk at the hotel swears that the person who checked into that room was a man; the signature on the book is 'Richard Williams,' probably a phony.

"The trouble is that these cheap hotels don't have any auto-identification systems, so there's nothing to go on.

"The cops checked with all the other hotels, and found that you and the girl had checked in at the Hilton the previous evening, so they did a little questioning and found out about your investigation of her room.

"It wouldn't have been so bad if you hadn't picked up that gun. When the police here found it on you, they knew they had something more than just a routine questioning on their hands. If you'd left that .300 where it was, you'd be in the clear by now."

Brad nodded, saying nothing.

"One other thing," the fat little lawyer said, "they gave your hands a nitrate test after they found the gun, didn't they?"

"Yes."

"Have you fired a gun in the past forty-eight hours?"

Brad laughed sharply. "I haven't fired a gun in the past forty-eight months."

"Good. You're clear on that, then. Of course, there are ways to remove that evidence, but the average man doesn't know that. At least it's a piece of evidence they *don't* have.

"What I'm going to do is get you out of here as soon as possible. I've already applied for a writ of *habeas corpus,* and I think—"

The cell-block door clanged again, and the guard let First Cop in. He came over to the cell, and Lew Bronson said, "I'm talking to my client, Sergeant Webley."

First Cop said, "That's all right, Mr. Bronson; you can talk to him outside. We're releasing him."

Bronson frowned. Brad knew that the *habeas corpus* writ hadn't come through yet; something like that took a little time.

"May I ask why this sudden realization of my client's innocence?" Bronson asked.

First Cop shrugged with one shoulder. "Sure. We checked on Mr. Stevens' movements, and he's got an alibi.

"The autopsy report on the girl came in, and it shows that she was killed late yesterday afternoon—before Mr. Stevens ever arrived in Chicago."

# CHAPTER SEVEN

Twenty minutes later, Brad Stevens and Lew Bronson were seated in a quiet bar over a pair of Scotch-and-waters. They had left the Municipal Building as rapidly as possible, without asking any more questions.

"They're looking for your girl friend now, of course," said Bronson. "If she had Lenora Douglas' papers, it's likely that she was mixed up in the killing."

Brad Stevens shook his head. "It sounds fishy, Lew. If she's an operative for Consolidated, why did they deny knowing anything about her?

"Why did they send for her suitcase and *not* the gun? Why was the gun left in the room, anyway? Did the gun belong to the real Lenora Douglas or to the murderer?"

Bronson took a sip of his drink before answering. "I don't know. The police aren't letting out any information."

"By the way, what about that Laurel Canyon address that the suitcase was sent to?" Brad asked. "The police must have gotten that from the hotel's assistant manager."

"I don't know," admitted Bronson. "Want me to check on it?" Without waiting for an answer, he got up and went to the pay phone over by the bar.

The call took about five minutes. When Lew Bronson came back, he said, "That's that. There's no such address."

"What about the check that was mailed to the Hilton to pay for her room?"

Lew Bronson snorted.

"That's easy. Anyone can go down to Western Union and send a telefac check under any name he wants to. As long as the money's paid in, they don't care who gives it to them. All they have to worry about is making sure the right person collects it."

"Damn!" said Brad. "I'd give a purty to know more about that check. Which office here in L. A. was it sent from? Did a man or a woman send it?"

"What makes you think it was a man? It looks to me as though the girl you met—whoever she was—knocked off the Douglas dame and then came here to L. A. to send the telefac."

"Yeah? What about the mysterious 'Richard Williams'? What's he got to do with it? I wish this thing made more sense." He finished his drink and lit a cigarette.

"Look here," he went on, "if the girl—call her Nora—killed Miss Douglas, why didn't she leave then? There would have been nothing to connect her with the killing; it would have been blamed on Williams. Instead, she sticks around, carrying the murder weapon, and using the dead woman's identification. She even checks into a hotel using it. That doesn't make much sense."

"No," said Bronson. "It doesn't."

FOR several minutes, neither of them said a word. Then Brad said, "Look, there are a few things that connect up. There are weird monsters in New York, Chicago, and Los Angeles. Then, we have Steadmann's in New York and Chicago. Ambulances and monsters. How do they connect?"

"What about that nursing home?" Bronson asked.

Brad nodded. "That's what I was coming to. Are there any private nursing homes in Chicago or in Los Angeles that are surrounded by high storm fencing?"

Bronson sighed gustily. "Several of them, I'd say. That's the usual procedure for 'nursing homes' that take care of mentally disturbed patients."

"Agreed. But I've got another tie-in. I'm not sure how it fits, but let's take a look at it.

"It was the private firefighting equipment of the Long Island Power Station that put out the fire in New York. When you come right down to it, that's more than just a little damned peculiar. The story about its being an accidental wrong number didn't sound right to me then, and it still doesn't.

"Now, there are five big nuclear power reactors in the United States, supplying eighty percent of the nation's power. Now where are the three biggest?"

Bronson exhaled pipe smoke slowly as he spoke. "New York, Chicago, and Los Angeles. That's a queer tie-up."

"Not too queer. Look, suppose someone wanted to take over the United States. If they could get control of our power system, they'd have us over a barrel wouldn't they?"

"Sure, sure," Bronson agreed. "But how are they going to do that? The U. S. Government knows that better than we do; those plants are well protected." He paused. "Besides, what country could pull off a coup like that? And how could they keep all the higher-ups clammed up?"

The newsman considered just exactly how he was going to put this. Finally he said, "Well, this sounds nutty, I know, but let's just try it for size and see what happens."

"Shoot," said the lawyer.

"Suppose we were being invaded by aliens from Mars or Venus or someplace like that. That would account for the monsters, wouldn't it?"

Bronson considered it. "It might. But it sounds pretty far-fetched. How do they go around getting all this cooperation from the higher-ups?"

"I don't know. Maybe they have hypnotic telepathy or something." He slammed his fist into his hand in a gesture of self-annoyance. "Oh, I know it sounds like something out of a kid's TV program, but then so does the rest of this set-up."

"Agreed," said the lawyer. "What are you going to do about it?"

"Keep investigating. What else can I do?"

"The police will still have a tail on you, you know," Bronson warned.

"Don't worry about that; I can ditch any tail they've got."

"Okay," the lawyer said. "If you get in another jam, just yell."

"Don't worry; I will. You can count on it."

At first, Brad made no attempt to get rid of the police officer he was sure was following him. He never looked around, or acted as though he suspected he was being followed; to do so would have made them harder to escape from when the time came.

He checked into a big hotel in downtown Los Angeles after buying a big map of the city and several magazines at a local bookstore. He had no intention of reading the magazines; they were simply to cover up the fact that he had gone in for only the map.

Once in his hotel room, he spread the map out on the floor and then opened the telephone book. First, he located the Southern California Power Station. Then, with his pencil, he began marking off the locations of the various hospitals and private nursing homes near the big reactor.

The Station itself was located near San Pedro, the harbor that connects Greater Los Angeles with the Pacific Ocean. Vast quantities of water are needed for the operation of a really high-powered atomic reactor, and all five of the Power Stations were located near big bodies of water.

There was only one private nursing home that actually filled the bill. It was located less than a mile from the area covered by the Power Station itself.

Just for the sake of curiosity, he looked up the Steadmann Emergency Service in the directory. It wasn't listed, but near it was a Steel Emergency Service.

He looked in the Yellow Pages, under "Ambulances," "Auto Repair," and "TV Repair." The Steel Emergency Service wasn't listed under any of them.

On a hunch, he called the number.

"I'm sorry, sir," said the operator, "that number has been disconnected."

The address for the Steel place was near that of the nursing home—Leadville Nursing Home.

*That cinches it,* Brad thought to himself. *The connection is there somewhere!*

The next step then was to check the Leadville Nursing Home.

And to do that, he'd have to elude the gentleman from the L. A. P. D. He'd wait until nightfall.

He took the express subway to San Pedro as the first step. Once there, he started walking toward old Fort MacArthur, as though he had a definite appointment with a definite person. After a few blocks, he turned and headed directly toward the waterfront.

It was just as he'd remembered it. There were several small boats—little tramp diesels—tied up against the dock. Most of them were less than forty feet long. He walked along as though he were looking for the name of the boat he was searching for. Actually, he was looking for a craft that was comparatively unguarded.

He finally found one. There was a lamp lit in the cabin, but the two men inside were playing cards and drinking beer; they weren't watching the deck. Why should they? There wasn't much aboard to steal.

Just as though he owned the craft, Brad Stevens walked up the gangway. As he turned, he could see a figure behind him out of the corner of his eye, but he didn't pause.

He walked quietly to the other side of the little ship, eased himself over the side until he was hanging by his hands. He let go and slid silently into the water.

He made his way silently through the water, sticking close to the sides of the anchored vessels. Once, as he passed between two of them, he saw a man watching the boat which he had boarded. He kept on moving.

Finally, when he was several hundred feet away, the curve of the dock had taken him out of sight of whoever was watching. He climbed up to the pier and took a look around. No one was in sight. Good. He started walking again. He hoped the cop kept a good eye on the innocent ship.

By the time he reached the Leadville Nursing Home, the warm evening air had completely dried his textron suit, leaving only a residue of salt, which could easily be shaken out.

From a block away, it was obvious that the Leadville place was quite similar to the Larchmont. And it was also obvious that there wasn't a light on in the building.

He walked up to the main gate. It was padlocked, and a sign read:

CLOSED.

Well, that left only one thing to do. He'd have to take a look at the Southern California Power Plant itself.

AT A distance, it was obvious that he wouldn't be able to sneak up on the power Plant. The area was well-lighted, and the double storm fence around it was probably electrified and loaded with alarms.

He spent forty-five minutes walking around the place, looking for some sort of loophole that he could get through. There were none.

The only way to conceivably get into the Power Station was through the main gates, and every one of them was watched by a pair of armed guards, one inside, one outside. He got up as close to the main gate as possible and tried to figure out a way to get into the enclosure, but it looked hopeless.

He was still wondering when he heard the sound of an automobile purring inside the compound. He looked at the road. A car was coming toward the plant.

No. Not a car. An ambulance.

And lettered neatly on the side were the words:

STEEL EMERGENCY SERVICE

It pulled up to the gate, and the guard went around to the rear and looked inside for several moments. Evidently they didn't want anyone getting into the Power Station in that manner.

"How many more loads?" asked the guard.

"Three more," said the driver. "Got to hurry; the *Oremus* sails at midnight."

The gate swung open, and the ambulance went on in. The guard pushed the gate closed after it.

Brad Stevens thought a moment, and then made a decision. If he couldn't get into the Southern California Power Plant, maybe he could get onto the *Oremus*.

He'd never heard of the ship before, but he knew several things about it. It would be a fairly large boat, but not a regular passenger liner. And it wouldn't be in any of the small docks.

He looked at his watch. He had just under two hours to find her and get aboard and get off again.

# CHAPTER EIGHT

The *Oremus* turned out to be a good-sized and fairly modern cargo vessel, probably not atomic powered, since the ban on using atomic power for seagoing vessels had come into effect before this ship was built.

Brad stayed well out of sight, looking for a way to get aboard her.

The loading ramp was out—flatly. It was brightly lit and there were several men working around her—two of them wearing uniforms and guns.

The *Oremus* was certainly ready to go. She floated low in the water, as though she was fully loaded, and a small remote-controlled tugboat was visible nearby, ready to pull her out to sea.

Brad wished he'd had time to check up on the sailing notices—and then reflected that they'd probably contain false information, anyway. He was rapidly reaching the point where he couldn't believe anything but the evidence of his own senses.

Was there any other way to get aboard besides the loading ramp?

Well, he might be able to climb the anchor chain, but the thought didn't appeal to him much.

There was one other way. The roof of the loading shed was about twenty feet higher than the deck of the *Oremus*. If he could get on top of the shed—

He'd have to chance it. He *had* to know what was aboard that ship! And *who!*

The piers themselves were paired off: 1-2, 3-4, 5-6, and so on. Actually, each pair was just one long, wide pier; the south side was the odd-numbered pier, the north side was even-numbered. The *Oremus* was in Pier 7. If he could get to the roof of the loading shed of Pier 8, he could make it.

There was no ship tied up to Pier 8; it was dark and unused at the time. Not completely dark, however; the light from Pier 7 reached it a little.

*Come on, boy,* he told himself, *don't yellow out now.*

Moving cautiously but rapidly, keeping well in the shadows, he made his way to the loading shed of Pier 8. And all the way, he knew that if one of the men on the other pier were to look his way, he stood a good chance of being seen.

But none of them did.

Getting to the roof was comparatively easy. There were a series of iron handholds going up the side for the convenience of the men who operated the loading machinery on the roof deck.

He hoped there wouldn't be anyone up there on the Pier 7 shed. There shouldn't be, since the *Oremus* was already loaded, but he couldn't be absolutely sure.

Again, he was in luck. The roof of the huge double shed was empty of life. He walked silently across it, lay flat on his stomach, and peered over the edge at the deck of the *Oremus.*

There were men on the deck; four of them, leaning on the rail, smoking and conversing in low tones. But, as Brad had hoped, they were not directly below him. When a man leans over a ship's rail, he wants to look at the sea or the city, not at the side of a loading shed.

He was in luck in another way. Because of the evident secrecy of this voyage, lights on the ship itself were being kept at a minimum. Only the pier was brightly illuminated.

Brad lifted himself back from the edge of the roof and looked around. There ought to be a rope around somewhere.

It required a little hunting, but eventually he found a coil of good, half-inch reinforced line. He secured it around a ringbolt and lowered the other end over the edge of the roof.

"Here comes another one," said a voice from the deck.

Brad froze. Had they seen his rope?

Then he heard the humming turboelectric engine of one of the ambulances. It was pulling up to discharge more of the mysterious cargo—or passengers—into the ship.

The men on deck were all looking at the new arrival now; they wouldn't be looking at the wall of the shed. Now was his chance.

Brad dropped the rest of the line over the edge, hoisted himself over, and slid down the rope.

Quickly, he moved into the comparative safety of the shadows of the superstructure. No one had seen him.

Crouching, he moved around to the stern of the ship.

"Who—who's there?" said a voice in the shadows beneath a lifeboat.

Again Brad froze in his tracks—but only for a moment. He recognized the voice.

It was that of the girl who had called herself Lenora Douglas.

Almost without pause, Brad's mind made its decision.

"It's me, Nora; Brad Stevens."

She gave a little gasp, then suddenly she was running across the deck and was in his arms. "Brad, Brad, I've been so frightened! Please! Get me off this terrible boat!"

He could feel that her face was wet with tears.

"Shhh! Be quiet! Get hold of yourself, Nora!"

She breathed heavily for a moment, then she seemed calmer. "I'm sorry," she said. "It's just that I've been scared stiff!"

"I don't blame you," Brad told her. "How did you get here? What happened?"

"I was kidnapped," she said in a low whisper. "I had barely stepped out of the hotel when two men walked up to me and stuck a gun in my ribs—right in broad daylight. There was nothing I could do; I got in their car, something jabbed me in the arm, and that's all I remember until I woke up here—on this ship."

"Where?"

"Down in the hold—in a cabin. They had handcuffed me to a bunk with my own handcuffs, but they didn't know I always carry a spare key pinned to the inside of my dress, right here." She patted the small of her back. Then she looked up at him, puzzled. "Brad, how did you get here?"

BRIEFLY, he told her what had happened to him since he'd last seen her. Then he added, "So, I'd like to know how it was that this woman was killed with your gun."

She shook her head. "That wasn't my gun. I don't know how it got there, but I had my own with me when I was picked up. It was in my purse, along with everything else."

"And why didn't Consolidated admit you were an agent of theirs?"

"They never do," she said. "At least to private individuals. If you'd been a policeman, they'd have identified me."

"Okay," Brad said. "Now what's going on aboard this ship?"

She shivered in his arms. "Oh, Brad! It's horrible! These people, whoever they are, have been kidnapping people and changing them into monsters! Terrible looking creatures with awful faces! Some of them have extra arms and legs and heads and—oh, all kinds of ugly things! Please, Brad, let's get off this boat before they catch us and do it to us!"

"No." Brad's voice was firm, the statement final. "I've got to see these things for myself. I can't leave after getting this far. You're pretty well hidden under that lifeboat where you were. I wouldn't have seen you if you hadn't called out. You get back under there and stay until I get back."

"But what if you don't get back?" she almost wailed. "How will I get off?"

"If necessary, dive overboard." Brad's voice was almost brutal.

"But I can't swim!"

"Get under there! I'll be back!"

She looked up at him with wide eyes, then nodded her head. Without another word, she returned to her hiding place.

The girl had obviously come up the companionway ladder that led below. Brad went to it and opened the hatch carefully. It was well lighted, but deserted. He knew he was sticking his neck out farther than any giraffe had ever dared, but—

Down he went.

# CHAPTER NINE

He was walking down one of the companionways toward the bow of the ship when he heard the thud of many feet coming toward him from around the turn ahead. Nearby was a cabin door that stood partially open.

Brad pushed the door open and stepped into the darkness of the cabin, then closed it. There were a series of ventilator slots at eye level in the door. Brad peered through them and saw four men in sailor's uniforms stride down the companionway toward the direction from which he had come. After they passed, Brad drew a deep breath. There was always the chance that they would be coming for the very cabin he was in.

Suddenly, the lights in the cabin went on. From behind him came an odd grunt. Brad whirled. His eyes widened, and his breath was jerked into his lungs in a harsh gasp.

Standing there, with one great hand on the light switch was one of the most shocking things he had ever seen.

It was not an ape; the brow, the brain case was much too large for any ape. Its face had no brow ridges, and the eyes were not set deeply into their sockets.

But the jaws were the great, fanged, bone-crunching jaws of a bull gorilla, and the hair that covered its body was long and shaggy.

The feet were not those of an ape, either. Instead of an opposed great toe, the toes were set like those in a human foot.

The most human thing about it was the fact that it was wearing a pair of white tennis shorts.

And the least human was that awesome face set above hairy shoulders that were all of three feet wide.

All this Brad saw and assimilated in a single, timeless second. Then he spun and was out the door.

Human antagonists he could fight, but the thing in that stateroom was too much for him. He started running up the companionway. Like Nora, his only thought now was to get off this hellish ship.

Perhaps, if he had met the creature in broad daylight, he might have stood his ground. If he had been warned of what he was to meet, he might have faced it bravely.

But there is panic in any man, and the shock of that brutal, inhuman face suddenly confronting him in the narrow confines of what he had assumed to be an unoccupied cabin had completely unnerved Bradley Stevens.

He ran. But not for long. As the first shock ebbed, the panic ebbed with it, and he saw that he was running almost directly into the path of the sailors who had just passed the door of the cabin he had left.

They had heard his running footsteps and turned. They had no time to be puzzled.

Brad had realized what that instant of panic had cost him, but he didn't slow his charge. His brain, although heated for a moment with blazing, unreasoning fear, had suddenly become the cold, logical brain of the seasoned fighter.

His charge carried him directly into the knot of men. One of his big fists slammed into a solar plexus, while the other thudded into the ribs over a man's heart.

The stricken men spun and dropped, getting in their companion's way. And Brad kept on running.

Behind him, he heard shouts. He turned a corner at full speed, and saw ahead of him another group of men.

And these men, having been warned, were ready for him.

In the melee that ensued, it didn't take long for Brad to realize that these men weren't just common sailors, practiced in bar battles and street fights; they were trained, hand-to-hand combat men.

Brad was trained, too, but there were more of them. The only reason it took them as long to get him as it did was because they were obviously trying hard *not* to kill him.

Brad never did remember feeling the blow. One minute he was there, fighting for his life; the next minute, he was plunged into a sea of nothingness.

THERE was something cold on his face. He had to think about it for what seemed a long time before he realized that someone was washing his face with a cold, wet washrag.

He opened his eyes, focused them, and looked around.

He was lying on a bunk in one of the staterooms of the ship. There were several sailors standing around watching him. One of them had been bathing his face with cold water.

On the other bunk, across the cabin, sat a fine-looking silver-haired man in his middle fifties. He was leaning forward his hands on his knees, looking intently at Brad. There was a half smile on his face.

"How do you feel?" the man asked.

"Like I'd been slugged," Brad admitted. "But that's all right. I'm getting used to sleeping that way in the evening."

The half smile became a smile. "So I understand. You've given us a little trouble, Mr. Stevens."

"I suppose I have. Do I get an explanation for my pains?"

"You might," the man said. "What do you think the answer is?"

"I don't know," Brad admitted. "But seeing your face clears up a lot of things."

"You know me?"

"Sure. I'm a newsman, remember? You're Dr. Edward FitzHugh. Director of the Atomic Research Commission." Brad sat up on the edge of the bed, holding his head in his hands. No one tried to stop him.

"Very well; what have you deduced?" asked FitzHugh.

"This is some sort of hush-hush top secret Government affair. It has something to do with—uh—monsters." He launched into an account of what he had discovered and surmised in the past two days.

"You were keeping these monsters in these phony nursing homes," he went on. "The 'emergency service' ambulances are used to transport them around—I suppose because an ambulance can get to places that an ordinary car couldn't.

"You've got these places set up near all five of the big atomic power stations. And I'll bet I could spot every one of them."

"You could?" FitzHugh didn't look surprised.

"Sure. It's a code. All the nursing homes start with the letter 'L,' and the emergency service name starts with 'S.'" He paused. "You want certain people to be able to find either one just by looking it up in the phone book."

"Do you know who these certain people are?" the scientist asked.

Brad shook his head and then wished he hadn't. "No," he said. "I was hoping you'd tell me." He winced again and looked up at the sailors. "Boy! You guys can fight!" He rubbed his chin.

"So can you," said one of them, grinning. "You got a couple of our boys before we got you."

"They should be able to fight," FitzHugh said dryly. "Gentlemen, meet Mr. Bradley Stevens of AmPress. Mr. Stevens, meet some of the finest officers in the United States Navy." He didn't bother to mention names. "This is probably the only civilian freighter in the world that has ever been commanded by a full admiral of the U. S. Navy."

"Wow. This would probably have made the greatest story of my career."

*"Would have?"* asked FitzHugh sharply.

"Sure," said Brad. "I won't print it if there's a good reason not to, and I've got a hunch there is."

"I hoped you'd say that. There *is* a good reason."

"Let's hear it," Brad said.

THE scientist offered Brad a cigarette and lit one for himself. "You know something about atomic radiations. I believe. You did some articles on it once.

"You know that there is a certain maximum dosage that the human body can take without serious damage to bodily tissues. That's been known for many decades.

"It's also been known that the dosage is cumulative. A lot of little exposures to radiation can be as bad as one massive dose of radiation.

"But it wasn't until about twenty years ago that we began to realize how damaging even very tiny dosages could be if they were allowed to accumulate over a long period of time. Especially if the radiation was directed toward the reproductive organs."

Brad's eyes widened. "I'm beginning to get it now. Mutation."

"Exactly," said FitzHugh. "Mutation of the human germ plasm, with the result that when the offspring were born, they weren't exactly human. The chromosomes and genes were affected; they were changed, with resulting changes in the inheritable characteristics of the children.

"Only those people who worked with really high-energy radiation, such as is used in our modern reactors, have been affected so far. But we still don't know what effect the lower energy radiation will have on the human race if it goes on long enough.

"That's why we took these—these mutations from their parents. Their parents were scientists and technicians who had worked around reactors that were thought to be adequately shielded. They weren't. Only in the past year have we been able to devise the suppressor fields, which stop *all* radiation.

"Even so, some damage has been done. Our technicians know about the danger. They know, too, that there is a chance that their children may be born—different.

"That was the reason for the nursing homes. The family of a scientist or technician who worked in one of the power stations or who ever had worked in one was able to call for aid in the event of pregnancy.

"Fortunately, the majority of children born are normal in every way. But it's sometimes difficult to tell when a child is different.

"In spite of what you may think, those poor creatures are not prisoners in the precise sense of the word. Most of them know that they would never be acceptable in the world. The older ones know perfectly well that their germ plasm must not be allowed to contaminate the human race."

"I can see that," Brad said. Then, changing the subject a little, he asked, "What caused that fire in New York?"

The scientist's brows drew down into a frown. "I'm afraid that some of the children—especially the young ones—don't understand why they're being kept segregated from the rest of humanity. One of them tried to burn the place down. Luckily, none of them were badly hurt."

"That, of course, explains why the nursing home called the Power Station fire department. You didn't want ordinary firemen seeing the kids." He paused. "But, wait a minute.

The Steadmann Emergency Service was located in Chicago. What were Steadmann ambulances doing on Long Island?"

"They'd been driven in from Chicago the day before, to pick up some of the children from New York. We would have changed the name to Salisbury Emergency Service, but the fire caught us unawares."

"I suppose the highway accident near Peoria was just an accident?" The pieces were rapidly coming together.

FitzHugh nodded. "Just an accident."

"What happened to the giant?"

"He ran into the woods and hid. We picked him up in a helicopter a few hours later."

"And what about the four-armed monster that was shot in Los Angeles?"

"He ran away," Dr. FitzHugh said sadly. "He was only fourteen—wanted to see the world, I suppose. We had a squad of our special police on his trail within ten minutes, but we were too late; he'd already been killed. The special squad covered up by pretending they were the city police. They took the boy away in an ambulance before the city police arrived. The woman's story, of course, was never believed."

"It seems to me that a lot of people must know about this already," Brad said. "Why not give it to the public?"

"Not many people know about it, and those who do won't talk. We have to apply pressure now and then to stop an investigation, but it usually works out well.

"Your friend, Inspector Costello, for instance, doesn't know anything. He was told by his superiors to stop investigating, that's all."

"By the way," Brad said, "you have the girl, don't you? If you don't, she's on deck, under Number Five lifeboat."

"We got her," FitzHugh said. "As soon as we found you aboard, we combed the ship."

"I'm not quite sure I see how she fits into the picture, though," the newsman admitted. "I'm fairly certain she killed the real Lenora Douglas, but I can't see why. And why would she carry the papers around with her?

"Her story was as full of holes as a fishnet; she couldn't even act the part of a female detective. I took her gun away from her, and she forgot I had it. And then she left it in the hotel room.

"She typed out that note, even her signature, but I knew it was from her. Nobody else would know what I had sent her after or know that we were on first name terms. And then tonight she tried to tell me she didn't write it.

"She's not a very good liar. What's the matter with her? Feeble minded?"

"No," said Dr. FitzHugh. "Actually, she's a very brilliant little girl. She just doesn't have enough experience, that's all.

"We have special operatives affiliated with the Consolidated agency. The agency doesn't know anything about this project, but they do know that certain of their employees are Government agents.

"Jeanette—that's her real name—escaped from the Los Angeles nursing home, and we sent Lenora Douglas after her, along with Richard Williams, another of our men.

"They found her, but when Williams went up to Evanston to help clear out the Steadmann group, Jeanette managed to get hold of the gun and in the struggle Lenora was killed."

Brad looked puzzled. "Then this Jeanette is a mutation, too? How?"

"There are other kinds than mere freakish mutations," the scientist told him. "Some of them are extremely hard to detect at first. Jeanette looked perfectly normal when she was born, but after four years, it became obvious that she was different.

"She grew up twice as fast as she should. She looked like an eight-year-old by the time she was four. And she had the high intelligence to keep up with her body growth."

"Good God!" said Brad. "How old is she now?"

"Just over nine years old," said Dr. FitzHugh.

"Then how did she get all that grown-up talk?"

"From books—from listening to adults talk—from everywhere she could pick it up. But she didn't have the perspective of an adult."

Brad silently thanked Heaven that he hadn't tried to make love to her.

"Williams picked her up when she was trying to get away from Chicago and brought her back here," said FitzHugh. "We have to keep her under observation. Perhaps, when she completely matures, the process will stop, but we don't think so. We believe that by the time she's thirty-five she'll look like a seventy-year-old woman. She'll probably die of old age before she's fifty."

To Brad, this was the most horrible nightmare of them all.

FitzHugh said, "Now, I'm afraid you'll have to leave, Mr. Stevens. The ship is ready to sail."

"Where to?"

"I can't tell you that, except that it's an island in the Pacific. We've brought all the mutants with us and closed up shop. No one else need ever know anything about them.

"You're an honest man, Mr. Stevens. We tried to keep you from finding out about this, but since you did, we don't think you'll say anything. We don't want the public to panic; I think you can see that."

"I can see it. There'd be monster lynchings and God only knows what else. No, I won't print it. I'll even destroy that picture Parker has." Then he grinned. "Besides, if I did try to print it, I couldn't prove it; you're taking all the evidence with you. And without evidence, I'd become such a laughingstock that I'd never be able to get a news job again."

There was a humorous glint in Dr. FitzHugh's eyes. "I think you may be right, Mr. Stevens. That's one reason why we can let you go.

"And by the way, it's because of people like you that we've had to leave the United States. No matter how well a secret is kept hidden by the Government, a newshawk like you can always dig it out, one way or another."

"Thanks for the compliment, Dr. FitzHugh. Good luck."

WHEN he reached the New York office the next morning, Bradley Stevens turned in his report to his editor.

"Wild goose chase," he said. "Nothing to it. Just like those flying saucer stories back in the forties and fifties."

Then he went back to his desk and sat down to look over the latest telefacs.

Suddenly he sat bolt upright in his chair.

*"Say! What about those flying saucers?"*

## THE END

*If you've enjoyed this book, you will not want to miss these terrific titles...*

## ARMCHAIR SCI-FI & HORROR DOUBLE NOVELS, $12.95 each

## ARMCHAIR SCIENCE FICTION CLASSICS, $12.95 each

*If you've enjoyed this book, you will not want to miss these terrific titles…*

## ARMCHAIR SCI-FI & HORROR DOUBLE NOVELS, $12.95 each

**D-71**   **THE DEEP END** by Gregory Luce
           **TO WATCH BY NIGHT** by Robert Moore Williams

**D-72**   **SWORDSMAN OF LOST TERRA** by Poul Anderson
           **PLANET OF GHOSTS** by David V. Reed

**D-73**   **MOON OF BATTLE** by J. J. Allerton
           **THE MUTANT WEAPON** by Murray Leinster

**D-74**   **OLD SPACEMEN NEVER DIE!** John Jakes
           **RETURN TO EARTH** by Bryan Berry

**D-75**   **THE THING FROM UNDERNEATH** by Milton Lesser
           **OPERATION INTERSTELLAR** by George O. Smith

**D-76**   **THE BURNING WORLD** by Algis Budrys
           **FOREVER IS TOO LONG** by Chester S. Geier

**D-77**   **THE COSMIC JUNKMAN** by Rog Phillips
           **THE ULTIMATE WEAPON** by John W. Campbell

**D-78**   **THE TIES OF EARTH** by James H. Schmitz
           **CUE FOR QUIET** by Thomas L. Sherred

**D-79**   **SECRET OF THE MARTIANS** by Paul W. Fairman
           **THE VARIABLE MAN** by Philip K. Dick

**D-80**   **THE GREEN GIRL** by Jack Williamson
           **THE ROBOT PERIL** by Don Wilcox

## ARMCHAIR SCIENCE FICTION CLASSICS, $12.95 each

**C-25**   **THE STAR KINGS**
           by Edmond Hamilton

**C-26**   **NOT IN SOLITUDE**
           by Kenneth Gantz

**C-32**   **PROMETHEUS II**
           by S. J. Byrne

## ARMCHAIR SCI-FI & HORROR GEMS SERIES, $12.95 each

**G-7**   **SCIENCE FICTION GEMS, Vol. Seven**
          Jack Sharkey and others

**G-8**   **HORROR GEMS, Vol. Eight**
          Seabury Quinn and others

*If you've enjoyed this book, you will not want to miss these terrific titles...*

## ARMCHAIR SCI-FI & HORROR DOUBLE NOVELS, $12.95 each

**D-101**   **CONQUEST OF THE PLANETS** by John W. Campbell
**THE MAN WHO ANNEXED THE MOON** by Bob Olsen

**D-102**   **WEAPON FROM THE STARS** by Rog Phillips
**THE EARTH WAR** by Mack Reynolds

**D-103**   **THE ALIEN INTELLIGENCE** by Jack Williamson
**INTO THE FOURTH DIMENSION** by Ray Cummings

**D-104**   **THE CRYSTAL PLANETOIDS** by Stanton A. Coblentz
**SURVIVORS FROM 9,000 B. C.** by Robert Moore Williams

**D-105**   **THE TIME PROJECTOR** by David H. Keller, M.D. and David Lasser
**STRANGE COMPULSION** by Philip Jose Farmer

**D-106**   **WHOM THE GODS WOULD SLAY** by Paul W. Fairman
**MEN IN THE WALLS** by William Tenn

**D-107**   **LOCKED WORLDS** by Edmond Hamilton
**THE LAND THAT TIME FORGOT** by Edgar Rice Burroughs

**D-108**   **STAY OUT OF SPACE** by Dwight V. Swain
**REBELS OF THE RED PLANET** by Charles L. Fontenay

**D-109**   **THE METAMORPHS** by S. J. Byrne
**MICROCOSMIC BUCCANEERS** by Harl Vincent

**D-110**   **YOU CAN'T ESCAPE FROM MARS** by E. K. Jarvis
**THE MAN WITH FIVE LIVES** by David V. Reed

## ARMCHAIR SCIENCE FICTION CLASSICS, $12.95 each

**C-34**   **30 DAY WONDER**
by Richard Wilson

**C-35**   **G.O.G. 666**
by John Taine

**C-36**   **RALPH 124C 41+**
by Hugo Gernsback

## ARMCHAIR SCI-FI & HORROR GEMS SERIES, $12.95 each

**G-11**   **SCIENCE FICTION GEMS, Vol. Six**
Edmond Hamilton and others

**G-12**   **HORROR GEMS, Vol. Six**
H. P. Lovecraft and others

*If you've enjoyed this book, you will not want to miss these terrific titles…*

## ARMCHAIR SCI-FI & HORROR DOUBLE NOVELS, $12.95 each

**D-111**   **THE MOON ERA** by Jack Williamson
**REVENGE OF THE ROBOTS** by Howard Browne

**D-112**   **SON OF THE BLACK CHALICE** by Milton Lesser
**SENTRY OF THE SKY** by Evelyn E. Smith

**D-113**   **OUTPOST ON THE MOON** by Joslyn Maxwell
**POTENTIAL ZERO** by S. J. Byrne

**D-114**   **OUTPOST INFINITY** by Raymond F. Jones
**THE WHITE INVADERS** by Ray Cummings

**D-115**   **TIME TRAP** by Rog Phillips
**THE COSMIC DESTROYER** by Alexander Blade

**D-116**   **THE OTHER SIDE OF THE MOON** by Edmond Hamilton
**SECRET INVASION** by Walter Kubilius

**D-117**   **DANGER MOON** by Frederik Pohl
**THE HIDDEN UNIVERSE** by Ralph Milne Farley

**D-118**   **THE WAILING ASTEROID** by Murray Leinster
**THE WORLD THAT COULDN'T BE** by Clifford D. Simak

**D-119**   **THE WHISPERING GORILLA** by Don Wilcox
**RETURN OF THE WHISPERING GORILLA** by David V. Reed

**D-120**   **SPECIAL EFFECT** by J. F. Bone
**WARLORD OF KOR** by Terry Carr

## ARMCHAIR SCIENCE FICTION CLASSICS, $12.95 each

**C-37**   **THE GREEN MAN RETURNS**
by Harold M. Sherman

**C-38**   **THE SHAVER MYSTERY, Book Five**
by Richard S, Shaver

**C-39**   **MARS CHILD**
by Cyril Judd

## ARMCHAIR MASTERS OF SCIENCE FICTION SERIES, $16.95 each

**MS-7**   **MASTERS OF SCIENCE FICTION AND FANTASY, Vol. Nine**
Poul Anderson, "The Star Beast" and other early tales

**MS-8**   **MASTERS OF SCIENCE FICTION, Vol. Ten**
Robert Moore Williams, "Time Tolls for Toro" and other tales

*If you've enjoyed this book, you will not want to miss these terrific titles...*

## ARMCHAIR SCI-FI & HORROR DOUBLE NOVELS, $12.95 each

**D-121**   **THE GENIUS BEASTS** by Frederik Pohl
   **THIS WORLD IS TABOO** by Murray Leinster

**D-122**   **THE COSMIC LOOTERS** by Edmond Hamilton
   **WANDL THE INVADER** by Ray Cummings

**D-123**   **ROBOT MEN OF BUBBLE CITY** by Rog Phillips
   **DRAGON ARMY** by William Morrison

**D-124**   **LAND BEYOND THE LENS** by S. J. Byrne
   **DIPLOMAT-AT-ARMS** by Keith Laumer

**D-125**   **VOYAGE OF THE ASTEROID, THE** by Laurence Manning
   **REVOLT OF THE OUTWORLDS** by Milton Lesser

**D-126**   **OUTLAW IN THE SKY** by Chester S. Geier
   **LEGACY FROM MARS** by Raymond Z. Gallun

**D-127**   **THE GREAT FLYING SAUCER INVASION** by Geoff St. Reynard
   **THE BIG TIME** by Fritz Leiber

**D-128**   **MIRAGE FOR PLANET X** by Stanley Mullen
   **POLICE YOUR PLANET** by Lester del Rey

**D-129**   **THE BRAIN SINNER** by Alan E. Nourse
   **DEATH FROM THE SKIES** by A. Hyatt Verrill

**D-130**   **CRY CHAOS** by Dwight V. Swain
   **THE DOOR THROUGH SPACE** By Marion Zimmer Bradley

## ARMCHAIR SCIENCE FICTION CLASSICS, $12.95 each

**C-55**   **UNDER THE TRIPLE SUNS**
   by Stanton A. Coblentz (single) 1950s, Fantasy Press

**C-56**   **STONE FROM THE GREEN STAR**
   by Jack Williamson, Amazing 10 & 11/31, (cleared by Eli)

**C-57**   **ALIEN MINDS**
   by E. Everett Evans

## ARMCHAIR SCI-FI & HORROR GEMS SERIES, $12.95 each

**G-13**   **SCIENCE FICTION GEMS, Vol. Seven**
   Jack Vance and others

**G-14**   **HORROR GEMS, Vol. Seven**
   Robert Bloch and others

*If you've enjoyed this book, you will not want to miss these terrific titles…*

*If you've enjoyed this book, you will not want to miss these terrific titles…*

## ARMCHAIR SCI-FI & HORROR DOUBLE NOVELS, $12.95 each

**D-141**   **ALL HEROES ARE HATED** by Milton Lesser
        **AND THE STARS REMAIN** by Bryan Berry

**D-142**   **LAST CALL FOR DOOMSDAY** by Edmond Hamilton
        **HUNTRESS OF AKKAN** by Robert Moore Williams

**D-143**   **THE MOON PIRATES** by Neil R. Jones
        **CALLISTO AT WAR** by Harl Vincent

**D-144**   **THUNDER IN THE DAWN** by Henry Kuttner
        **THE UNCANNY EXPERIMENTS OF DR. VARSAG** by David V. Reed

**D-145**   **A PATTERN FOR MONSTERS** by Randall Garrett
        **STAR SURGEON** by Alan E Nourse

**D-146**   **THE ATOM CURTAIN** by Nick Boddie Williams
        **WARLOCK OF SHARRADOR** by Gardner F. Fox

**D-147**   **SECRET OF THE LOST PLANET** by David Wright O'Brien
        **TELEVISION HILL** by George McLociard

**D-148**   **INTO THE GREEN PRISM** by A Hyatt Verrill
        **WANDERERS OF THE WOLF-MOON** by Nelson S. Bond

**D-149**   **MINIONS OF THE TIGER** by Chester S. Geier
        **FOUNDING FATHER** by J. F. Bone

**D-150**   **THE INVISIBLE MAN** by H. G. Wells
        **THE ISLAND OF DR. MOREAU** by H. G. Wells

## ARMCHAIR SCIENCE FICTION CLASSICS, $12.95 each

**C-61**   **THE SHAVER MYSTERY, Book Six**
        by Richard. S. Shaver

**C-62**   **CADUCEUS WILD**
        by Ward Moore & Robert Bradford

## ARMCHAIR MYSTERY-CRIME DOUBLE NOVELS, $12.95 each

**B-1**   **THE DEADLY PICK-UP** by Milton Ozaki
        **KILLER TAKE ALL** by James O. Causey

**B-2**   **THE VIOLENT ONES** by E. Howard Hunt
        **HIGH HEEL HOMICIDE** by Frederick C. Davis

**B-3**   **FURY ON SUNDAY** by Richard Matheson
        **THE AGONY COLUMN** by Earl Derr Biggers

# A DOCTOR TO THE STARS...

*Back in the 1950s when the original version of "Star Surgeon" was first written (Amazing Stories, 12/59), space opera rarely varied from the usual science fiction formulas of the day. That's why when "Star Surgeon" came out it was such a breath of fresh air to fans of the genre. Here you had a grand tale of intergalactic medicine and the men who practiced it. In fact, the tale's main character, Dal Timgar, wasn't even from good old Earth, but a non-human from the faraway planet of Garv II. Timgar had grown up wanting to be a doctor, but unfortunately only humans had ever been trained to serve in the Galactic Confederation of Worlds. This proved to be a challenge that pitted Timgar against both friends and enemies, and at times…even himself.*

*Alan E. Nourse's "Star Surgeon" is a science fiction gem that gives the reader many exciting space opera thrills, interwoven with a unique brand of medical intrigue.*

# ALAN E. NOURSE (1928-1992)

Alan E. Nourse was one of the most respected sci-fi authors of his day, writing over a dozen novels and short novels, including what is perhaps his most famous work, "The Bladerunner," which, along with a Philip K. Dick story, were the roots for Ridley Scott's epic sci-fi film, *Blade Runner*. Nourse also wrote other notable tales like "Raiders of the Rings," "Scavengers in Space," and "The Fourth Horseman."

# STAR
# SURGEON

By
ALAN E.  NOURSE

ARMCHAIR FICTION
PO Box 4369, Medford, Oregon 97504

*For more information about Armchair Books and products, visit our
website at…*

**www.armchairfiction.com**

*Or email us at…*

**armchairfiction@yahoo.com**

# CHAPTER ONE
## *The Intruder*

The shuttle plane from the port of Philadelphia to Hospital Seattle had already gone when Dal Timgar arrived at the loading platform, even though he had taken great pains to be at least thirty minutes early for the boarding.

"You'll just have to wait for the next one," the clerk at the dispatcher's desk told him unsympathetically. "There's nothing else you can do."

"But I *can't* wait," Dal said. "I have to be in Hospital Seattle by morning." He pulled out the flight schedule and held it under the clerk's nose. "Look there! The shuttle wasn't supposed to leave for another forty-five minutes!"

The clerk blinked at the schedule, and shrugged. "The seats were full, so it left," he said. "Graduation time, you know. Everybody has to be somewhere else, right away. The next shuttle goes in three hours."

"But I had a reservation on this one," Dal insisted.

"Don't be silly," the clerk said sharply. "Only graduates can get reservations this time of year—" He broke off to stare at Dal Timgar, a puzzled frown on his face. "Let me see that reservation."

Dal fumbled in his pants pocket for the yellow reservation slip. He was wishing now that he'd kept his mouth shut. He was acutely conscious of the clerk's suspicious stare, and suddenly he felt extremely awkward. The Earth-cut trousers had never really fit Dal very well; his legs were too long and spindly, and his hips too narrow to hold the pants up properly. The tailor in the Philadelphia shop had tried three times to make a jacket fit across Dal's narrow shoulders, and finally had given up in despair. Now, as he handed the reservation slip across the counter, Dal saw the clerk staring at the fine gray fur that coated the back of his hand and arm. "Here it is," he said angrily. "See for yourself."

The clerk looked at the slip and handed it back indifferently. "It's a valid reservation, all right, but there won't be another shuttle to Hospital Seattle for three hours," he said, "unless you have a priority card, of course."

"No, I'm afraid I don't," Dal said. It was a ridiculous suggestion, and the clerk knew it. Only physicians in the Black Service of Pathology and a few Four-star Surgeons had the power to commandeer public aircraft whenever they wished. "Can I get on the next shuttle?"

"You can try," the clerk said, "but you'd better be ready when they start loading. You can wait up on the ramp if you want to."

Dal turned and started across the main concourse of the great airport. He felt a stir of motion at his side, and looked down at the small pink fuzz-ball sitting in the crook of his arm. "Looks like we're out of luck, pal," he said gloomily. "If we don't get on the next plane, we'll miss the hearing altogether. Not that it's going to do us much good to be there anyway."

The little pink fuzz-ball on his arm opened a pair of black shoe-button eyes and blinked up at him, and Dal absently stroked the tiny creature with a finger. The fuzz-ball quivered happily and clung closer to Dal's side as he started up the long ramp to the observation platform. Automatic doors swung open as he reached the top, and Dal shivered in the damp night air. He could feel the gray fur that coated his back and neck rising to protect him from the coldness and dampness that his body was never intended by nature to endure.

Below him the bright lights of the landing fields and terminal buildings of the port of Philadelphia spread out in panorama, and he thought with a sudden pang of the great space-port in his native city, so very different from this one and so unthinkably far away. The field below was teeming with activity, alive with men and vehicles. Moments before, one of Earth's great hospital ships had landed, returning from a cruise deep into the heart of the galaxy, bringing in the gravely ill from a dozen star systems for care in one of Earth's hospitals. Dal watched as the long line of stretchers poured from the ship's hold with white-clad orderlies in nervous attendance. Some of the stretchers were encased in special atmosphere tanks; a siren wailed across the field as an emergency truck raced up with fresh gas bottles for a chlorine-breather from the Betelgeuse system, and a derrick crew spent fifteen minutes lifting down the special liquid ammonia tank housing a native of Aldebaran's massive sixteenth planet.

All about the field were physicians supervising the process of disembarcation, resplendent in the colors that signified their medical specialties. At the foot of the landing crane a Three-star Internist in the green cape of the Medical Service—obviously the commander of the ship—was talking with the welcoming dignitaries of Hospital Earth. Half a dozen doctors in the Blue Service of Diagnosis were checking new lab supplies ready to be loaded aboard. Three young Star Surgeons swung by just below Dal with their bright scarlet capes fluttering in the breeze, headed for customs and their first Earthside liberty in months. Dal watched them go by, and felt the sick, bitter feeling in the pit of his stomach that he had felt so often in recent months.

He had dreamed, once, of wearing the scarlet cape of the Red Service of Surgery too, with the silver star of the Star Surgeon on his collar. That had been a long time ago, over eight Earth years ago; the dream had faded slowly, but now the last vestige of hope was almost gone. He thought of the long years of intensive training he had just completed in the medical school of Hospital Philadelphia, the long nights of studying for exams, the long days spent in the laboratories and clinics in order to become a physician of Hospital Earth, and a wave of bitterness swept through his mind.

*A dream*, he thought hopelessly, *a foolish idea and nothing more. They knew before I started that they would never let me finish. They had no intention of doing so, it just amused them to watch me beat my head on a stone wall for these eight years.* But then he shook his head and felt a little ashamed of the thought. It wasn't quite true, and he knew it. He had known that it was a gamble from the very first. Black Doctor Arnquist had warned him the day he received his notice of admission to the medical school. "I can promise you nothing," the old man had said, "except a slender chance. There are those who will fight to the very end to prevent you from succeeding, and when it's all over, you may not win. But if you are willing to take that risk, at least you have a chance."

Dal had accepted the risk with his eyes wide open. He had done the best he could do, and now he had lost. True, he had not received the final, irrevocable word that he had been expelled from the medical service of Hospital Earth, but he was certain now that it was waiting for him when he arrived at Hospital Seattle the following morning.

The loading ramp was beginning to fill up, and Dal saw half a dozen of his classmates from the medical school burst through the door from the station below, shifting their day packs from their shoulders and chattering among themselves. Several of them saw him, standing by himself against the guard rail. One or two nodded coolly and turned away; the others just ignored him. Nobody greeted him, nor even smiled. Dal turned away and stared down once again at the busy activity on the field below.

"Why so gloomy, friend?" a voice behind him said. "You look as though the ship left without you."

Dal looked up at the tall, dark-haired young man, towering at his side, and smiled ruefully. "Hello, Tiger! As a matter of fact, it *did* leave. I'm waiting for the next one."

"Where to?" Frank Martin frowned down at Dal. Known as "Tiger" to everyone but the professors, the young man's nickname fit him well. He was big, even for an Earthman, and his massive shoulders and stubborn jaw only served to emphasize his bigness. Like the other recent graduates on the platform, he was wearing the colored cuff and collar of the probationary physician, in the bright green of the Green Service of Medicine. He reached out a huge hand and gently rubbed the pink fuzz-ball sitting on Dal's arm. "What's the trouble, Dal? Even Fuzzy looks worried. Where's your cuff and collar?"

"I didn't get any cuff and collar," Dal said.

"Didn't you get an assignment?" Tiger stared at him. "Or are you just taking a leave first?"

Dal shook his head. "A permanent leave, I guess," he said bitterly. "There's not going to be any assignment for me. Let's face it, Tiger. I'm washed out."

"Oh, now look here—"

"I mean it. I've been booted, and that's all there is to it."

"But you've been in the top ten in the class right through!" Tiger protested. "You know you passed your finals. What is this, anyway?"

Dal reached into his jacket and handed Tiger a blue paper envelope. "I should have expected it from the first. They sent me this instead of my cuff and collar."

Tiger opened the envelope. "From Doctor Tanner," he grunted. "The Black Plague himself. But what is it?"

"Read it," Dal said.

"'You are hereby directed to appear before the medical training council in the council chambers in Hospital Seattle at 10:00 A.M., Friday, June 24, 2375, in order that your application for assignment to a General Practice Patrol ship may be reviewed. Insignia will not be worn. Signed, Hugo Tanner, Physician, Black Service of Pathology.'" Tiger blinked at the notice and handed it back to Dal. "I don't get it," he said finally. "You applied, you're as qualified as any of us—"

"Except in one way," Dal said, "and that's the way that counts. They don't want me, Tiger. They have never wanted me. They only let me go through school because Black Doctor Arnquist made an issue of it, and they didn't quite dare to veto him. But they never intended to let me finish, not for a minute."

For a moment the two were silent, staring down at the busy landing procedures below. A warning light was flickering across the field, signaling the landing of an incoming shuttle ship, and the supply cars broke from their positions in center of the field and fled like beetles for the security of the garages. A loudspeaker blared, announcing the incoming craft. Dal Timgar turned, lifting Fuzzy gently from his arm into a side jacket pocket and shouldering his day pack. "I guess this is my flight, Tiger. I'd better get in line."

Tiger Martin gripped Dal's slender four-fingered hand tightly. "Look," he said intensely, "this is some sort of mistake that the training council will straighten out. I'm sure of it. Lots of guys have their applications reviewed. It happens all the time, but they still get their assignments."

"Do you know of any others in this class? Or the last class?"

"Maybe not," Tiger said. "But if they were washing you out, why would the council be reviewing it? Somebody must be fighting for you."

"But Black Doctor Tanner is on the council," Dal said.

"He's not the only one on the council. It's going to work out. You'll see."

"I hope so," Dal said without conviction. He started for the loading line, then turned. "But where are *you* going to be? What ship?"

Tiger hesitated. "Not assigned yet. I'm taking a leave. But you'll be hearing from me."

The loading call blared from the loudspeaker. The tall Earthman seemed about to say something more, but Dal turned away and headed across toward the line for the shuttle plane. Ten minutes later, he was aloft as the tiny plane speared up through the black night sky and turned its needle nose toward the west.

He tried to sleep, but couldn't. The shuttle trip from the Port of Philadelphia to Hospital Seattle was almost two hours long because of passenger stops at Hospital Cleveland, Eisenhower City, New Chicago, and Hospital Billings. In spite of the help of the pneumatic seats and a sleep-cap, Dal could not even doze. It was one of the perfect clear nights that often occurred in midsummer now that weather control could modify Earth's air currents so well; the stars glittered against the black velvet backdrop above, and the North American continent was free of clouds. Dal stared down at the patchwork of lights that flickered up at him from the ground below.

Passing below him were some of the great cities, the hospitals, the research and training centers, the residential zones and supply centers of Hospital Earth, medical center to the powerful Galactic Confederation, physician in charge of the health of a thousand intelligent races on a thousand planets of a thousand distant star systems. Here, he knew, was the ivory tower of galactic medicine, the hub from which the medical care of the confederation arose. From the huge hospitals, research centers, and medical schools here, the physicians of Hospital Earth went out to all corners of the galaxy. In the permanent outpost clinics, in the gigantic hospital ships that served great sectors of the galaxy, and in the

General Practice Patrol ships that roved from star system to star system, they answered the calls for medical assistance from a multitude of planets and races, wherever and whenever they were needed.

Dal Timgar had been on Hospital Earth for eight years, and still he was a stranger here. To him this was an alien planet, different in a thousand ways from the world where he was born and grew to manhood. For a moment now he thought of his native home, the second planet of a hot yellow star which Earthmen called "Garv" because they couldn't pronounce its full name in the Garvian tongue. Unthinkably distant, yet only days away with the power of the star-drive motors that its people had developed thousands of years before, Garv II was a warm planet, teeming with activity, the trading center of the galaxy and the governmental headquarters of the powerful Galactic Confederation of Worlds. Dal could remember the days before he had come to Hospital Earth, and the many times he had longed desperately to be home again.

He drew his fuzzy pink friend out of his pocket and rested him on his shoulder, felt the tiny silent creature rub happily against his neck. It had been his own decision to come here, Dal knew; there was no one else to blame. His people were not physicians. Their instincts and interests lay in trading and politics, not in the life sciences, and plague after plague had swept across his home planet in the centuries before Hospital Earth had been admitted as a probationary member of the Galactic Confederation.

But as long as Dal could remember, he had wanted to be a doctor. From the first time he had seen a General Practice Patrol ship landing in his home city to fight the plague that was killing his people by the thousands, he had known that this was what he wanted more than anything else: to be a physician of Hospital Earth, to join the ranks of the doctors who were serving the galaxy.

Many on Earth had tried to stop him from the first. He was a Garvian, alien to Earth's climate and Earth's people. The physical differences between Earthmen and Garvians were small, but just enough to set him apart and make him easily identifiable as an alien. He had one too few digits on his hands; his body was small and spindly, weighing a bare ninety pounds, and the coating of fine gray fur that covered all but his face and palms annoyingly grew longer and thicker as soon as he came to the comparatively cold climateof Hospital Earth to live. The bone structure of his face gave his cheeks and nose a flattened appearance, and his pale gray eyes seemed abnormally large and wistful. And even though it had long been known that Earthmen and Garvians were equal in range of intelligence, his classmates still assumed just from his appearance that he was either unusually clever or unusually stupid.

The gulf that lay between him and the men of Earth went beyond mere physical differences, however. Earthmen had differences of skin color, facial contour and physical size among them, yet made no sign of distinction. Dal's alienness went deeper. His classmates had been civil enough, yet with one or two exceptions, they had avoided him carefully. Clearly they resented his presence in their lecture rooms and laboratories. Clearly they felt that he did not belong there, studying medicine.

From the first they had let him know unmistakably that he was unwelcome, an intruder in their midst, the first member of an alien race ever to try to earn the insignia of a physician of Hospital Earth.

And now, Dal knew he had failed after all. He had been allowed to try only because a powerful physician in the Black Service of Pathology had befriended him. If it had not been for the friendship and support of another Earthman in the class, Tiger Martin, the eight years of study would have been unbearably lonely.

But now, he thought, it would have been far easier never to have started than to have his goal snatched away at the last minute. The notice of the council meeting left no doubt in his mind. He had failed. There would be lots of talk, some perfunctory debate for the sake of the record, and the medical council would wash their hands of him once and for all. The decision, he was certain, was already made. It was just a matter of going through the formal motions.

Dal felt the motors change in pitch, and the needle-nosed shuttle plane began to dip once more toward the horizon. Ahead he could see the sprawling lights of Hospital Seattle, stretching from the Cascade Mountains to the sea and beyond, north to Alaska and south toward the great California metropolitan centers. Somewhere down there was a council room where a dozen of the most powerful physicians on Hospital Earth, now sleeping soundly, would be meeting tomorrow for a trial that was already over, to pass a judgment that was already decided.

He slipped Fuzzy back into his pocket, shouldered his pack, and waited for the ship to come down for its landing. It would be nice, he thought wryly, if his reservations for sleeping quarters in the students' barracks might at least be honored, but now he wasn't even sure of that.

In the port of Seattle he went through the customary baggage check. He saw the clerk frown at his ill-fitting clothes and not-quite-human face, and then read his passage permit carefully before brushing him on through. Then he joined the crowd of travelers heading for the city subways. He didn't hear the loudspeaker blaring until the announcer had stumbled over his name half a dozen times.

"*Doctor Dal Timgar, please report to the information booth.*"

He hurried back to central information. "You were paging me. What is it?"

"Telephone message, sir," the announcer said, his voice surprisingly respectful. "A top priority call. Just a minute."

Moments later he had handed Dal the yellow telephone message sheet, and Dal was studying the words with a puzzled frown:

CALL AT MY QUARTERS ON ARRIVAL REGARDLESS OF HOUR STOP URGENT THAT I SEE YOU STOP REPEAT URGENT

The message was signed THORVOLD ARNQUIST, BLACK SERVICE and carried the priority seal of the Four-star Pathologist. Dal read it again, shifted his pack, and started once more for the subway ramp. He thrust the message into his pocket, and his step quickened as he heard the whistle of the pressure-tube trains up ahead.

Black Doctor Arnquist, the man who had first defended his right to study medicine on Hospital Earth, now wanted to see him before the council meeting took place.

For the first time in days, Dal Timgar felt a new flicker of hope.

# CHAPTER TWO
*Hospital Seattle*

It was a long way from the students' barracks to the pathology sector where Black Doctor Arnquist lived. Dal Timgar decided not to try to go to the barracks first. It was after midnight, and even though the message had said "regardless of hour," Dal shrank from the thought of awakening a physician of the Black Service at two o'clock in the morning. He was already later arriving at Hospital Seattle than he had expected to be, and quite possibly Black Doctor Arnquist would be retiring. It seemed better to go there without delay.

But one thing took priority. He found a quiet spot in the waiting room near the subway entrance and dug into his day pack for the pressed biscuit and the canister of water he had there. He broke off a piece of the biscuit and held it up for Fuzzy to see.

Fuzzy wriggled down onto his hand, and a tiny mouth appeared just below the shoe-button eyes. Bit by bit Dal fed his friend the biscuit, with squirts of water in between bites. Finally, when the biscuit was gone, Dal squirted the rest of the water into Fuzzy's mouth and rubbed him between the eyes. "Feel better now?" he asked.

The creature seemed to understand; he wriggled in Dal's hand and blinked his eyes sleepily. "All right, then," Dal said. "Off to sleep."

Dal started to tuck him back into his jacket pocket, but Fuzzy abruptly sprouted a pair of forelegs and began struggling fiercely to get out again. Dal grinned and replaced the little creature in the crook of his arm. "Don't like that idea so well, eh? Okay, friend. If you want to watch, that suits me."

He found a map of the city at the subway entrance, and studied it carefully. Like other hospital cities on Earth, Seattle was primarily a center for patient care and treatment rather than a supply or administrative center. Here in Seattle special facilities existed for the care of the intelligent marine races that required specialized hospital care. The depths of Puget Sound served as a vast aquatic ward system where creatures which normally lived in salt-water oceans on their native planets could be cared for, and the specialty physicians who worked with marine races had facilities here for research and teaching in their specialty. The dry-land sectors of the hospital were organized to support the aquatic wards; the surgeries, the laboratories, the pharmacies and living quarters all were arranged on the periphery of the salt-water basin, and rapid-transit tubes carried medical workers, orderlies, nurses and physicians to the widespread areas of the hospital city.

The pathology sector lay to the north of the city, and Black Doctor Arnquist was the chief pathologist of Hospital Seattle. Dal found a northbound express tube, climbed into an empty capsule, and pressed the buttons for the pathology sector. Presently the capsule was shifted automatically into the pressure tube that would carry him thirty miles north to his destination.

It was the first time Dal had ever visited a Black Doctor in his quarters, and the idea made him a little nervous. Of all the medical services on Hospital Earth, none had the power of the Black Service of Pathology. Traditionally in Earth medicine, the pathologists had always occupied a position of power and discipline. The autopsy rooms had always been the "Temples of Truth" where the final, inarguable answers in medicine were ultimately found, and for centuries pathologists had been the judges and inspectors of the profession of medicine.

And when Earth had become Hospital Earth, with status as a probationary member of the Galactic Confederation of Worlds, it was natural that the Black Service of Pathology had become the governors and policy-makers, regimenting every aspect of the medical services provided by Earth physicians.

Dal knew that the medical training council, which would be reviewing his application in just a few hours, was made up of physicians from all the services—the Green Service of Medicine, the Blue Service of Diagnosis, the Red Service of Surgery, as well as the Auxiliary Services—but the Black Doctors who sat on the council would have the final say, the final veto power.

He wondered now why Black Doctor Arnquist wanted to see him. At first he had thought there might be special news for him, word perhaps that his assignment had come through after all, that the interview tomorrow would not be held. But on reflection, he realized that didn't make sense. If that were the case, Doctor Arnquist would have said so, and directed him to report to a ship. More likely, he thought, the Black Doctor wanted to see him only to soften the blow, to help him face the decision that seemed inevitable.

He left the pneumatic tube and climbed on the jitney that wound its way through the corridors of the pathology sector and into the quiet, austere quarters of the resident pathologists. He found the proper concourse, and moments later he was pressing his thumb against the identification plate outside the Black Doctor's personal quarters.

Black Doctor Thorvold Arnquist looked older now than when Dal had last seen him. His silvery gray hair was thinning, and there were tired lines around his eyes and mouth that Dal did not remember from before. The old man's body seemed more wispy and frail than ever, and the black cloak across his shoulders rustled as he led Dal back into a book-lined study.

The Black Doctor had not yet gone to bed. On a desk in the corner of the study several books lay open, and a roll of paper was inserted in the dicto-typer. "I knew you would get the message when you arrived," he said as he took Dal's pack, "and I thought you might be later than you planned. A good trip, I trust. And your friend here? He enjoys shuttle travel?" He smiled and stroked Fuzzy with a gnarled finger. "I suppose you wonder why I wanted to see you."

Dal Timgar nodded slowly. "About the interview tomorrow?"

"Ah, yes. The interview." The Black Doctor made a sour face and shook his head. "A bad business for you, that interview. How do you feel about it?"

Dal spread his hands helplessly. As always, the Black Doctor's questions cut through the trimming to the heart of things. They were always difficult questions to answer.

"I...I suppose it's something that's necessary," he said finally.

"Oh?" the Black Doctor frowned. "But why necessary for you if not for the others? How many were there in your class, including all the services? Three hundred? And out of the three hundred only one was refused assignment." He looked up sharply at Dal, his pale blue eyes very alert in his aged face. "Right?"

"Yes, sir."

"And you really feel it's just normal procedure that your application is being challenged?"

"No, sir."

"How *do* you feel about it, Dal? Angry, maybe?"

Dal squirmed. "Yes, sir. You might say that."

"Perhaps even bitter," the Black Doctor said.

"I did as good work as anyone else in my class," Dal said hotly. "I did my part as well as anyone could, I didn't let up once all the way through. Bitter! Wouldn't you feel bitter?"

The Black Doctor nodded slowly. "Yes, I imagine I would," he said, sinking down into the chair behind the desk with a sigh. "As a matter of fact, I do feel a little bitter about it, even though I was afraid that it might come to this in the end. I can't blame you for your feelings." He took a deep breath. "I wish I could promise you that everything would be all right tomorrow, but I'm afraid I can't. The council has a right to review your qualifications, and it holds the power to assign you to a patrol ship on the spot, if it sees fit. Conceivably, a Black Doctor might force the council's approval, if he were the only representative of the Black service there. But I will not be the only Black Doctor sitting on the council tomorrow."

"I know that," Dal said.

Doctor Arnquist looked up at Dal for a long moment. "Why do you want to be a doctor in the first place, Dal? This isn't the calling of your people. You must be the one Garvian out of millions with the patience and peculiar mental make-up to permit you to master the scientific disciplines involved in studying medicine. Either you are different from the rest of your people—which I doubt—or else you are driven to force yourself into a pattern foreign to your nature for very compelling reasons. What are they? Why do you want medicine?"

It was the hardest question of all, the question Dal had dreaded. He knew the answer, just as he had known for most of his life that he wanted to be a doctor above all else. But he had never found a way to put the reasons into words. "I can't say," he said slowly. "I *know*, but I can't express it, and whenever I try, it just sounds silly."

"Maybe your reasons don't make reasonable sense," the old man said gently.

"But they do! At least to me, they do," Dal said. "I've always wanted to be a doctor. There's nothing else I want to do. To work at home, among my people."

"There was a plague on Garv II, wasn't there?" Doctor Arnquist said. "A cyclic thing that came back again and again. The cycle was broken just a few years ago, when the virus that caused it was finally isolated and destroyed."

"By the physicians of Hospital Earth," Dal said.

"It's happened again and again," the Black Doctor said. "We've seen the same pattern repeated a thousand times across the galaxy, and it has always puzzled us, just a little." He smiled. "You see, our knowledge and understanding of the life sciences here on Earth have always grown hand in hand with the physical sciences. We had always assumed that the same thing would happen on *any* planet where a race has developed intelligence and scientific methods of study. We were wrong, of course, which is the reason for the existence of Hospital Earth and her physicians today, but it still amazes us that with all the technology and civilization in the galaxy, we Earthmen are the only people yet discovered who have developed a broad knowledge of the processes of life and illness and death."

The old man looked up at his visitor, and Dal felt his pale blue eyes searching his face. "How badly do you want to be a doctor?"

"More than anything else I know," Dal said.

"Badly enough to do anything to achieve your goal?"

Dal hesitated, and stroked Fuzzy's head gently. "Well...almost anything."

The Black Doctor nodded. "And that, of course, is the reason I had to see you before this interview. I know you've played the game straight right from the beginning, up to this point. Now I beg of you not to do the thing that you are thinking of doing."

For a moment Dal just stared at the little old man in black, and felt the fur on his arms and back rise up. A wave of panic flooded his mind. *He knows!* he thought frantically. *He must be able to read minds!* But he thrust the idea away. There was no way that the Black Doctor could know. No race of creatures in the galaxy had *that* power. And yet there was no doubt that Black Doctor Arnquist knew what Dal had been thinking, just as surely as if he had said it aloud.

Dal shook his head helplessly. "I don't know what you mean."

"I think you do," Doctor Arnquist said. "Please, Dal. Trust me. This is not the time to lie. The thing that you were planning to do at the interview would be disastrous, even if it won you an assignment. It would be dishonest and unworthy."

*Then he does know!* Dal thought. *But how? I couldn't have told him, or given him any hint.* He felt Fuzzy give a frightened shiver on his arm, and then words were tumbling out of his mouth. "I don't know what you're talking about, there wasn't anything I was thinking of. I mean, what could I do? If the council wants to assign me to a ship, they will, and if they don't, they won't. I don't know what you're thinking of."

"Please." Black Doctor Arnquist held up his hand. "Naturally you defend yourself," he said. "I can't blame you for that, and I suppose this is an unforgivable breach of diplomacy even to mention it to you, but I think it must be done. Remember that we have been studying and observing your people very carefully over the past two hundred years, Dal. It is no accident that you have such a warm attachment to your little pink friend here, and it is no accident that wherever a Garvian is found, his Fuzzy is with him, isn't that so? And it is no accident that your people are such excellent tradesmen, that you are so remarkably skillful in driving bargains favorable to yourselves...that you are in fact the most powerful single race of creatures in the whole Galactic Confederation."

The old man walked to the bookshelves behind him and brought down a thick, bound manuscript. He handed it across the desk as Dal watched him. "You may read this if you like, at your leisure. Don't worry, it's not for publication, just a private study which I have never mentioned before to anyone, but the pattern is unmistakable. This peculiar talent of your people is difficult to describe: not really telepathy, but an ability to create the emotional responses in others that will be most favorable to you. Just what part your Fuzzies play in this ability of your people I am not sure, but I'm quite certain that without them you would not have it."

He smiled at Dal's stricken face. "A forbidden topic, eh? And yet perfectly true. You know right now that if you wanted to you could virtually paralyze me with fright, render me helpless to do anything but stand here and shiver, couldn't you? Or if I were hostile to your wishes, you could suddenly force me to sympathize with you and like you enormously, until I was ready to agree to anything you wanted—"

"No," Dal broke in. "Please, you don't understand! I've never done it, not once since I came to Hospital Earth."

"I know that. I've been watching you."

"And I wouldn't think of doing it."

"Not even at the council interview?"

"Never!"

"Then let me have Fuzzy now. He is the key to this special talent of your people. Give him to me now, and go to the interview without him."

Dal drew back, trembling, trying to fight down panic. He brought his hand around to the soft fur of the little pink fuzz-ball. "I...can't do that," he said weakly.

"Not even if it meant your assignment to a patrol ship?"

Dal hesitated, then shook his head. "Not even then. But I won't do what you're saying, I promise you."

For a long moment Black Doctor Arnquist stared at him. Then he smiled. "Will you give me your word?"

"Yes, I promise."

"Then I wish you good luck. I will do what I can at the interview. But now there is a bed for you here. You will need sleep if you are to present your best appearance."

## CHAPTER THREE
### *The Inquisition*

The interview was held in the main council chambers of Hospital Seattle, and Dal could feel the tension the moment he stepped into the room. He looked at the long semicircular table, and studied the impassive faces of the four-star Physicians across the table from him.

Each of the major medical services was represented this morning. In the center, presiding over the council, was a physician of the White Service, a Four-star Radiologist whose insignia gleamed on his shoulders. There were two physicians each, representing the Red Service of Surgery, the Green Service of Medicine, the Blue Service of Diagnosis, and finally, seated at either end of the table, the representatives of the Black Service of Pathology. Black Doctor Thorvold Arnquist sat to Dal's left; he smiled faintly as the young Garvian stepped forward, then busied himself among the papers on the desk before him. To Dal's right sat another Black Doctor who was not smiling.

Dal had seen him before—the chief co-ordinator of medical education on Hospital Earth, the "Black Plague" of the medical school jokes. Black Doctor Hugo Tanner was large and florid of face, blinking owlishly at Dal over his heavy horn-rimmed glasses. The glasses were purely decorative; with modern eye-cultures and transplant techniques, no Earthman had really needed glasses to correct his vision for the past two hundred years, but on Hugo Tanner's angry face they added a look of gravity and solemnity that the Black Doctor could not achieve without them. Still glaring at Dal, Doctor Tanner leaned over to speak to the Blue Doctor on his right, and they nodded and laughed unpleasantly at some private joke.

There was no place for him to sit, so Dal stood before the table, as straight as his five-foot height would allow him. He had placed Fuzzy almost defiantly on his shoulder, and from time to time he could feel the little creature quiver and huddle against his neck as though to hide from sight under his collar.

The White Doctor opened the proceedings, and at first the questions were entirely medical. "We are meeting to consider this student's application for assignment to a General Practice Patrol ship, as a probationary physician in the Red Service of Surgery. I believe you are all acquainted with his educational qualifications?"

There was an impatient murmur around the table. The White Doctor looked up at Dal. "Your name, please?"

"Dal Timgar, sir."

"Your *full* name," Black Doctor Tanner rumbled from the right-hand end of the table.

Dal took a deep breath and began to give his full Garvian name. It was untranslatable and unpronounceable to Earthmen, who could not reproduce the sequence of pops and whistles that made up the Garvian tongue. The doctors listened, blinking, as the complex family structure and ancestry which entered into every Garvian's full name continued to roll from Dal's lips. He was entering into the third generation removed of his father's lineage when Doctor Tanner held up his hand.

"All right, all right! We will accept the abbreviated name you have used on Hospital Earth. Let it be clear on the record that the applicant is a native of the second planet of the Garv system." The Black Doctor settled back in his chair and began whispering again to the Blue Doctor next to him.

A Green Doctor cleared his throat. "Doctor Timgar, what do you consider to be the basic principle that underlies the work and services of physicians of Hospital Earth?"

It was an old question, a favorite on freshman medical school examinations. "The principle that environments and life forms in the universe may be dissimilar, but that biochemical reactions are universal throughout creation," Dal said slowly.

"Well memorized," Black Doctor Tanner said sourly. "What does it mean?"

"It means that the principles of chemistry, physiology, pathology and the other life sciences, once understood, can be applied to any living creature in the universe, and will be found valid," Dal said. "As different as the various life forms may be, the basic life processes in one life form are the same, under different conditions, as the life processes in any other life form, just as hydrogen and oxygen will combine to form water anywhere in the universe where the proper physical conditions prevail."

"Very good, very good," the Green Doctor said. "But tell me this: what in your opinion is the place of surgery in a Galactic practice of medicine?"

A more difficult question, but one that Dal's training had prepared him well to answer. He answered it, and faced another question, and another. One by one, the doctors interrogated him,

Black Doctor Arnquist among them. The questions came faster and faster; some were exceedingly difficult. Once or twice Dal was stopped cold, and forced to admit that he did not know the answer. Other questions which he knew would stop other students happened to fall in fields he understood better than most, and his answers were full and succinct.

But finally the questioning tapered off, and the White Doctor shuffled his papers impatiently. "If there are no further medical questions, we can move on to another aspect of this student's application. Certain questions of policy have been raised. Black Doctor Tanner had some things to say, I believe, as co-ordinator of medical education."

The Black Doctor rose ponderously to his feet. "I have some things to say, you can be sure of that," he said, "but they have nothing to do with this Dal Timgar's educational qualifications for assignment to a General Practice Patrol ship." Black Doctor Tanner paused to glare in Dal's direction. "He has been trained in a medical school on Hospital Earth, and apparently has passed his final qualifying examinations for the Red Service of Surgery. I can't argue about that."

Black Doctor Arnquist's voice came across the room. "Then why are we having his review, Hugo? Dal Timgar's classmates all received their assignments automatically."

"Because there are other things to consider here than educational qualifications," Hugo Tanner said. "Gentlemen, consider our position for a moment. We have thousands of probationary physicians abroad in the galaxy at the present time, fine young men and women who have been trained in medical schools on Hospital Earth, and now are gaining experience and judgment while fulfilling our medical service contracts in every part of the confederation. They are probationers, but we must not forget that we physicians of Hospital Earth are also probationers. We are seeking a permanent place in this great Galactic Confederation, which was in existence many thousands of years before we even knew of its existence. It was not until our own scientists discovered the Koenig star-drive, enabling us to break free of our own solar system, that we were met face to face with a confederation of intelligent races inhabiting the galaxy—among others, the people from whom this same Dal Timgar has come."

"The history is interesting," Black Doctor Arnquist broke in, "but really, Hugo, I think most of us know it already."

"Maybe we do," Doctor Tanner said, flushing a little. "But the history is significant. Permanent membership in the confederation is contingent on two qualifications. First, we must have developed a star-drive of our own, a qualification of intelligence, if you will. The confederation has ruled that only races having a certain level of intelligence can become members. A star-drive could only be developed with a far-reaching understanding of the physical sciences, so this is a valid criterion of intelligence. But the second qualification for confederation membership is nothing more nor less than a question of usefulness."

The presiding White Doctor looked up, frowning. "Usefulness?"

"Exactly. The Galactic Confederation, with its exchange of ideas and talents, and all the wealth of civilization it has to offer, is based on a division of labor. Every member must have something to contribute, some special talent. For Earthmen, the talent was obvious very early. Our technology was primitive, our manufacturing skills mediocre, our transport and communications systems impossible. But in our understanding of the life sciences, we have far outstripped any other race in the galaxy. We had already solved the major problems of disease and longevity among our own people, while some of the most advanced races in the confederation were being reduced to helplessness by cyclic plagues which slaughtered their populations, and were caused by nothing more complex than a simple parasitic virus. Garv II is an excellent example."

One of the Red Doctors cleared his throat. "I'm afraid I don't quite see the connection. Nobody is arguing about our skill as doctors."

"Of course not," Black Doctor Tanner said. "The point is that in all the galaxy, Earthmen are by their very nature the *best* doctors, outstripping the most advanced physicians on any other planet. And this, gentlemen, is our bargaining point. We are useful to the Galactic Confederation only as physicians. The confederation needed us badly enough to admit us to probational membership, but if we ever hope to become full members of the confederation, we must demonstrate our usefulness, our unique skill, as physicians. We have worked hard to prove ourselves. We have made Hospital Earth the galactic center of study and treatment of diseases of many races. Earthmen on the General Practice Patrol ships visit planets in the remotest sections, and their reputation as physicians has grown. Every year new planets are writing full medical service contracts with us...as Earthmen serving the galaxy—"

"As *physicians* serving the galaxy," Black Doctor Arnquist's voice shot across the room.

"As far as the confederation has been concerned, the two have been synonymous," Hugo Tanner roared. "*Until now.* But now we have an alien among us. We have allowed a non-Earthman to train in our medical schools. He has completed the required work, his qualifications are acceptable, and now he proposes to go out on a patrol ship as a physician of the Red Service of Surgery. But think of what you are doing if you permit him to go! You will be proving to every planet in the confederation that they don't really need Earthmen after all, that any race from any planet might produce physicians just as capable as Earthmen."

The Black Doctor turned slowly to face Dal, his mouth set in a grim line. As he talked, his face had grown dark with anger. "Understand that I have nothing against this creature as an individual. Perhaps he would prove to be a competent physician, although I cannot believe it. Perhaps he would carry on the traditions of medical service we have worked so long to establish, although I doubt it. But I do know that if we permit him to become a qualified physician, it will be the beginning of the end for Hospital Earth. We will be selling out our sole bargaining position. We can forget our hopes for membership in the confederation, because one like him this year will mean two next year, and ten the next, and there will be no end to it. We should have stopped it eight years ago, but certain ones prevailed to admit Dal Timgar to training. If we do not stop it now, for all time, we will never be able to stop it."

Slowly the Black Doctor sat down, motioning to an orderly at the rear of the room. The orderly brought a glass of water and a small capsule which Black Doctor Tanner gulped down. The other doctors were talking heatedly among themselves as Black Doctor Arnquist rose to his feet. "Then you are claiming that our highest calling is to keep medicine in the hands of Earthmen alone?" he asked softly.

Doctor Tanner flushed. "Our highest calling is to provide good medical care for our patients," he said.

"The best possible medical care?"

"I never said otherwise."

"And yet you deny the ancient tradition that a physician's duty is to help his patients help themselves," Black Doctor Arnquist said.

"I said no such thing!" Hugo Tanner cried, jumping to his feet. "But we must protect ourselves. We have no other power, nothing else to sell."

"And I say that if we must sell our medical skill for our own benefit first, then we are not worthy to be physicians to anyone," Doctor Arnquist snapped. "You make a very convincing case, but if we examine it closely, we see that it amounts to nothing but fear and selfishness."

"Fear?" Doctor Tanner cried. "What do we have to fear if we can maintain our position? But if we must yield to a Garvian who has no business in medicine in the first place, what can we have left but fear?"

"If I were really convinced that Earthmen were the best physicians in the galaxy," Black Doctor Arnquist replied, "I don't think I'd have to be afraid."

The Black Doctor at the end of the table stood up, shaking with rage. "Listen to him!" he cried to the others. "Once again he is defending this creature and turning his back on common sense. All I ask is that we keep our skills among our own people and avoid the contamination that will surely result—"

Doctor Tanner broke off, his face suddenly white. He coughed, clutching at his chest, and sank down groping for his medicine box and the water glass. After a moment he caught his breath and shook his head. "There's nothing more I can say," he said weakly.

"I have done what I could, and the decision is up to the rest of you." He coughed again, and slowly the color came back into his face. The Blue Doctor had risen to help him, but Tanner waved him aside. "No, no, it's nothing. I allowed myself to become angry."

Black Doctor Arnquist spread his hands. "Under the circumstances, I won't belabor the point," he said, "although I think it would be good if Doctor Tanner would pause in his activities long enough for the surgery that would make his anger less dangerous to his own life. But he represents a view, and his right to state it is beyond reproach." Doctor Arnquist looked from face to face along the council table. "The decision is yours, gentlemen, I would ask only that you consider what our highest calling as physicians really is—a duty that overrides fear and selfishness. I believe Dal Timgar would be a good physician, and that this is more important than the planet of his origin. I think he would uphold the honor of Hospital Earth wherever he went, and give us his loyalty as well as his service. I will vote to accept his application, and thus cancel out my colleague's negative vote. The deciding votes will be cast by the rest of you."

He sat down, and the White Doctor looked at Dal Timgar. "It would be good if you would wait outside," he said. "We will call you as soon as a decision is reached."

Dal waited in an anteroom, feeding Fuzzy and trying to put out of his mind for a moment the heated argument still raging in the council chamber. Fuzzy was quivering with fright; unable to speak, the tiny creature nevertheless clearly experienced emotions, even though Dal himself did not know how he received impressions, nor why.

But Dal knew that there was a connection between the tiny pink creature's emotions and the peculiar talent that Black Doctor Arnquist had spoken of the night before. It was not a telepathic power that Dal and his people possessed. Just *what* it was, was difficult to define, yet Dal knew that every Garvian depended upon it to some extent in dealing with people around him. He knew that when Fuzzy was sitting on his arm he could sense the emotions of those around him—the anger, the fear, the happiness, the suspicion—and he knew that under certain circumstances, in a way he did not clearly understand, he could wilfully change the feelings of others toward himself. Not a great deal, perhaps, nor in any specific way, but just enough to make them look upon him and his wishes more favorably than they otherwise might.

Throughout his years on Hospital Earth he had vigilantly avoided using this strange talent. Already he was different enough from Earthmen in appearance, in ways of thinking, in likes and dislikes. But these differences were not advantages, and he had realized that if his classmates had ever dreamed of the advantage that he had, minor as it was, his hopes of becoming a physician would have been destroyed completely.

And in the council room he had kept his word to Doctor Arnquist. He had felt Fuzzy quivering on his shoulder; he had sensed the bitter anger in Black Doctor Tanner's mind, and the temptation deliberately to mellow that anger had been almost overwhelming, but he had turned it aside. He had answered questions that were asked him, and listened to the debate with a growing sense of hopelessness.

And now the chance was gone. The decision was being made.

He paced the floor, trying to remember the expressions of the other doctors, trying to remember what had been said, how many had seemed friendly and how many hostile, but he knew that only intensified the torture. There was nothing he could do now but wait.

At last the door opened, and an orderly nodded to him. Dal felt his legs tremble as he walked into the room and faced the semi-circle of doctors. He tried to read the answer on their faces, but even Black Doctor Arnquist sat impassively, doodling on the pad before him, refusing to meet Dal's eyes.

The White Doctor took up a sheet of paper. "We have considered your application, and have reached a decision. You will be happy to know that your application for assignment has been tentatively accepted."

Dal heard the words, and it seemed as though the room were spinning around him. He wanted to shout for joy and throw his arms around Black Doctor Arnquist, but he stood perfectly still, and suddenly he noticed that Fuzzy was very quiet on his shoulder.

"You will understand that this acceptance is not irrevocable," the White Doctor went on. "We are not willing to guarantee your ultimate acceptance as a fully qualified Star Surgeon at this point. You will be allowed to wear a collar and cuff, uniform and insignia of a probationary physician, in the Red Service, and will be assigned aboard the General Practice Patrol ship *Lancet*, leaving from Hospital Seattle next Tuesday. If you prove your ability in that post, your performance will once again be reviewed by this board, but you alone will determine our decision then. Your final acceptance as a Star Surgeon will depend entirely upon your conduct as a member of the patrol ship's crew." He smiled at Dal, and set the paper down. "The council wishes you well. Do you have any questions?"

"Just one," Dal managed to say. "Who will my crewmates be?"

"As is customary, a probationer from the Green Service of Medicine and one from the Blue Service of Diagnosis. Both have been specially selected by this council. Your Blue Doctor will be Jack Alvarez, who has shown great promise in his training in diagnostic medicine."

"And the Green Doctor?"

"A young man named Frank Martin," the White Doctor said. "Known to his friends, I believe, as 'Tiger.'"

## CHAPTER FOUR
### *The Galatic Pill Peddlers*

The ship stood tall and straight on her launching pad, with the afternoon sunlight glinting on her hull. Half a dozen crews of check-out men were swarming about her, inspecting her engine and fuel supplies, riding up the gantry crane to her entrance lock, and guiding the great cargo nets from the loading crane into her afterhold. High up on her hull Dal Timgar could see a golden caduceus emblazoned, the symbol of the General Practice Patrol, and beneath it the ship's official name:

GPPS 238

*LANCET*

Dal shifted his day pack down from his shoulders, ridiculously pleased with the gleaming scarlet braid on the collar and cuff of his uniform, and lifted Fuzzy up on his shoulder to see. It seemed to Dal that everyone he had passed in the terminal had been looking at the colorful insignia; it was all he could do to keep from holding his arm up and waving it like a banner.

"You'll get used to it," Tiger Martin chuckled as they waited for the jitney to take them across to the launching pad. "At first you think everybody is impressed by the colors, until you see some guy go past with the braid all faded and frazzled at the edges, and then you realize that you're just the latest greenhorn in a squad of two hundred thousand men."

"It's still good to be wearing it," Dal said. "I couldn't really believe it until Black Doctor Arnquist turned the collar and cuff over to me." He looked suspiciously at Tiger. "You must have known a lot more about that interview than you let on. Or, was it just coincidence that we were assigned together?"

"Not coincidence, exactly." Tiger grinned. "I didn't know what was going to happen. I'd requested assignment with you on my application, and then when yours was held up, Doctor Arnquist asked me if I'd be willing to wait for assignment until the interview was over. So I said okay. He seemed to think you had a pretty good chance."

"I'd never have made it without his backing," Dal said.

"Well, anyway, he figured that if you *were* assigned, it would be a good idea to have a friend on the patrol ship team."

"I won't argue about *that*," Dal said. "But who is the Blue Service man?"

Tiger's face darkened. "I don't know much about him," he said. "He trained in California, and I met him just once, at a diagnosis and therapy conference. He's supposed to be plenty smart, according to the grapevine. I guess he'd have to be, to pass Diagnostic Service finals." Tiger chuckled. "Any dope can make it in the Medical or Surgical Services, but diagnosis is something else again."

"Will he be in command?"

"On the *Lancet*? Why should he? We'll share command, just like any patrol ship crew. If we run into problems we can't agree on, we holler for help. But if he acts like most of the Blue Doctors I know, he'll *think* he's in command."

A jitney stopped for them, and then zoomed out across the field toward the ship. The gantry platform was just clanging to the ground, unloading three technicians and a Four-bar Electronics Engineer. Tiger and Dal rode the platform up again and moments later stepped through the entrance lock of the ship that would be their home base for months and perhaps years.

They found the bunk room to the rear of the control and lab sections. A duffel bag was already lodged on one of the bunks; one of the foot lockers was already occupied, and a small but expensive camera and a huge pair of field glasses were hanging from one of the wall brackets.

"Looks like our man has already arrived," Tiger said, tossing down his own duffel bag and looking around the cramped quarters. "Not exactly a luxury suite, I'd say. Wonder where he is?"

"Let's look up forward," Dal said. "We've plenty to do before we take off. Maybe he's just getting an early start."

They explored the ship, working their way up the central corridor past the communications and computer rooms and the laboratory into the main control and observation room. Here they found a thin, dark-haired young man in a bright blue collar and cuff, sitting engrossed with a tape-reader.

For a moment they thought he hadn't heard them. Then, as though reluctant to tear himself away, the Blue Doctor sighed, snapped off the reader, and turned on the swivel stool.

"So!" he said. "I was beginning to wonder if you were ever going to get here."

"We ran into some delays," Tiger said. He grinned and held out his hand. "Jack Alvarez? Tiger Martin. We met each other at that conference in Chicago last year."

"Yes, I remember," the Blue Doctor said. "You found some holes in a paper I gave. Matter of fact, I've plugged them up very nicely since then. You'd have trouble finding fault with the work now." Jack Alvarez turned his eyes to Dal. "And I suppose this is the Garvian I've been hearing about, complete with his little pink stooge."

The moment they had walked in the door, Dal had felt Fuzzy crouch down tight against his shoulder. Now a wave of hostility struck his mind like a shower of ice water. He had never seen this thin, dark-haired youth before, or even heard of him, but he recognized this sharp impression of hatred and anger unmistakably. He had felt it a thousand times among his medical school classmates during the past eight years, and just hours before he had felt it in the council room when Black Doctor Tanner had turned on him.

"It's really a lucky break that we have Dal for a Red Doctor," Tiger said. "We almost didn't get him."

"Yes, I heard all about how lucky we are," Jack Alvarez said sourly. He looked Dal over from the gray fur on the top of his head to the spindly legs in the ill-fitting trousers. Then the Blue Doctor shrugged in disgust and turned back to the tape-reader. "A Garvian and his Fuzzy!" he muttered. "Let's hope one or the other knows something about surgery."

"I think we'll do all right," Dal said slowly.

"I think you'd better," Jack Alvarez replied.

Dal and Tiger looked at each other, and Tiger shrugged. "It's all right," he said. "We know our jobs, and we'll manage."

Dal nodded, and started back for the bunk room. No doubt, he thought, they would manage.

But if he had thought before that the assignment on the *Lancet* was going to be easy, he knew now that he was wrong.

Tiger Martin may have been Doctor Arnquist's selection as a crewmate for him, but there was no question in his mind that the Blue Doctor on the *Lancet*'s crew was Black Doctor Hugo Tanner's choice.

The first meeting with Jack Alvarez hardly seemed promising to either Dal or Tiger, but if there was trouble coming, it was postponed for the moment by common consent. In the few days before blast-off there was no time for conflict, or even for much talk. Each of the three crewmen had two full weeks of work to accomplish in two days; each knew his job and buried himself in it with a will.

The ship's medical and surgical supplies had to be inventoried, and missing or required supplies ordered up. New supplies coming in had to be checked, tested, and stored in the ship's limited hold space. It was like preparing for an extended pack trip into wilderness country; once the *Lancet* left its home base on Hospital Earth it was a world to itself, equipped to support its physician-crew and provide the necessary equipment and data they would need to deal with the problems they would face. Like all patrol ships, the *Lancet* was equipped with automatic launching, navigation and drive mechanisms; no crew other than the three doctors was required, and in the event of mechanical failures, maintenance ships were on continual call.

The ship was responsible for patrolling an enormous area, including hundreds of stars and their planetary systems—yet its territory was only a tiny segment of the galaxy. Landings were to be made at various specified planets maintaining permanent clinic outposts of Hospital Earth; certain staple supplies were carried for each of these check points. Aside from these lonely clinic contacts, the nearest port of call for the *Lancet* was one of the hospital ships that continuously worked slow orbits through the star systems of the confederation.

But a hospital ship, with its staff of Two-star and Three-star Physicians, was not to be called except in cases of extreme need. The probationers on the patrol ships were expected to be self-sufficient. Their job was to handle diagnosis and care of all but the most difficult problems that arose in their travels. They were the first to answer the medical calls from any planet with a medical service contract with Hospital Earth.

It was an enormous responsibility for doctors-in-training to assume, but over the years it had proven the best way to train and weed out new doctors for the greater responsibilities of hospital ship and Hospital Earth assignments. There was no set period of duty on the patrol ships; how long a young doctor remained in the General Practice Patrol depended to a large extent upon how well he handled the problems and responsibilities that faced him; and since the first years of Hospital Earth, the fledgling doctors in the General Practice Patrol, the self-styled "Galactic Pill Peddlers," had lived up to their responsibilities. The reputation of Hospital Earth rested on their shoulders, and they never forgot it.

As he worked on his inventories, Dal Timgar thought of Doctor Arnquist's words to him after the council had handed down its decision. "Remember that judgment and skill are two different things," he had said. "Without skill in the basic principles of diagnosis and treatment, medical judgment isn't much help, but skill without the judgment to know how and when to use it can be downright dangerous. You'll be judged both on the judgment you use in deciding the right thing to do, and on the skill you use in doing it." He had given Dal the box with the coveted collar and cuff. "The colors are pretty, but never forget what they stand for. Until you can convince the council that you have both the skill and the judgment of a good physician, you will never get your Star. And you will be watched closely; Black Doctor Tanner and certain others will be waiting for the slightest excuse to recall you from the *Lancet*. If you give them the opportunity, nothing I can do will stop it."

And now, as they worked to prepare the ship for service, Dal was determined that the opportunity would not arise. When he was not working in the storerooms, he was in the computer room, reviewing the thousands of tapes that carried the basic information about the contract planets where they would be visiting, and the races that inhabited them. If errors and fumbles and mistakes were made by the crew of the *Lancet*, he thought grimly, it would not be Dal Timgar who made them.

The first night they met in the control room to divide the many extracurricular jobs involved in maintaining a patrol ship.

Tiger's interest in electronics and communications made him the best man to handle the radio; he accepted the post without comment. "Jack, you should be in charge of thecomputer," he said, "because you'll be the one who'll need the information first. The lab is probably your field too. Dal can be responsible for stores and supplies as well as his own surgical instruments."

Jack shrugged. "I'd just as soon handle supplies, too," he said.

"Well, there's no need to overload one man," Tiger said.

"I wouldn't mind that. But when there's something I need, I want to be sure it's going to be there without any goof-ups," Jack said.

"I can handle it all right," Dal said.

Jack just scowled. "What about the contact man when we make landings?" he asked Tiger.

"Seems to me Dal would be the one for that, too," Tiger said. "His people are traders and bargainers; right, Dal? And first contact with the people on unfamiliar planets can be important."

"It sure can," Jack said. "Too important to take chances with. Look, this is a ship from Hospital Earth. When somebody calls for help, they expect to see an Earthman turn up in response. What are they going to think when a patrol ship lands and *he* walks out?"

Tiger's face darkened. "They'll be able to see his collar and cuff, won't they?"

"Maybe. But they may wonder what he's doing wearing them."

"Well, they'll just have to learn," Tiger snapped. "And you'll have to learn, too, I guess."

Dal had been sitting silently. Now he shook his head. "I think Jack is right on this one," he said. "It would be better for one of you to be contact man."

"Why?" Tiger said angrily. "You're as much of a doctor from Hospital Earth as we are, and the sooner we get your position here straight, the better. We aren't going to have any ugly ducklings on this ship, and we aren't going to hide you in the hold every time we land on a planet. If we want to make anything but a mess of this cruise, we've got to work as a team, and that means everybody shares the important jobs."

"That's fine," Dal said, "but I still think Jack is right on this point. If we are walking into a medical problem on a planet where the patrol isn't too well known, the contact man by rights ought to be an Earthman."

Tiger started to say something, and then spread his hands helplessly. "Okay," he said. "If you're satisfied with it, let's get on to these other things." But obviously he wasn't satisfied, and when Jack disappeared toward the storeroom, Tiger turned to Dal. "You shouldn't have given in," he said. "If you give that guy as much as an inch, you're just asking for trouble."

"It isn't a matter of giving in," Dal insisted. "I think he was right, that's all. Don't let's start a fight where we don't have to."

Tiger yielded the point, but when Jack returned, Tiger avoided him, keeping to himself the rest of the evening. And later, as he tried to get to sleep, Dal wondered for a moment. Maybe Tiger was right. Maybe he was just dodging a head-on clash with the Blue Doctor now and setting the stage for a real collision later.

Next day the argument was forgotten in the air of rising excitement as embarkation orders for the *Lancet* came through. Preparations were completed, and only last-minute double-checks were required before blast-off.

But an hour before count-down began, a jitney buzzed across the field, and a Two-star Pathologist climbed aboard with his three black-cloaked orderlies. "Shakedown inspection," he said curtly. "Just a matter of routine." And with that he stalked slowly through the ship, checking the storage holds, the inventories, the lab, the computer with its information banks, and the control room. As he went along he kept firing medical questions at Dal and Tiger, hardly pausing long enough for the answers, and ignoring Jack Alvarez completely. "What's the normal range of serum cholesterol in a vegetarian race with Terran environment? How would you run a Wenberg electrophoresis? How do you determine individual radiation tolerance? How would you prepare a heart culture for cardiac transplant on board this ship?" The questions went on until Tiger and Dal were breathless, as count-down time grew closer and closer. Finally the Black Doctor turned back toward the entrance lock. He seemed vaguely disappointed as he checked the record sheets the orderlies had been keeping. With an odd look at Dal, he shrugged. "All right, here are your clearance papers," he said to Jack. "Your supply of serum globulin fractions is up to black-book requirements, but you'll run short if you happen to hit a virus epidemic; better take on a couple of more cases. And check central information just before leaving. We've signed two new contracts in the past week, and the co-ordinator's office has some advance information on both of them."

When the inspector had gone, Tiger wiped his forehead and sighed. "That was no routine shakedown!" he said. "What *is* a Wenberg electrophoresis?"

"A method of separating serum proteins," Jack Alvarez said. "You ran them in third year biochemistry. And if we *do* hit a virus epidemic, you'd better know how, too."

He gave Tiger an unpleasant smile, and started back down the corridor as the count-down signal began to buzz.

But for all the advance arrangements they had made to divide the ship's work, it was Dal Timgar who took complete control of the *Lancet* for the first two weeks of its cruise. Neither Tiger nor Jack challenged his command; not a word was raised in protest. The Earthmen were too sick to talk, much less complain about anything.

For Dal the blast-off from the port of Seattle and the conversion into Koenig star-drive was nothing new. His father owned a fleet of Garvian trading ships that traveled to the far corners of the galaxy by means of a star-drive so similar to the Koenig engines that only an electronic engineer could tell them apart. All his life Dal had traveled on the outgoing freighters with his father; star-drive conversion was no surprise to him.

But for Jack and Tiger, it was their first experience in a star-drive ship. The *Lancet*'s piloting and navigation were entirely automatic; its destination was simply coded into the drive computers, and the ship was ready to leap across light years of space in a matter of hours. But the conversion to star-drive, as the *Lancet* was wrenched, crew and all, out of the normal space-time continuum, was far outside of normal human experience. The physical and emotional shock of the conversion hit Jack and Tiger like a sledge hammer, and during the long hours while the ship was traveling through the time-less, distance-less universe of the drive to the pre-set co-ordinates where it materialized again into conventional space-time, the Earthmen were retching violently, too sick to budge from the bunk room. It took over two weeks, with stops at half a dozen contract planets, before Jack and Tiger began to adjust themselves to the frightening and confusing sensations of conversion to star-drive. During this time Dal carried the load of the ship's work alone, while the others lay gasping and exhausted in their bunks, trying to rally strength for the next shift.

To his horror, Dal discovered that the first planetary stop-over was traditionally a hazing stop. It had been a well-kept patrol secret; the outpost clinic on Tempera VI was waiting eagerly for the arrival of the new "green" crew, knowing full well that the doctors aboard would hardly be able to stumble out of their bunks, much less to cope with medical problems. The outpost men had concocted a medical "crisis" of staggering proportions to present to the *Lancet*'s crew; they were so clearly disappointed to find the ship's Red Doctor in full command of himself that Dal obligingly became violently ill too, and did his best to mimick Jack and Tiger's floundering efforts to pull themselves together and do *something* about the "problem" that suddenly descended upon them.

Later, there was a party and celebration, with music and food, as the clinic staff welcomed the pale and shaken doctors into the joke. The outpost men plied Dal for the latest news from Hospital Earth. They were surprised to see a Garvian aboard the *Lancet*, but no one at the outpost showed any sign of resentment at the scarlet braid on Dal's collar and cuff.

Slowly Jack and Tiger got used to the peculiarities of popping in and out of hyperspace. It was said that immunity to star-drive sickness was hard to acquire, but lasted a lifetime, and would never again bother them once it was achieved. Bit by bit the Earthmen crept out of their shells, to find the ship in order and a busy Dal Timgar relieved and happy to have them aboard again.

Fortunately, the medical problems that came to the *Lancet* in the first few weeks were largely routine. The ship stopped at the specified contact points—some far out near the rim of the galactic constellation, others in closer to the densely star-populated center. At each outpost clinic the *Lancet* was welcomed with open arms. The outpost men were hungry for news from home, and happy to see fresh supplies; but they were also glad to review the current medical problems on their planets with the new doctors, exchanging opinions and arguing diagnosis and therapy into the small hours of the night.

Occasionally calls came in to the ship from contract planets in need of help. Usually the problems were easy to handle. On Singall III, a tiny planet of a cooling giant star, help was needed to deal with a new outbreak of a smallpox-like plague that had once decimated the population; the disease had finally been controlled after a Hospital Earth research team had identified the organism that caused it, determined its molecular structure, and synthesized an antibiotic that could destroy it without damaging the body of the host. But now a flareup had occurred. The *Lancet* brought in supplies of the antibiotic, and Tiger Martin spent two days showing

Singallese physicians how to control further outbreaks with modern methods of immunization and antisepsis.

Another planet called for a patrol ship when a bridge-building disaster occurred; one of the beetle-like workmen had been badly crushed under a massive steel girder. Dal spent over eighteen hours straight with the patient in the *Lancet*'s surgery, carefully repairing the creature's damaged exoskeleton and grafting new segments of bone for regeneration of the hopelessly ruined parts, with Tiger administering anaesthesia and Jack preparing the grafts from the freezer.

On another planet Jack faced his first real diagnostic challenge and met the test with flying colors. Here a new cancer-like degenerative disease had been appearing among the natives of the planet. It had never before been noted. Initial attempts to find a causative agent had all three of the *Lancet*'s crew spending sleepless nights for a week, but Jack's careful study of the pattern of the disease and the biochemical reactions that accompanied it brought out the answer: the disease was caused by a rare form of genetic change which made crippling alterations in an essential enzyme system. Knowing this, Tiger quickly found a drug which could be substituted for the damaged enzyme, and the problem was solved. They left the planet, assuring the planetary government that laboratories on Hospital Earth would begin working at once to find a way actually to rebuild the damaged genes in the embryonic cells, and thus put a permanent end to the disease.

These were routine calls, the kind of ordinary general medical work that the patrol ships were expected to handle. But the visits to the various planets were welcome breaks in the pattern of patrol ship life. The *Lancet* was fully equipped, but her crew's quarters and living space were cramped. Under the best conditions, the crewmen on patrol ships got on each other's nerves; on the *Lancet* there was an additional focus of tension that grew worse with every passing hour.

From the first Jack Alvarez had made no pretense of pleasure at Dal's company, but now it seemed that he deliberately sought opportunities to annoy him. The thin Blue Doctor's face set into an angry mold whenever Dal was around. He would get up and leave when Dal entered the control room, and complained loudly and bitterly at minor flaws in Dal's shipboard work. Nothing Dal did seemed to please him.

But Tiger had a worse time controlling himself at the Blue Doctor's digs and slights than Dal did. "It's like living in an armed camp," he complained one night when Jack hadstalked angrily out of the bunk room. "Can't even open your mouth without having him jump down your throat."

"I know," Dal said.

"And he's doing it on purpose."

"Maybe so. But it won't help to lose your temper."

Tiger clenched a huge fist and slammed it into his palm. "He's just deliberately picking at you and picking at you," he said. "You can't take that forever. Something's got to break."

"It's all right," Dal assured him. "I just ignore it."

But when Jack began to shift his attack to Fuzzy, Dal could ignore it no longer.

One night in the control room Jack threw down the report he was writing and turned angrily on Dal. "Tell your friend there to turn the other way before I lose my temper and splatter him all over the wall," he said, pointing to Fuzzy. "All he does is sit there and stare at me and I'm getting fed up with it."

Fuzzy drew himself up tightly, shivering on Dal's shoulder. Dal reached up and stroked the tiny creature, and Fuzzy's shoe-button eyes disappeared completely. "There," Dal said. "Is that better?"

Jack stared at the place the eyes had been, and his face darkened suspiciously. "Well, what happened to them?" he demanded.

"What happened to what?"

"To his eyes, you idiot!"

Dal looked down at Fuzzy. "I don't see any eyes."

Jack jumped up from the stool. He scowled at Fuzzy as if commanding the eyes to come back again. All he saw was a small ball of pink fur. "Look, he's been blinking them at me for a week," he snarled. "I thought all along there was something funny about him. Sometimes he's got legs and sometimes he hasn't. Sometimes he looks fuzzy, and other times he hasn't got any hair at all."

"He's a pleomorph," Dal said. "No cellular structure at all, just a protein-colloid matrix."

Jack glowered at the inert little pink lump. "Don't be silly," he said, curious in spite of himself. "What holds him together?"

"Who knows? I don't. Some kind of electro-chemical cohesive force. The only reason he has 'eyes' is because he thinks I want him to have eyes. If you don't like it, he won't have them any more."

"Well, that's very obliging," Jack said. "But why do you keep him around? What good does he do you, anyhow? All he does is eat and drink and sleep."

"Does he have to do something?" Dal said evasively. "He isn't bothering you. Why pick on him?"

"He just seems to worry you an awful lot," Jack said unpleasantly. "Let's see him a minute." He reached out for Fuzzy, then jerked his finger back with a yelp. Blood dripped from the finger tip.

Jack's face slowly went white. "Why, he—he *bit* me!"

"Yes, and you're lucky he didn't take a finger off," Dal said, trembling with anger. "He doesn't like you any more than I do, and you'll get bit every time you come near him, so you'd better keep your hands to yourself."

"Don't worry," Jack Alvarez said, "he won't get another chance. You can just get rid of him."

"Not a chance," Dal said. "You leave him alone and he won't bother you, that's all. And the same thing goes for me."

"If he isn't out of here in twelve hours, I'll get a warrant," Jack said tightly. "There are laws against keeping dangerous pets on patrol ships."

Somewhere in the main corridor an alarm bell began buzzing. For a moment Dal and Jack stood frozen, glaring at each other. Then the door burst open and Tiger Martin's head appeared. "Hey, you two, let's get moving! We've got a call coming in, and it looks like a tough one. Come on back here!"

They headed back toward the radio room. The signal was coming through frantically as Tiger reached for the pile of punched tape running out on the floor. But as they crowded into the radio room, Dal felt Jack's hand on his arm. "If you think I was fooling, you're wrong," the Blue Doctor said through his teeth. "You've got twelve hours to get rid of him."

# CHAPTER FIVE
*Crisis on Morua VIII*

The three doctors huddled around the teletype, watching as the decoded message was punched out on the tape. "It started coming in just now," Tiger said. "And they've been beaming the signal in a spherical pattern, apparently trying to pick up the nearest ship they could get. There's certainly some sort of trouble going on."

The message was brief, repeated over and over: REQUIRE MEDICAL AID URGENT REPLY AT ONCE. This was followed by the code letters that designated the planet, its location, and the number of its medical service contract.

Jack glanced at the code. "Morua VIII," he said. "I think that's a grade I contract." He began punching buttons on the reference panel, and several screening cards came down the slot from the information bank. "Yes. The eighth planet of a large Sol-type star, the only inhabited planet in the system with a single intelligent race, ursine evolutionary pattern." He handed the cards to Tiger. "Teddy-bears, yet!"

"Mammals?" Tiger said.

"Looks like it. And they even hibernate."

"What about the contract?" Dal asked.

"Grade I," said Tiger. "And they've had a thorough survey. Moderately advanced in their own medical care, but they have full medical coverage any time they think they need it. We'd better get an acknowledgment back to them. Jack, get the ship ready to star-jump while Dal starts digging information out of the bank. If this race has its own doctors, they'd only be hollering for help if they're up against a tough one."

Tiger settled down with earphones and transmitter to try to make contact with the Moruan planet, while Jack went forward to control and Dal started to work with the tape reader. There was no argument now, and no dissension. The procedure to be followed was a well-established routine: acknowledge the call, estimate arrival time, relay the call and response to the programmers on

Hospital Earth, prepare for star-drive, and start gathering data fast. With no hint of the nature of the trouble, their job was to get there, equipped with as much information about the planet and its people as time allowed.

The Moruan system was not distant from the *Lancet*'s present location. Tiger calculated that two hours in Koenig drive would put the ship in the vicinity of the planet, with another hour required for landing procedures. He passed the word on to the others, and Dal began digging through the mass of information in the tape library on Morua VIII and its people.

There was a wealth of data. Morua VIII had signed one of the first medical service contracts with Hospital Earth, and a thorough medical, biochemical, social and psychological survey had been made on the people of that world. Since the original survey, much additional information had been amassed, based on patrol ship reports and dozens of specialty studies that had been done there.

And out of this data, a picture of Morua VIII and its inhabitants began to emerge.

The Moruans were moderately intelligent creatures, warm-blooded air breathers with an oxygen-based metabolism. Their planet was cold, with 17 per cent oxygen and much water vapor in its atmosphere. With its vast snow-fields and great mountain ranges, the planet was a popular resort area for oxygen-breathing creatures; most of the natives were engaged in some work related to winter sports. They were well fitted anatomically for their climate, with thick black fur, broad flat hind feet and a four-inch layer of fat between their skin and their vital organs.

Swiftly Dal reviewed the emergency file, checking for common drugs and chemicals that were poisonous to Moruans, accidents that were common to the race, and special problems that had been met by previous patrol ships. The deeper he dug into the mass of data, the more worried he became. Where should he begin? Searching in the dark, there was no way to guess what information would be necessary and what part totally useless.

He buzzed Tiger. "Any word on the nature of the trouble?" he asked.

"Just got through to them," Tiger said. "Not too much to go on, but they're really in an uproar. Sounds like they've started some kind of organ-transplant surgery and their native surgeon got cold feet halfway through and wants us to bail him out." Tiger paused. "I think this is going to be your show, Dal. Better check up on Moruan anatomy."

It was better than no information, but not much better. Fuzzy huddled on Dal's shoulder as if he could sense his master's excitement. Very few races under contract with Hospital Earth ever attempted their own major surgery. If a Moruan surgeon had walked into a tight spot in the operating room, it could be a real test of skill to get him—and his patient—out of it, even on a relatively simple procedure. But organ-transplantation, with the delicate vascular surgery and micro-surgery that it entailed, was never simple. In incompetent hands, it could turn into a nightmare.

Dal took a deep breath and began running the anatomical atlas tapes through the reader, checking the critical points of Moruan anatomy. Oxygen-transfer system, circulatory system, renal filtration system—at first glance, there was little resemblance to any of the "typical" oxygen-breathing mammals Dal had studied in medical school. But then something struck a familiar note, and he remembered studying the peculiar Moruan renal system, in which the creature's chemical waste products were filtered from the bloodstream in a series of tubules passing across the peritoneum, and re-absorbed into the intestine for excretion. Bit by bit other points of the anatomy came clear, and in half an hour of intense study Dal began to see how the inhabitants of Morua VIII were put together.

Satisfied for the moment, he then pulled the tapes that described the Moruans' own medical advancement. What were they doing attempting organ-transplantation, anyway? That was the kind of surgery that even experienced Star Surgeons preferred to take aboard the hospital ships, or back to Hospital Earth, where the finest equipment and the most skilled assistants were available.

There was a signal buzzer, the two-minute warning before the Koenig drive took over. Dal tossed the tape spools back into the bin for refiling, and went forward to the control room.

Just short of two hours later, the *Lancet* shifted back to normal space drive, and the cold yellow sun of the Moruan system swam into sight in the viewscreen. Far below, the tiny eighth planet glistened like a snowball in the reflection of the sun, with only occasional rents in the cloud blanket revealing the ragged surface below. The doctors watched as the ship went into descending orbit, skimming the outer atmosphere and settling into a landing pattern.

Beneath the cloud blanket, the frigid surface of the planet spread out before them. Great snow-covered mountain ranges rose up on either side. A forty-mile gale howled across the landing field, sweeping clouds of powdery snow before it.

A huge gawky vehicle seemed to be waiting for the ship to land; it shot out from the huddle of gray buildings almost the moment they touched down. Jack slipped into the furs that he had pulled from stores, and went out through the entrance lock and down the ladder to meet the dark furry creatures that were bundling out of the vehicle below. The electronic language translator was strapped to his chest.

Five minutes later he reappeared, frost forming on his blue collar, his face white as he looked at Dal. "You'd better get down there right away," he said, "and take your micro-surgical instruments. Tiger, give me a hand with the anaesthesia tanks. They're keeping a patient alive with a heart-lung machine right now, and they can't finish the job. It looks like it might be bad."

The Moruan who escorted them across the city to the hospital was a huge shaggy creature who left no question of the evolutionary line of his people. Except for the flattened nose, the high forehead and the fur-less hand with opposing thumb, he looked for all the world like a mammoth edition of the Kodiak bears Dal had seen displayed at the natural history museum in Hospital Philadelphia. Like all creatures with oxygen-and-water based metabolisms, the Moruans could trace their evolutionary line to minute one-celled salt-water creatures; but with the bitter cold of the planet, the first land-creatures to emerge from the primeval swamp of Morua VIII had developed the heavy furs and the hibernation characteristics of bear-like mammals. They towered over Dal, and even Tiger seemed dwarfed by their immense chest girth and powerful shoulders.

As the surface car hurried toward the hospital, Dal probed for more information. The Moruan's voice was a hoarse growl which nearly deafened the Earthmen in the confined quarters of the car but Dal with the aid of the translator could piece together what had happened.

More sophisticated in medical knowledge than most races in the galaxy, the Moruans had learned a great deal from their contact with Hospital Earth physicians. They actually did have a remarkable grasp of physiology and biochemistry, and constantly sought to learn more. They had already found ways to grow replacement organs from embryonic grafts, the Moruan said, and by copying the techniques used by the surgeons of Hospital Earth, their own surgeons had attempted the delicate job of replacing a diseased organ with a new, healthy one in a young male afflicted with cancer.

Dal looked up at the Moruan doctor. "What organ were you replacing?" he asked suspiciously.

"Oh, not the entire organ, just a segment," the Moruan said. "The tumor had caused an obstructive pneumonia—"

"Are you talking about a segment of *lung*?" Dal said, almost choking.

"Of course. That's where the tumor was."

Dal swallowed hard. "So you just decided to replace a segment."

"Yes. But something has gone wrong, we don't know what."

"I see." It was all Dal could do to keep from shouting at the huge creature. The Moruans had no duplication of organs, such as Earthmen and certain other races had. A tumor of the lung would mean death...but the technique of grafting a culture-grown lung segment to a portion of natural lung required enormous surgical skill, and the finest microscopic instruments that could be made in order to suture together the tiny capillary walls and air tubules. And if one lung were destroyed, a Moruan had no other to take its place. "Do you have any micro-surgical instruments at all?"

"Oh, yes," the Moruan rumbled proudly. "We made them ourselves, just for this case."

"You mean you've never attempted this procedure before?"

"This was the first time. We don't know where we went wrong."

"You went wrong when you thought about trying it," Dal muttered. "What anaesthesia?"

"Oxygen and alcohol vapor."

This was no surprise. With many species, alcohol vapor was more effective and less toxic than other anaesthetic gases. "And you have a heart-lung machine?"

"The finest available, on lease from Hospital Earth."

All the way through the city Dal continued the questioning, and by the time they reached the hospital he had an idea of the task that was facing him. He knew now that it was going to be bad; he didn't realize just how bad until he walked into the operating room.

The patient was barely alive. Recognizing too late that they were in water too deep for them, the Moruan surgeons had gone into panic, and neglected the very fundamentals of physiological support for the creature on the table. Dal had to climb up on a platform just to see the operating field; the faithful wheeze of the heart-lung machine that was sustaining the creature continued in Dal's ears as he examined the work already done, first with the naked eye, then scanning the operative field with the crude microscopic eyepiece.

"How long has he been anaesthetized?" he asked the shaggy operating surgeon.

"Over eighteen hours already."

"And how much blood has he received?"

"A dozen liters."

"Any more on hand?"

"Perhaps six more."

"Well, you'd better get it into him. He's in shock right now."

The surgeon scurried away while Dal took another look at the micro field. The situation was bad; the anaesthesia had already gone on too long, and the blood chemistry record showed progressive failure.

He stepped down from the platform, trying to clear his head and decide the right thing to do.

He had done micro-surgery before, plenty of it, and he knew the techniques necessary to complete the job, but the thought of attempting it chilled him. At best, he was on unfamiliar ground, with a dozen factors that could go wrong. By now the patient was a dreadful risk for any surgeon. If he were to step in now, and the patient died, how would he explain not calling for help?

He stepped out to the scrub room where Tiger was waiting. "Where's Jack?" he said.

"Went back to the ship for the rest of the surgical pack."

Dal shook his head. "I don't know what to do. I think we should get him to a hospital ship."

"Is it more than you can handle?" Tiger said.

"I could probably do it all right—but I could lose him, too."

A frown creased Tiger's face. "Dal, it would take six hours for a hospital ship to get here."

"I know that. But on the other hand..." Dal spread his hands. He felt Fuzzy crouching in a tight frightened lump in his pocket. He thought again of the delicate, painstaking microscopic work that remained to be done to bring the new section of lung into position to function, and he shook his head. "Look, these creatures hibernate," he said. "If we could get him cooled down enough, we could lighten the anaesthesia and maintain him as is, indefinitely."

"This is up to you," Tiger said. "I don't know anything about surgery. If you think we should just hold tight, that's what we'll do."

"All right. I think we'd better. Have them notify Jack to signal for a hospital ship. We'll just try to stick it out."

Tiger left to pass the word, and Dal went back into the operating room. Suddenly he felt as if a great weight had been lifted from his shoulders. There would be Three-star Surgeons on a Hospital Ship to handle this; it seemed an enormous relief to have the task out of his hands. Yet something was wriggling uncomfortably in the back of his mind, a quiet little voice saying *this isn't right, you should be doing this yourself right now instead of wasting precious time...*

He thrust the thought away angrily and ordered the Moruan physicians to bring in ice packs to cool the patient's huge hulk down to hibernation temperatures. "We're going to send for help," Dal told the Moruan surgeon who had met them at the ship. "This man needs specialized care, and we'd be taking too much chance to try to do it this way."

"You mean you're sending for a hospital ship?"

"That's right," Dal said.

This news seemed to upset the Moruans enormously. They began growling among themselves, moving back from the operating table.

"Then you can't save him?" the operating surgeon said.

"I think he can be saved, certainly!"

"But we thought you could just step in—"

"I could, but that would be taking chances that we don't need to take. We can maintain him until the hospital ship arrives."

The Moruans continued to growl ominously, but Dal brushed past them, checking the vital signs of the patient as his body temperature slowly dropped. Tiger had taken over the anaesthesia, keeping the patient under as light a dosage of medication as was possible.

"What's eating them?" he asked Dal quietly.

"They don't want a hospital ship here very much," Dal said. "Afraid they'll look like fools all over the Confederation if the word gets out. But that's their worry. Ours is to keep this bruiser alive until the ship gets here."

They settled back to wait.

It was an agonizing time for Dal. Even Fuzzy didn't seem to be much comfort. The patient was clearly not doing well, even with the low body temperatures Dal had induced. His blood pressure was sagging, and at one time Tiger sat up sharply, staring at his anaesthesia dials and frowning in alarm as the nervous-system reactions flagged. The Moruan physicians hovered about, increasingly uneasy as they saw the doctors from Hospital Earth waiting and doing nothing. One of them, unable to control himself any longer, tore off his sterile gown and stalked angrily out of the operating suite.

A dozen times Dal was on the verge of stepping in. It was beginning to look now like a race with time, and precious minutes were passing by. He cursed himself inwardly for not taking the bit in his teeth at the beginning and going ahead the best he could; it had been a mistake in judgment to wait. Now, as minutes passed into hours it looked more and more like a mistake that was going to cost the life of a patient.

Then there was a murmur of excitement outside the operating room, and word came in that another ship had been sighted making landing maneuvers. Dal clenched his fists, praying that the patient would last until the hospital ship crew arrived.

But the ship that was landing was not a hospital ship. Someone turned on a TV scanner and picked up the image of a small ship hardly larger than a patrol ship, with just two passengers stepping down the ladder to the ground. Then the camera went close-up. Dal saw the faces of the two men, and his heart sank.

One was a Four-star Surgeon, resplendent in flowing red cape and glistening silver insignia. Dal did not recognize the man, but the four stars meant that he was a top-ranking physician in the Red Service of Surgery.

The other passenger, gathering his black cloak and hood around him as he faced the blistering wind on the landing field, was Black Doctor Hugo Tanner.

Moments after the Four-star Surgeon arrived at the hospital, he was fully and unmistakably in command of the situation. He gave Dal an icy stare, then turned to the Moruan operating surgeon, whom he seemed to know very well. After a short barrage of questions and answers, he scrubbed and gowned, and stalked past Dal to the crude Moruan micro-surgical control table.

It took him exactly fifteen seconds to scan the entire operating field through the viewer, discussing the anatomy as the Moruan surgeon watched on a connecting screen. Then, without hesitation, he began manipulating the micro-instruments. Once or twice he murmured something to Tiger at the anaesthesia controls, and occasionally he nodded reassurance to the Moruan surgeon. He did not even invite Dal to observe.

Ten minutes later he rose from the control table and threw the switch to stop the heart-lung machine. The patient took a gasping breath on his own, then another and another. The Four-star Surgeon stripped off his gown and gloves with a flourish. "It will be all right," he said to the Moruan physician. "An excellent job,

Doctor, excellent!" he said. "Your technique was flawless, except for the tiny matter you have just observed."

It was not until they were outside the operating room and beyond earshot of the Moruan doctors that the Four-star surgeon turned furiously to Dal. "Didn't you even bother to examine the operating field, Doctor? Where did you study surgery? Couldn't you tell that the fools had practically finished the job themselves? All that was needed was a simple great-vessel graft, which an untrained idiot could have done blindfolded. And for this you call me clear from Hospital Earth!"

The surgeon threw down his mask in disgust and stalked away, leaving Dal and Tiger staring at each other in dismay.

## CHAPTER SIX
### Tiger Makes a Promise

"I think," Black Doctor Hugo Tanner said ominously, "that an explanation is in order. I would now like to hear it. And believe me, gentlemen, it had better be a very sensible explanation, too."

The pathologist was sitting in the control room of the *Lancet*, his glasses slightly askew on his florid face. He had climbed through the entrance lock ten minutes before, shaking snow off his cloak and wheezing like a boiler about to explode; now he faced the patrol ship's crew like a small but ominous black thundercloud. Across the room, Jack Alvarez was staring through the viewscreen at the blizzard howling across the landing field below, a small satisfied smile on his face, while Tiger sulked with his hands jammed into his trousers. Dal sat by himself feeling very much alone, with Fuzzy peering discreetly out of his jacket pocket.

He knew the Black Doctor was speaking to him, but he didn't try to reply. He had known from the moment the surgeon came out of the operating room that he was in trouble. It was just a matter of time before he would have to answer for his decision here, and it was even something of a relief that the moment came sooner rather than later.

And the more Dal considered his position, the more indefensible it appeared. Time after time he had thought of Dr. Arnquist's words about judgment and skill. Without one the other was of little value to a doctor, and whatever his skill as a surgeon might have been in the Moruan operating room, he now realized that his judgment had been poor. He had allowed himself to panic at a critical moment, and had failed to see how far the surgery had really progressed. By deciding to wait for help to arrive instead of taking over at once, he had placed the patient in even greater jeopardy than before. In looking back, Dal could see clearly that it would have been far better judgment to proceed on his own.

But that was how it looked *now*, not *then*, and there was an old saying that the "retrospectoscope" was the only infallible instrument in all medicine.

In any event, the thing was done, and couldn't be changed, and Dal knew that he could only stand on what he had done, right or wrong.

"Well, I'm waiting," Black Doctor Tanner said, scowling at Dal through his thick-rimmed glasses. "I want to know who was responsible for this fiasco, and why it occurred in the first place."

Dal spread his hands hopelessly. "What do you want me to say?" he asked. "I took a careful history of the situation as soon as we arrived here, and then I examined the patient in the operating room. I thought the surgery might be over my head, and couldn't see attempting it if a hospital ship could be reached in time. I thought the patient could be maintained safely long enough for us to call for help."

"I see," the Black Doctor said. "You've done micro-surgery before?"

"Yes, sir."

"And organ transplant work?"

"Yes, sir."

The Black Doctor opened a folder and peered at it over his glasses. "As a matter of fact, you spent two solid years in micro-surgical training in Hospital Philadelphia, with all sorts of glowing reports from your preceptors about what a flair you had for the work."

Dal shook his head. "I—I did some work in the field, yes, but not on critical cases under field conditions."

"You mean that this case required some different kind of technique than the cases you've worked on before?"

"No, not really, but—"

"But you just couldn't quite shoulder the responsibility the job involved when you got into a pinch without any help around," the Black Doctor growled.

"I just thought it would be safer to wait," Dal said helplessly.

"A good conservative approach," Dr. Tanner sneered. "Of course, you realized that prolonged anaesthesia in itself could threaten that patient's life?"

"Yes, sir."

"And you saw the patient's condition steadily deteriorating while you waited, did you not?"

"It was too late to change my mind then," Dal said desperately. "We'd sent for you. We knew that it would be only a matter of hours before you arrived."

"Indeed," the Black Doctor said. "Unfortunately, it takes only seconds for a patient to cross the line between life and death, not hours. And I suppose you would have stood therequietly and allowed him to expire if we had not arrived at the time we did?"

Dal shook his head miserably. There was nothing he could answer to that, and he realized it. What could he say? That the situation seemed quite different now than it had under pressure in the Moruan operating room? That he would have been blamed just as much if he had gone ahead, and then lost the case? His fingers stole down to Fuzzy's soft warm body for comfort, and he felt the little creature cling closer to his side.

The Black Doctor looked up at the others. "Well? What do the rest of you have to say?"

Jack Alvarez shrugged his shoulders. "I'm not a surgeon," he said, "but even I could see that *something* should be done without delay."

"And what does the Green Doctor think?"

Tiger shrugged. "We misjudged the situation, that's all. It came out fortunately for the patient, why make all this fuss about it?"

"Because there are other things at stake than just medical considerations," the Black Doctor shot back. "This planet has a grade I contract with Hospital Earth. We guarantee them full medical coverage of all situations and promise them immediate response to any call for medical help that they may send us. It is the most favorable kind of contract we have; when Morua VIII calls for help they expect their call to be answered by expert medical attention, not by inept bungling."

The Black Doctor leafed through the folder in his hands. "We have built our reputation in the Galactic Confederation on this kind of contract, and our admission to full membership in the Confederation will ultimately depend upon how we fulfill our promises. Poor medical judgment cannot be condoned under any circumstances—but above all, we cannot afford to jeopardize a contract."

Dal stared at him. "I—I had no intention of jeopardizing a contract," he faltered.

"Perhaps not," the Black Doctor said. "But you were the doctor on the spot, and you were so obviously incompetent to handle the situation that even these clumsy Moruan surgeons could see it. Their faith in the doctors from Hospital Earth has been severely shaken. They are even talking of letting their contract lapse at the end of this term."

Tiger Martin jumped to his feet. "Doctor Tanner, even Four-star Surgeons lose patients sometimes. These people should be glad that the doctor they call has sense enough to call for help if he needs it."

"But no help was needed," the Black Doctor said angrily. "Any half-decent surgeon would have handled the case. If the Moruans see a patrol ship bring in one incompetent doctor, what are they going to expect the next time they have need for help? How can they feel sure that their medical needs are well taken care of?" He shook his head grimly. "This is the sort of responsibility that doctors on the patrol ships are expected to assume. If you call for help where there is need for help, no one will ever complain; but when you turn and run the moment things get tough, you are not fit for patrol ship service."

The Black Doctor turned to Dal Timgar. "You had ample warning," he said. "It was clearly understood that your assignment on this ship depended upon the fulfillment of the duties of Red Doctor here, and now at the first real test you turn and run instead of doing your job. All right. You had your opportunity. You can't complain that we haven't given you a chance. According to the conduct code of the General Practice Patrol, section XIV, paragraph 2, any physician in the patrol on probationary status who is found delinquent in executing his duties may be relieved of his assignment at the order of any Black Doctor, or any other physician of four-star rank." Doctor Tanner closed the folder with a snap of finality. "It seems to me that the case is clear. Dal Timgar, on the authority of the Code, I am now relieving you of duty—"

"Just a minute," Tiger Martin burst out.

The Black Doctor looked up at him. "Well?"

"This is ridiculous," Tiger said. "Why are you picking on *him*? Or do you mean that you're relieving all three of us?"

"Of course I'm not relieving all three of you," the Black Doctor snapped. "You and Dr. Alvarez will remain on duty and conduct the ship's program without a Red Doctor until a man is sent to replace this bungler. That also is provided for in the code."

"But I understood that we were operating as a diagnostic and therapeutic team," Tiger protested. "And I seem to remember something in the code about fixing responsibility before a man can be relieved."

"There's no question where the responsibility lies," the Black Doctor said, his face darkening. "This was a surgical problem, and Dal Timgar made the decisions. I don't see anything to argue."

"There's plenty to argue," Tiger said. "Dal, don't you see what he's trying to do?"

Across the room Dal shook his head wearily. "You'd better keep out of it, Tiger," he said.

"Why should I keep out of it and let you be drummed out of the patrol for something that wasn't even your fault?" Tiger said. He turned angrily to the Black Doctor. "Dal wasn't the one that wanted the hospital ship called," he said. "I was. If you're going to relieve somebody, you'd better make it me."

The Black Doctor pulled off his glasses and glared at Tiger. "Whatever are you talking about?" he said.

"Just what I said. We had a conference after he'd examined the patient in the operating room, and I insisted that we call the hospital ship. Why, Dal—Dal wanted to go ahead and try to finish the case right then, and I wouldn't let him," Tiger blundered on. "I didn't think the patient could take it. I thought that it would be too great a risk with the facilities we had here."

Dal was staring at Tiger, and he felt Fuzzy suddenly shivering violently in his pocket. "Tiger, don't be foolish—"

The Black Doctor slammed the file down on the table again. "Is this true, what he's saying?" he asked Dal.

"No, not a word of it," Dal said. "I wanted to call the hospital ship."

"Of course he won't admit it," Tiger said angrily. "He's afraid you'll kick me out too, but it's true just the same in spite of what he says."

"And what do *you* say?" the Black Doctor said, turning to Jack Alvarez.

"I say it's carrying this big brother act too far," Jack said. "I didn't notice any conferences going on."

"You were back at the ship getting the surgical pack," Tiger said. "You didn't know anything about it. You didn't hear us talking, and we didn't see any reason to consult you about it."

The Black Doctor stared from Dal to Tiger, his face growing angrier by the minute. He jerked to his feet, and stalked back and forth across the control room, glaring at them. Then he took a capsule from his pocket, gulped it down with some water, and sat back down. "I ought to throw you both out on your ears," he snarled. "But I am forced to control myself. I mustn't allow myself to get angry—" He crashed his fist down on the control panel. "I suppose that you would swear to this statement of yours if it came to that?" he asked Tiger.

Tiger nodded and swallowed hard. "Yes, sir, I certainly would."

"All right," the Black Doctor said tightly. "Then you win this one. The code says that two opinions can properly decide any course of action. If you insist that two of you agreed on this decision, then I am forced to support you officially. I will make a report of the incident to patrol headquarters, and it will go on the permanent records of all three of this ship's crew—including my personal opinion of the decision." He looked up at Dal. "But be very careful, my young friend. Next time you may not have a technicality to back you up, and I'll be watching for the first plausible excuse to break you, and your Green Doctor friend as well. One misstep, and you're through. And I assure you that is not just an idle threat. I mean every word of it."

And trembling with rage, the Black Doctor picked up the folder, wrapped his cape around him, and marched out of the control room.

"Well, you put on a great show," Jack Alvarez said later as they prepared the ship for launching from the snow-swept landing field on Morua VIII. An hour before the ground had trembled as the Black Doctor's ship took off with Dr. Tanner and the Four-star Surgeon aboard; now Jack broke the dark silence in the *Lancet*'s control room for the first time. "A really great show. You missed your calling, Tiger. You should have been on the stage. If you think you fooled Dr. Tanner with that story for half a second, you're crazy,but I guess you got what you wanted. You kept your pal's cuff and collar for him, and you put a black mark on all of our records, including mine. I hope you're satisfied."

Tiger Martin took off his earphones and set them carefully on the control panel. "You know," he said to Jack, "you're lucky."

"Really?"

"You're lucky I don't wipe that sneer off your face and scrub the walls with it. And you'd better not crowd your luck, because all I need right now is an invitation." He stood up, towering over the dark-haired Blue Doctor. "You bet I'm satisfied. And if you got a black mark along with the rest of us, you earned it all the way."

"That still doesn't make it right," Dal said from across the room.

"You just keep out of this for a minute," Tiger said. "Jack has got to get a couple of things straight, and this is the time for it right now."

Dal shook his head. "I can't keep out of it," he said. "You got me off the hook by shifting the blame, but you put yourself in trouble doing it. Dr. Tanner could just as well have thrown us both out of the service as not."

Tiger snorted. "On what grounds? For a petty little error like this? He wouldn't dare! You ought to read the log books of some of the other GPP ships some time and see the kind of bloopers they pull without even a reprimand. Don't worry, he was mad enough to throw us both out if he thought he could make it stick, but he knew he couldn't. He knew the council would just review the case and reverse his decision."

"It was still my error, not yours," Dal protested. "I should have gone ahead and finished the case on the spot. I knew it at the time, and I just didn't quite dare."

"So you made a mistake," Tiger said. "You'll make a dozen more before you get your Star, and if none of them amount to any more than this one, you can be very happy." He scowled at Jack. "It's only thanks to our friend here that the Black Doctor heard about this at all. A hospital ship would have come to take the patient aboard, and the local doctors would have been quieted down and that would have been all there was to it. This business about losing a contract is a lot of nonsense."

"Then you think this thing was just used as an excuse to get at me?"

"Ask him," Tiger said, looking at Jack again. "Ask him why a Black Doctor and a Four-star Surgeon turned up when we just called for a hospital ship."

"I called the hospital ship," Jack said sullenly.

"But you called Dr. Tanner too," said Tiger. "Your nose has been out of joint ever since Dal came aboard this ship. You've made things as miserable for him as you could, and you just couldn't wait for a chance to come along to try to scuttle him."

"All right," Jack said, "but he was making a mistake. Anybody could see that. What if the patient had died while he was standing around waiting? Isn't that important?"

Tiger started to answer, and then threw up his hands in disgust. "It's important—but something else is more important. We've got a job to do on this ship, and we can't do it fighting each other. Dal misjudged a case and got in trouble. Fine, he won't make that mistake again. It could just as well have been you, or me. We'll all make mistakes, but if we can't work as a team, we're sunk. We'll all be drummed out of the patrol before a year is out." Tiger stopped to catch his breath, his face flushed with anger. "Well, I'm fed up with this back-stabbing business. I don't want a fight any more than Dal does, but if I have to fight, I'll fight to get it over with, and you'd better be careful. If you pull any more sly ones, you'd better include me in the deal, because if Dal goes, I go too. And that's a promise."

There was silence for a moment as Jack stared up at Tiger's angry face. He shook his head and blinked, as though he couldn't quite believe what he was hearing. He looked across at Dal, and then back at Tiger again. "You mean you'd turn in your collar and cuff?" he said.

"If it came to that."

"I see." Jack sat down at the control panel, still shaking his head. "I think you really mean it," he said soberly. "This isn't just a big brother act. You really like the guy, don't you?"

"Maybe I do," Tiger said, "but I don't like to watch anybody get kicked around just because somebody else doesn't happen to like him."

The control room was very quiet. Then somewhere below a motor clicked on, and the ventilation fan made a quiet whirring sound. The teletype clicked sporadically down the corridor in the communications room. Dal sat silently, rubbing Fuzzy between the eyes and watching the two Earthmen. It seemed suddenly as if they were talking about somebody a million miles away, as if he were not even in the room.

Then the Blue Doctor shrugged and rose to his feet. "All right," he said to Tiger. "I guess I just didn't understand where you stood, and I suppose it wasn't my job to let the Black Doctor know about the situation here. I don't plan to be making all the mistakes you think we're going to make, and I won't take the blame for anybody else's, but I guess we've got to work together in the tight spots." He gave Dal a lop-sided grin. "Welcome aboard," he said. "We'd better get this crate airborne before the people here come and cart it away."

They moved then, and the subject was dropped. Half an hour later the *Lancet* lifted through the atmospheric pull of the Moruan planet and moved on toward the next contact point, leaving the recovering patient in the hands of the native physicians. It was not until hours later that Dal noticed that Fuzzy had stopped quivering, and was resting happily and securely on his shoulder even when the Blue Doctor was near.

## CHAPTER SEVEN
*Alarums and Excursions*

Once more the crew of the *Lancet* settled down to routine, and the incident on Morua VIII seemed almost forgotten.

But a change had come about in the relations between the three doctors, and in every way the change was for the better. If Jack Alvarez was not exactly cordial to Dal Timgar, at least he had dropped the open antagonism that he had shown before. Apparently Tiger's angry outburst had startled Jack, as though he had never really considered that the big Earthman might honestly be attached to his friend from Garv II, and the Blue Doctor seemed sincere in his agreement to work with Dal and Tiger as a team.

But bit by bit Dal could sense that the change in Jack's attitude went deeper than the surface. "You know, I really think he was *scared* of me," Dal said one night when he and Tiger were alone. "Sounds silly, but I think it's true. He pretends to be so sure of himself, but I think he's as worried about doing things wrong as we are, and just won't admit it.And he really thought I was a threat when I came aboard."

"He probably had a good thorough briefing from Black Doctor Tanner before he got the assignment," Tiger said grimly.

"Maybe—but somehow I don't think he cares for the Black Doctor much more than we do."

But whatever the reason, much of the tension was gone when the *Lancet* had left the Moruan system behind. A great weight seemed to have been lifted, and if there was not quite peace on board, at least there was an uneasy truce. Tiger and Jack were almost friendly, talking together more often and getting to know each other better. Jack still avoided Dal and seldom included him in conversations, but the open contempt of the first few weeks on the ship now seemed tempered somewhat.

Once again the *Lancet*'s calls fell into a pattern. Landings on the outpost planets became routine, bright spots in a lonely and wandering existence. The calls that came in represented few real problems. The ship stopped at one contract planet to organize a mass inoculation program against a parasitic infestation resembling malaria. They paused at another place to teach the native doctors the use of some new surgical instruments that had been developed in Hospital Earth laboratories just for them. Frantic emergency calls usually proved to involve trivial problems, but once or twice potentially serious situations were spotted early, before they could develop into real trouble.

And as the three doctors got used to the responsibilities of a patrol ship's rounds, and grew more confident of their ability to handle the problems thrust upon them, they found themselves working more and more efficiently as a team.

This was the way the General Practice Patrol was supposed to function. Each doctor had unsuspected skills that came to light. There was no questioning Jack Alvarez's skill as a diagnostician, but it seemed uncanny to Dal the way the slender, dark-haired Earthman could listen carefully to a medical problem of an alien race on a remote planet, and then seem to know exactly which questions to ask to draw out the significant information about the situation. Tiger was not nearly as quick and clever as Jack; he needed more time to ponder a question of medical treatment, and he would often spend long hours poring over the data tapes before deciding what to do in a given case—but he always seemed to come up with an answer, and his answers usually worked. Above all, Tiger's relations with the odd life-forms they encountered were invariably good; the creatures seemed to like him, and would follow his instructions faithfully.

Dal, too, had opportunities to demonstrate that his surgical skill and judgment was not universally faulty in spite of the trouble on Morua VIII. More than once he succeeded in almost impossible surgical cases where there was no time to call for help, and little by little he could sense Jack's growing confidence in his abilities, grudging though it might be.

Dal had ample time to mull over the thing that had happened on Morua VIII and to think about the interview with Black Doctor Tanner afterward. He knew he was glad that Tiger had intervened even on the basis of a falsehood; until Tiger had spoken up Dal had been certain that the Black Doctor fully intended to use the incident as an excuse to discharge him from the General Practice Patrol. There was no question in his mind that the Black Doctor's charges had been exaggerated into a trumped-up case against him, and there was no question that Tiger's insistence on taking the blame had saved him; he could not help being thankful.

Yet there was something about it that disturbed Dal, nibbling away persistently at his mind. He couldn't throw off the feeling that his own acceptance of Tiger's help had been wrong.

Part of it, he knew, was his native, inbred loathing for falsehood. Fair or unfair, Dal had always disliked lying. Among his people, the truth might be bent occasionally, but frank lying was considered a deep disgrace, and there was a Garvian saying that "a false tongue wins no true friends." Garvian traders were known throughout the Galaxy as much for their rigid adherence to their word as they were for the hard bargains they could drive; Dal had been enormously confused during his first months on Hospital Earth by the way Earthmen seemed to accept lying as part of their daily life, unconcerned about it as long as the falsehood could not be proven.

But something else about Tiger's defense of him bothered Dal far more than the falsehood—something that had vaguely disturbed him ever since he had known the big Earthman, and that now seemed to elude him every time he tried to pinpoint it. Lying in his bunk during a sleep period, Dal remembered vividly the first time he had met Tiger, early in the second year of medical school. Dal had almost despaired by then of making friends with his hostile and resentful classmates and had begun more and more to avoid contact with them, building up a protective shell and relying on Fuzzy for company or comfort. Then Tiger had found him eating lunch by himself in the medical school lounge one day and flopped down in the seat beside him and began talking as if Dal were just another classmate. Tiger's open friendliness had been like a spring breeze to Dal who was desperately lonely in this world of strangers; their friendship had grown rapidly, and gradually others in the class had begun to thaw enough at least to be civil when Dal was around. Dal had sensed that this change of heart was largely because of Tiger and not because of him, yet he had welcomed it as a change from the previous intolerable coldness even though it left him feeling vaguely uneasy. Tiger was well liked by the others in the class; Dal had been grateful more than once when Tiger had risen in hot defense of the Garvian's right to be studying medicine among Earthmen in the school on Hospital Earth.

But that had been in medical school, among classmates. Somehow that had been different from the incident that occurred on Morua VIII, and Dal's uneasiness grew stronger than ever the more he thought of it. Talking to Tiger about it was no help; Tiger just grinned and told him to forget it, but even in the rush of shipboard activity it stubbornly refused to be forgotten.

One minor matter also helped to ease the tension between the doctors as they made their daily rounds. Tiger brought a pink dispatch sheet in to Dal one day, grinning happily. "This is from the weekly news capsule," he said. "It ought to cheer you up."

It was a brief news note, listed under "incidental items." "The Black Service of Pathology," it said, "has announced that Black Doctor Hugo Tanner will enter Hospital Philadelphia within the next week for prophylactic heart surgery. In keeping with usual Hospital Earth administrative policy, the Four-star Black Doctor will undergo a total cardiac transplant to halt the Medical education administrator's progressively disabling heart disease." The note went on to name the surgeons who would officiate at the procedure.

Dal smiled and handed back the dispatch. "Maybe it will improve his temper," he said, "even if it does give him another fifty years of active life."

"Well, at least it will take him out of *our* hair for a while," Tiger said. "He won't have time to keep us under too close scrutiny."

Which, Dal was forced to admit, did not make him too unhappy.

Shipboard rounds kept all three doctors busy. Often, with contact landings, calls, and studying, it seemed only a brief time from sleep period to sleep period, but still they had some time for minor luxuries. Dal was almost continuously shivering, with the ship kept at a temperature that was comfortable for Tiger and Jack; he missed the tropical heat of his home planet, and sometimes it seemed that he was chilled down to the marrow of his bones in spite of his coat of gray fur. With a little home-made plumbing and ingenuity, he finally managed to convert one of the ship's shower units into a steam bath. Once or twice each day he would retire for a blissful half hour warming himself up to Garv II normal temperatures.

Fuzzy also became a part of shipboard routine. Once he grew accustomed to Tiger and Jack and the surroundings aboard the ship, the little creature grew bored sitting on Dal's shoulder and wanted to be in the middle of things. Since the early tension had eased, he was willing to be apart from his master from time to time, so Dal and Tiger built him a platform that hung from the ceiling of the control room. There Fuzzy would sit and swing by the hour, blinking happily at the activity going on all around him.

But for all the appearance of peace and agreement, there was still an undercurrent of tension on board the *Lancet* which flared up from time to time when it was least expected, between Dal and Jack. It was on one such occasion that a major crisis almost developed, and once again Fuzzy was the center of the contention.

Dal Timgar knew that disaster had struck at the very moment it happened, but he could not tell exactly what was wrong. All he knew was that something fearful had happened to Fuzzy.

There was a small sound-proof cubicle in the computer room, with a chair, desk and a tape-reader for the doctors when they had odd moments to spend reading up on recent medical bulletins or reviewing their textbooks. Dal spent more time here than the other two; the temperature of the room could be turned up, and he had developed a certain fondness for the place with its warm gray walls and its soft relaxing light. Here on the tapes were things that he could grapple with, things that he could understand. If a problem here eluded him, he could study it out until he had mastered it. The hours he spent here were a welcome retreat from the confusing complexities of getting along with Jack and Tiger.

These long study periods were boring for Fuzzy who wasn't much interested in the oxygen-exchange mechanism of the intelligent beetles of Aldebaran VI. Frequently Dal would leave him to swing on his platform or explore about the control cabin while he spent an hour or two at the tape-reader. Today Dal had been working for over an hour, deeply immersed in a review of the intermediary metabolism of chlorine-breathing mammals, when something abruptly wrenched his attention from the tape.

It was as though a light had snapped off in his mind, or a door slammed shut. There was no sound, no warning; yet, suddenly, he felt dreadfully, frighteningly alone, as if in a split second something inside him had been torn away. He sat bolt upright, staring, and he felt his skin crawl and his fingers tremble as he listened, trying to spot the source of the trouble.

And then, almost instinctively, he knew what was wrong. He leaped to his feet, tore open the door to the cubicle and dashed down the hallway toward the control room. "Fuzzy!" he shouted. "Fuzzy, *where are you*?"

Tiger and Jack were both at the control panel dictating records for filing. They looked up in surprise as the Red Doctor burst into the room. Fuzzy's platform was hanging empty, gently swaying back and forth. Dal peered frantically around the room. There was no sign of the small pink creature.

"Where is he?" he demanded. "What's happened to Fuzzy?"

Jack shrugged in disgust. "He's up on his perch. Where else?"

"He's not either! Where is he?"

Jack blinked at the empty perch. "He was there just a minute ago. I saw him."

"Well, he's not there now, and something's wrong!" In a panic, Dal began searching the room, knocking over stools, scattering piles of paper, peering in every corner where Fuzzy might be concealed.

For a moment the others sat frozen, watching him. Then Tiger jumped to his feet. "Hold it, hold it! He probably just wandered off for a minute. He does that all the time."

"No, it's something worse than that." Dal was almost choking on the words. "Something terrible has happened. I know it."

Jack Alvarez tossed the recorder down in disgust. "You and your miserable pet!" he said. "I knew we shouldn't have kept him on board."

Dal stared at Jack. Suddenly all the anger and bitterness of the past few weeks could no longer be held in. Without warning he hurled himself at the Blue Doctor's throat. "Where is he?" he cried. "What have you done with him? What have you done to

Fuzzy? You've done something to him! You've hated him every minute just like you hate me, only he's easier to pick on. Now where is he? What have you done to him?"

Jack staggered back, trying to push the furious little Garvian away. "Wait a minute! Get away from me! I didn't do anything!"

"You did too! Where is he?"

"I don't know." Jack struggled to break free, but there was powerful strength in Dal's fingers for all his slight body build. "I tell you, he was here just a minute ago."

Dal felt a hand grip his collar then, and Tiger was dragging them apart like two dogs in a fight. "Now stop this!" he roared, holding them both at arm's length. "I said *stop it!* Jack didn't do anything to Fuzzy, he's been sitting here with me ever since you went back to the cubicle. He hasn't even budged."

"But he's *gone*," Dal panted. "Something's happened to him. I *know* it."

"How do you know?"

"I—I just know. I can feel it."

"All right, then let's find him," Tiger said. "He's got to be somewhere on the ship. If he's in trouble, we're wasting time fighting."

Tiger let go, and Jack brushed off his shirt, his face very white. "I saw him just a little while ago," he said. "He was sitting up on that silly perch watching us, and then swinging back and forth and swinging over to that cabinet and back."

"Well, let's get started looking," Tiger said.

They fanned out, with Jack still muttering to himself, and searched the control room inch by inch. There was no sign of Fuzzy. Dal had control of himself now, but he searched with a frantic intensity. "He's not in here," he said at last, "he must have gone out somewhere."

"There was only one door open," Tiger said. "The one you just came through, from the rear corridor. Dal, you search the computer room. Jack, check the lab and I'll go back to the reactors."

They started searching the compartments off the rear corridor. For ten minutes there was no sound in the ship but the occasional slamming of a hatch, the grate of a desk drawer, the bang of a cabinet door. Dal worked through the maze of cubby-holes in the computer room with growing hopelessness. The frightening sense of loneliness and loss in his mind was overwhelming; he was almost physically ill. The warm, comfortable feeling of *contact* that he had always had before with Fuzzy was gone. As the minutes passed, hopelessness gave way to despair.

Then Jack gave a hoarse cry from the lab. Dal tripped and stumbled in his haste to get down the corridor, and almost collided with Tiger at the lab door.

"I think we're too late," Jack said. "He's gotten into the formalin."

He lifted one of the glass beakers down from the shelf to the work bench. It was obvious what had happened. Fuzzy had gone exploring and had found the laboratory a fascinating place. Several of the reagents bottles had been knocked over as if he had been sampling them. The glass lid to the beaker of formalin which was kept for tissue specimens had been pushed aside just enough to admit the little creature's two-inch girth. Now Fuzzy lay in the bottom of the beaker, immersed in formalin, a formless, shapeless blob of sickly gray jelly.

"Are you sure it's formalin?" Dal asked.

Jack poured off the fluid, and the acrid smell of formaldehyde that filled the room answered the question. "It's no good, Dal," he said, almost gently. "The stuff destroys protein, and that's about all he was. I'm sorry—I was beginning to like the little punk, even if he did get on my nerves. But he picked the one thing to fall into that could kill him. Unless he had some way to set up a protective barrier…"

Dal took the beaker. "Get me some saline," he said tightly. "And some nutrient broth."

Jack pulled out two jugs and poured their contents into an empty beaker. Dal popped the tiny limp form into the beaker and began massaging it. Layers of damaged tissue peeled off in his hand, but he continued massaging and changing the solutions, first saline, then nutrient broth. "Get me some sponges and a blade."

Tiger brought them in. Carefully Dal began debriding the damaged outer layers. Jack and Tiger watched; then Jack said, "Look, there's a tinge of pink in the middle."

Slowly the faint pink in the center grew more ruddy. Dal changed solutions again, and sank down on a stool. "I think he'll make it," he said. "He has enormous regenerative powers as long as any fragment of him is left." He looked up at Jack who was still watching the creature in the beaker almost solicitously. "I guess I made a fool of myself back there when I jumped you."

Jack's face hardened, as though he had been caught off guard. "I guess you did, all right."

"Well, I'm sorry. I just couldn't think straight. It was the first time I'd ever been—apart from him."

"I still say he doesn't belong aboard," Jack said. "This is a medical ship, not a menagerie. And if you ever lay your hands on me again, you'll wish you hadn't."

"I said I was sorry," Dal said.

"I heard you," Jack said. "I just don't believe you, that's all."

He gave Fuzzy a final glance, and then headed back to the control room.

Fuzzy recovered, a much abashed and subdued Fuzzy, clinging timorously to Dal's shoulder and refusing to budge for three days, but apparently basically unharmed by his inadvertent swim in the deadly formalin bath. Presently he seemed to forget the experience altogether, and once again took his perch on the platform in the control room.

But Dal did not forget. He said little to Tiger and Jack, but the incident had shaken him severely. For as long as he could remember, he had always had Fuzzy close at hand. He had never before in his life experienced the dreadful feeling of emptiness and desertion, the almost paralyzing fear and helplessness that he had felt when Fuzzy had lost contact with him. It had seemed as though a vital part of him had suddenly been torn away, and the memory of the panic that followed sent chills down his back and woke him up trembling from his sleep. He was ashamed of his unwarranted attack on Jack, yet even this seemed insignificant in comparison to the powerful fear that had been driving him.

Happily, the Blue Doctor chose to let the matter rest where it was, and if anything, seemed more willing than before to be friendly. For the first time he seemed to take an active interest in

Fuzzy, "chatting" with him when he thought no one was around, and bringing him occasional tid-bits of food after meals were over.

Once more life on the *Lancet* settled back to routine, only to have it shattered by an incident of quite a different nature. It was just after they had left a small planet in the Procyon system, one of the routine check-in points, that they made contact with the Garvian trading ship.

Dal recognized the ship's design and insignia even before the signals came in, and could hardly contain his excitement. He had not seen a fellow countryman for years except for an occasional dull luncheon with the Garvian ambassador to Hospital Earth during medical school days. The thought of walking the corridors of a Garvian trading ship again brought an overwhelming wave of homesickness. He was so excited he could hardly wait for Jack to complete the radio-sighting formalities. "What ship is she?" he wanted to know. "What house?"

Jack handed him the message transcript. "The ship is the *Teegar*," he said. "Flagship of the SinSin trading fleet. They want permission to approach us."

Dal let out a whoop. "Then it's a space trader, and a big one. You've never seen ships like these before."

Tiger joined them, staring at the message transcript. "A SinSin ship! Send them the word, Jack, and be quick, before they get disgusted and move on."

Jack sent out the approach authorization, and they watched with growing excitement as the great trading vessel began its close-approach maneuvers.

The name of the house of SinSin was famous throughout the galaxy. It was one of the oldest and largest of the great trading firms that had built Garv II into its position of leadership in the Confederation, and the SinSin ships had penetrated to every corner of the galaxy, to every known planet harboring an intelligent life-form.

Tiger and Jack had seen the multitudes of exotic products in the Hospital Earth stores that came from the great Garvian ships on their frequent visits. But this was more than a planetary trader loaded with a few items for a single planet. The space traders roamed from star system to star system, their holds filled with treasures beyond number. Such ships as these might be out from Garv II for decades at a time, tempting any ship they met with the magnificent variety of wares they carried.

Slowly the trader approached, and Dal took the speaker, addressing the commander of the *Teegar* in Garvian. "This is the General Practice Patrol Ship *Lancet*," he said, "out from Hospital Earth with three physicians aboard, including a countryman of yours."

"Is that Dal Timgar?" the reply came back. "By the Seven Moons! We'd heard that there was now a Garvian physician, and couldn't believe our ears. Come aboard, all of you, you'll be welcome. We'll send over a lifeboat!"

The *Teegar* was near now, a great gleaming ship with the sign of the house of SinSin on her hull. A lifeboat sprang from a launching rack and speared across to the *Lancet*. Moments later the three doctors were climbing into the sleek little vessel and moving across the void of space to the huge Garvian ship.

It was like stepping from a jungle outpost village into a magnificent, glittering city. The Garvian ship was enormous; she carried a crew of several hundred, and the wealth and luxury of the ship took the Earthmen's breath away. The cabins and lounges were paneled with expensive fabrics and rare woods, the furniture inlaid with precious metals. Down the long corridors goods of the traders were laid out in resplendent display, surpassing the richest show cases in the shops on Hospital Earth.

They received a royal welcome from the commander of the *Teegar*, an aged, smiling little Garvian with a pink fuzz-ball on his shoulder that could have been Fuzzy's twin. He bowed low to Tiger and Jack, leading them into the reception lounge where a great table was spread with foods and pastries of all varieties. Then he turned to Dal and embraced him like a long-lost brother. "Your father Jai Timgar has long been an honored friend of the house of SinSin, and anyone of the house of Timgar is the same as my own son and my son's son! But this collar! This cuff! Is it really possible that a man of Garv has become a physician of Hospital Earth?"

Dal touched Fuzzy to the commander's fuzz-ball in the ancient Garvian greeting. "It's possible, and true," he said. "I studied there. I am the Red Doctor on this patrol ship."

"Ah, but this is good," the commander said. "What better way to draw our worlds together, eh? But come, you must look and see what we have in our storerooms, feast your eyes on the splendors we carry. For all of you, a thousand wonders are to be found here."

Jack hesitated as the commander led them back toward the display corridors. "We'd be glad to see the ship, but you should know that patrol ship physicians have little money to spend."

"Who speaks of money?" the commander cried. "Did I speak of it? Come and look! Money is nothing. The Garvian traders are not mere money-changers. Look and enjoy; if there is something that strikes your eye, something that would fulfill the desires of your heart, it will be yours." He gave Dal a smile and a sly wink. "Surely our brother here has told you many times of the wonders to be seen in a space trader, and terms can be arranged that will make any small purchase a painless pleasure."

He led them off, like a head of state conducting visiting dignitaries on a tour, with a retinue of Garvian underlings trailing behind them. For two delirious hours they wandered the corridors of the great ship, staring hungrily at the dazzling displays. They had been away from Hospital Earth and its shops and stores for months; now it seemed they werewalking through an incredible treasure-trove stocked with everything that they could possibly have wanted.

For Jack there was a dress uniform, specially tailored for a physician in the Blue Service of Diagnosis, the insignia woven into the cloth with gold and platinum thread. Reluctantly he turned away from it, a luxury he could never dream of affording. For Tiger, who had been muttering for weeks about getting out of condition in the sedentary life of the ship, there was a set of bar bells and gymnasium equipment ingeniously designed to collapse into a unit no larger than one foot square, yet opening out into a completely equipped gym. Dal's eyes glittered at the new sets of surgical instruments, designed to the most rigid Hospital Earth specifications, which appeared almost without his asking to see them. There were clothes and games, precious stones and exotic rings, watches set with Arcturian dream-stones, and boots inlaid with silver.

They made their way through the corridors, reluctant to leave one display for the next. Whenever something caught their eyes, the commander snapped his fingers excitedly, and the item was unobtrusively noted down by one of the underlings. Finally, exhausted and glutted just from looking, they turned back toward the reception room.

"The things are beautiful," Tiger said wistfully, "but impossible. Still, you were very kind to take your time—"

"Time? I have nothing but time." The commander smiled again at Dal. "And there is an old Garvian proverb that to the wise man 'impossible' has no meaning. Wait, you will see!"

They came out into the lounge, and the doctors stopped short in amazement. Spread out before them were all of the items that had captured their interest earlier.

"But this is ridiculous," Jack said staring at the dress uniform. "We couldn't possibly buy these things, it would take our salaries for twenty years to pay for them."

"Have we mentioned price even once?" the commander protested. "You are the crewmates of one of our own people! We would not dream of setting prices that we would normally set for such trifles as these. And as for terms, you have no worry. Take the goods aboard your ship, they are already yours. We have drawn up contracts for you which require no payment whatever for five years, and then payments of only a fiftieth of the value for each successive year. And for each of you, with the compliments of the house of SinSin, a special gift at no charge whatever."

He placed in Jack's hands a small box with the lid tipped back. Against a black velvet lining lay a silver star, and the official insignia of a Star Physician in the Blue Service. "You cannot wear it yet, of course," the commander said. "But one day you will need it."

Jack blinked at the jewel-like star. "You are very kind," he said. "I—I mean perhaps—" He looked at Tiger, and then at the display of goods on the table. "Perhaps there are *some*things—"

Already two of the Garvian crewmen were opening the lock to the lifeboat, preparing to move the goods aboard. Then Dal

Timgar spoke up sharply. "I think you'd better wait a moment," he said.

"And for you," the commander continued, turning to Dal so smoothly that there seemed no break in his voice at all, "as one of our own people, and an honored son of Jai Timgar, who has been kind to the house of SinSin for many years, I have something out of the ordinary. I'm sure your crewmates would not object to a special gift at my personal expense."

The commander lifted a scarf from the table and revealed the glittering set of surgical instruments, neatly displayed in a velvet-lined carrying case. The commander took it up from the table and thrust it into Dal's hands. "It is yours, my friend. And for this, there will be no contract whatever."

Dal stared down at the instruments. They were beautiful. He longed just to touch them, to hold them in his hands, but he shook his head and set the case back on the table. He looked up at Tiger and Jack. "You should be warned that the prices on these goods are four times what they ought to be, and the deferred-payment contracts he wants you to sign will permit as much as 24 per cent interest on the unpaid balance, with no closing-out clause. That means you would be paying many times the stated price for the goods before the contract is closed. You can go ahead and sign if you want but understand what you're signing."

The Garvian commander stared at him, and then shook his head, laughing. "Of course your friend is not serious," he said. "These prices can be compared on any planet and you will see their fairness. Here, read the contracts, see what they say and decide for yourselves." He held out a sheaf of papers.

"The contracts may sound well enough," Dal said, "but I'm telling you what they actually say."

Jack looked stricken. "But surely just one or two things—"

Tiger shook his head. "Dal knows what he's talking about. I don't think we'd better buy anything at all."

The Garvian commander turned to Dal angrily. "What are you telling them? There is nothing false in these contracts!"

"I didn't say there was. I just can't see them taking a beating with their eyes shut, that's all. Your contracts are legal enough, but the prices and terms are piracy, and you know it."

The commander glared at him for a moment. Then he turned away scornfully. "So what I have heard is true, after all," he said. "You really have thrown in your lot with these pill-peddlers, these idiots from Earth who can't even wipe their noses without losing in a trade." He signaled the lifeboat pilot. "Take them back to their ship, we're wasting our time. There are better things to do than to deal with traitors."

The trip back to the *Lancet* was made in silence. Dal could sense the pilot's scorn as he dumped them off in their entrance lock, and dashed back to the *Teegar* with the lifeboat. Gloomily Jack and Tiger followed Dal into the control room, a drab little cubby-hole compared to the *Teegar*'s lounge.

"Well, it was fun while it lasted," Jack said finally, looking up at Dal. "But the way that guy slammed you, I wish we'd never gone."

"I know," Dal said. "The commander just thought he saw a perfect setup. He figured you'd never question the contracts if I backed him up."

"It would have been easy enough. Why didn't you?"

Dal looked at the Blue Doctor. "Maybe I just don't like people who give away surgical sets," he said. "Remember, I'm not a Garvian trader any more. I'm a doctor from Hospital Earth."

Moments later, the great Garvian ship was gone, and the red light was blinking on the call board. Tiger started tracking down the call while Jack went back to work on the daily log book and Dal set up food for dinner. The pleasant dreams were over; they were back in the harness of patrol ship doctors once again.

Jack and Dal were finishing dinner when Tiger came back with a puzzled frown on his face. "Finally traced that call. At least I think I did. Anybody ever hear of a star called 31 Brucker?"

"Brucker?" Jack said. "It isn't on the list of contracts. What's the trouble?"

"I'm not sure," Tiger said. "I'm not even certain if it's a call or not. Come on up front and see what you think."

# CHAPTER EIGHT
*Plague!*

In the control room the interstellar radio and teletype-translator were silent. The red light on the call board was still blinking; Tiger turned it off with a snap. "Here's the message that just came in, as near as I can make out," he said, "and if you can make sense of it, you're way ahead of me."

The message was a single word, teletyped in the center of a blue dispatch sheet:

GREETINGS

"This is all?" Jack said.

"That's every bit of it. They repeated it half a dozen times, just like that."

"*Who* repeated it?" Dal asked. "Where are the identification symbols?"

"There weren't any," said Tiger. "Our own computer designated 31 Brucker from the direction and intensity of the signal. The question is, what do we do?"

The message stared up at them cryptically. Dal shook his head. "Doesn't give us much to go on, that's certain. Even the location could be wrong if the signal came in on an odd frequency or from a long distance. Let's beam back at the same direction and intensity and see what happens."

Tiger took the earphones and speaker, and turned the signal beam to coincide with the direction of the incoming message.

"We have your contact. Can you hear me? Who are you and what do you want?"

There was a long delay and they thought the contact was lost. Then a voice came whispering through the static. "Where is your ship now? Are you near to us?"

"We need your co-ordinates in order to tell," Tiger said. "Who are you?"

Again a long pause and a howl of static. Then: "If you are far away it will be too late. We have no time left, we are dying..."

Abruptly the voice message broke off and co-ordinates began coming through between bursts of static. Tiger scribbled them down, piecing them together through several repetitions. "Check these out fast," he told Jack. "This sounds like real trouble." He tossed Dal another pair of earphones and turned back to the speaker. "Are you a contract planet?" he signaled. "Do we have a survey on you?"

There was a much longer pause. Then the voice came back, "No, we have no contract. We are all dying, but if you must have a contract to come…"

"Not at all," Tiger sent back. "We're coming. Keep your frequency open. We will contact again when we are closer."

He tossed down the earphones and looked excitedly at Dal. "Did you hear that? A planet calling for help, with no Hospital Earth contract!"

"They sound desperate," Dal said. "We'd better go there, contract or no contract."

"Of course we'll go there, you idiot. See if Jack has those co-ordinates charted, and start digging up information on them, everything you can find. We need all of the dope we can get and we need it fast. This is our golden chance to seal a contract with a new planet."

All three of the doctors fell to work trying to identify the mysterious caller. Dal began searching the information file for data on 31 Brucker, punching all the reference tags he could think of, as well as the galactic co-ordinates of the planet. He could hardly control his fingers as the tapes with possible references began plopping down into the slots. Tiger was right; this was almost too good to be true. When a planet without a medical service contract called a GPP Ship for help, there was always hope that a brand new contract might be signed if the call was successful. And no greater honor could come to a patrol craft crew than to be the originators of a new contract for Hospital Earth.

But there were problems in dealing with uncontacted planets. Many star systems had never been explored by ships of the Confederation. Many races, like Earthmen at the time their star-drive was discovered, had no inkling of the existence of a Galactic Confederation of worlds. There might be no information whatever about the special anatomical and physiological characteristics of the inhabitants of an uncontacted planet, and often a patrol crew faced insurmountable difficulties, coming in blind to solve a medical problem.

Dal had his information gathered first—a disappointingly small amount indeed. Among the billions of notes on file in the *Lancet*'s data bank, there were only two scraps of data available on the 31 Brucker system.

"Is this all you could find?" Tiger said, staring at the information slips.

"There's just nothing else there," Dal said. "This one is a description and classification of the star, and it doesn't sound like the one who wrote it had even been near it."

"He hadn't," Tiger said. "This is a routine radio-telescopic survey report. The star is a red giant. Big and cold, with three— possibly four—planets inside the outer envelope of the star itself, and only one outside it. Nothing about satellites. None of the planets thought to be habitable by man. What's the other item?"

"An exploratory report on the outer planet, done eight hundred years ago. Says it's an Earth-type planet, and not much else. Gives reference to the full report in the Confederation files. Not a word about an intelligent race living there."

"Well, maybe Jack's got a bit more for us," Tiger said. "If the place has been explored, there must be *some* information about the inhabitants."

But Jack also came up with a blank. Central Records on Hospital Earth sent back a physical description of a tiny outer planet of the star, with a thin oxygen-nitrogen atmosphere, very little water, and enough methane mixed in to make the atmosphere deadly to Earthmen.

"Then there's never been a medical service contract?" Tiger asked.

"Contract!" Jack said. "It doesn't even say there are any people there. Not a word about any kind of life form."

"Well, that's ridiculous," Dal said. "If we're getting messages from there, somebody must be sending them. But if a Confederation ship explored there, there's a way to find out. How soon can we convert to star-drive?"

"As soon as we can get strapped down," Tiger said.

"Then send our reconversion co-ordinates to the Confederation headquarters on Garv II and request the Confederation records on the place."

Jack stared at him. "You mean just ask to see Confederation records? We can't do that, they'd skin us alive. Those records are closed to everyone except full members of the Confederation."

"Tell them it's an emergency," Dal said. "If they want to be legal about it, give them my Confederation serial number. Garv II is a member of the Confederation, and I'm a native-born citizen."

Tiger got the request off while Jack and Dal strapped down for the conversion to Koenig drive. Five minutes later Tiger joined them, grinning from ear to ear. "Didn't even have to pull rank," he said. "When they started to argue, I just told them it was an emergency, and if they didn't let us see any records they had, we would file their refusal against claims that might come up later. They quit arguing. We'll have the records as soon as we reconvert."

The star that they were seeking was a long distance from the current location of the *Lancet*. The ship was in Koenig drive for hours before it reconverted, and even Dal was beginning to feel the first pangs of drive-sickness before they felt the customary jolting vibration of the change to normal space, and saw bright stars again in the viewscreen.

The star called 31 Brucker was close then. It was indeed a red giant; long tenuous plumes of gas spread out for hundreds of millions of miles on all sides of its glowing red core. This mammoth star did not look so cold now, as they stared at it in the viewscreen, yet among the family of stars it was a cold, dying giant with only a few moments of life left on the astronomical time scale. From the *Lancet*'s position, no planets at all were visible to the naked eye, but with the telescope Jack soon found two inside the star's envelope of gas and one tiny one outside. They would have to be searched for, and the one that they were hoping to reach located before centering and landing maneuvers could be begun.

Already the radio was chattering with two powerful signals coming in. One came from the Galactic Confederation headquarters on Garv II; the other was a good clear signal from very close range, unquestionably beamed to them from the planet in distress.

They watched as the Confederation report came clacking off the teletype, and they stared at it unbelieving.

"It just doesn't make sense," Jack said. "There *must* be intelligent creatures down there. They're sending radio signals."

"Then why a report like this?" Tiger said. "This was filed by a routine exploratory ship that came here eight hundred years ago. You can't tell me that any intelligent race could develop from scratch in less than eight centuries' time."

Dal picked up the report and read it again. "This red giant star," he read, "was studied in the usual fashion. It was found to have seven planets, all but one lying within the tenuous outer gas envelope of the star itself. The seventh planet has an atmosphere of its own, and travels an orbit well outside the star surface. This planet was selected for landing and exploration."

Following this was a long, detailed and exceedingly dull description of the step-by-step procedure followed by a Confederation exploratory ship making a first landing on a barren planet. There was a description of the atmosphere, the soil surface, the land masses and major water bodies. Physically, the planet was a desert, hot and dry, and barren of vegetation excepting in two or three areas of jungle along the equator. "The planet is inhabited by numerous small unintelligent animal species which seem well-adapted to the semi-arid conditions. Of higher animals and mammals only two species were discovered, and of these the most highly developed was an erect biped with an integrated central nervous system and the intelligence level of a Garvian *drachma*."

"How small is that?" Jack said.

"Idiot-level," Dal said glumly. "I.Q. of about 20 on the human scale. I guess the explorers weren't much impressed; they didn't even put the planet down for a routine colonization survey."

"Well, *something* has happened down there since then. Idiots can't build interstellar radios." Jack turned to Tiger. "Are you getting them?"

Tiger nodded. A voice was coming over the speaker, hesitant and apologetic, using the common tongue of the Galactic

Confederation. "How soon can you come?" the voice was asking clearly, still with the sound of great reticence. "There is not much time."

"But who are you?" Tiger asked. "What's wrong down there?"

"We are sick, dying, thousands of us. But if you have other work that is more pressing, we would not want to delay you—"

Jack shook his head, frowning. "I don't get this," he said. "What are they afraid of?"

Tiger spoke into the microphone again. "We will be glad to help, but we need information about you. You have our position—can you send up a spokesman to tell us your problem?"

A long pause, and then the voice came back wearily. "It will be done. Stand by to receive him."

Tiger snapped off the radio receiver and looked up triumphantly at the others. "Now we're getting somewhere. If the people down there can send a ship out with a spokesman to tell us about their troubles, we've got a chance to sew up a contract, and that could mean a Star for every one of us."

"Yes, but who are they?" Dal said. "And where were they when the Confederation ship was here?"

"I don't know," Jack said, "but I'll bet you both that we have quite a time finding out."

"Why?" Tiger said. "What do you mean?"

"I mean we'd better be very careful here," Jack said darkly. "I don't know about you, but I think this whole business has a very strange smell."

There was nothing strange about the Bruckian ship when it finally came into view. It was a standard design, surface-launching interplanetary craft, with separated segments on either side suggesting atomic engines. They saw the side jets flare as the ship maneuvered to come in alongside the *Lancet*.

Grapplers were thrown out to bind the emissary ship to the *Lancet*'s hull, and Jack threw the switches to open the entrance lock and decontamination chambers. They had taken pains to describe the interior atmosphere of the patrol ship and warn the spokesman to keep himself in a sealed pressure suit. On the intercom viewscreens they saw the small suited figure cross from his ship into the *Lancet*'s lock, and watched as the sprays of formalin washed down the outside of the suit.

Moments later the creature stepped out of the decontamination chamber. He was small and humanoid, with tiny fragile bones and pale, hairless skin. He stood no more than four feet high. More than anything else, he looked like a very intelligent monkey with a diminutive space suit fitting his fragile body. When he spoke the words came through the translator in English; but Dal recognized the flowing syllables of the universal language of the Galactic Confederation.

"How do you know the common tongue?" he said. "There is no record of your people in our Confederation, yet you use our own universal language."

The Bruckian nodded. "We know the language well. My people dread outside contact—it is a racial characteristic—but we hear the Confederation broadcasts and have learned to understand the common tongue." The space-suited stranger looked at the doctors one by one. "We also know of the good works of the ships from Hospital Earth, and now we appeal to you."

"Why?" Jack said. "You gave us no information, nothing to go on."

"There was no time," the creature said. "Death is stalking our land, and the people are falling at their plows. Thousands of us are dying, tens of thousands. Even I am infected and soon will be dead. Unless you can find a way to help us quickly, it will be too late, and my people will be wiped from the face of the planet."

Jack looked grimly at Tiger and Dal. "Well," he said, "I guess that answers our question, all right. It looks as if we have a plague planet on our hands, whether we like it or not."

## CHAPTER NINE
### *The Incredible People*

Slowly and patiently they drew the story from the emissary from the seventh planet of 31 Brucker.

The small, monkey-like creature was painfully shy; he required constant reassurance that the doctors did not mind being called, that they wanted to help, and that a contract was not necessary in an emergency. Even at that the spokesman was reluctant to give details about the plague and about his stricken people. Every bit of information had to be extracted with patient questioning.

By tacit consent the doctors did not even mention the strange fact that this very planet had been explored by a Confederation ship eight hundred years before and no sign of intelligent life had been found. The little creature before them seemed ready to turn and bolt at the first hint of attack or accusation. But bit by bit, a picture of the current situation on the planet developed.

Whoever they were and wherever they had been when the Confederation ship had landed, there was unquestionably an intelligent race now inhabiting this lonely planet in the outer reaches of the solar system of 31 Brucker. There was no doubt of their advancement; a few well-selected questions revealed that they had control of atomic power, a working understanding of the nature and properties of contra-terrene matter, and a workable star drive operating on the same basic principle as Earth's Koenig drive but which the Bruckians had never really used because of their shyness and fear of contact with other races. They also had an excellent understanding, thanks to their eavesdropping on Confederation interstellar radio chatter, of the existence and functions of the Galactic Confederation of worlds, and of Hospital Earth's work as physician to the galaxy.

But about Bruckian anatomy, physiology or biochemistry, the little emissary would tell them nothing. He seemed genuinely frightened when they pressed him about the physical make-up of his people, as though their questions were somehow scraping a raw nerve. He insisted that his people knew nothing about the nature of the plague that had stricken them, and the doctors could not budge him an inch from his stand.

But a plague had certainly struck.

It had begun six months before, striking great masses of the people. It had walked the streets of the cities and the hills and valleys of the countryside. First three out of ten had been stricken, then four, then five. The course of the disease, once started, was invariably the same: first illness, weakness, loss of energy and interest, then gradually a fading away of intelligent responses, leaving thousands of creatures walking blank-faced and idiot-like about the streets and countryside. Ultimately even the ability to take food was lost, and after an interval of a week or so, death invariably ensued.

Finally the doctors retired to the control room for a puzzled conference. "It's got to be an organism of some sort that's doing it," Dal said. "There couldn't be an illness like this that wasn't caused by some kind of a parasitic germ or virus."

"But how do we know?" Jack said. "We know nothing about these people except what we can see. We're going to have to do a complete biochemical and medical survey before we can hope to do anything."

"But we aren't equipped for a real survey," Tiger protested.

"We've got to do it anyway," Jack said. "If we can just learn enough to be sure it's an infectious illness, we might stand a chance of finding a drug that will cure it. Or at least a way to immunize the ones that aren't infected yet. If this is a virus infection, we might only need to find an antibody for inoculation to stop it in its tracks. But first we need a good look at the planet and some more of the people—both infected and healthy ones. We'd better make arrangements as fast as we can."

An hour later they had reached an agreement with the Bruckian emissary. The *Lancet* would be permitted to land on the planet's surface as soon as the doctors were satisfied that it was safe. For the time being the initial landings would be made in the patrol ship's lifeboats, with the *Lancet* in orbit a thousand miles above the surface. Unquestionably the first job was diagnosis, discovering the exact nature of the illness and studying the afflicted people. This responsibility rested squarely on Jack's shoulders; he was the diagnostician, and Dal and Tiger willingly yielded to him in organizing the program.

It was decided that Jack and Tiger would visit the planet's surface at once, while Dal stayed on the ship and set up the reagents and examining techniques that would be needed to measure the basic physical and biochemical characteristics of the Bruckians.

Yet in all the excitement of planning, Dal could not throw off the lingering shadow of doubt in his mind, some instinctive voice of caution that seemed to say *watch out, be careful, go slowly! This may not be what it seems to be; you may be walking into a trap...*

But it was only a faint voice, and easy to thrust aside as the planning went ahead full speed.

It did not take very long for the crew of the *Lancet* to realize that there was something very odd indeed about the small, self-effacing inhabitants of 31 Brucker VII.

In fact, "odd" was not really quite the proper word for these creatures at all. No one knew better than the doctors of Hospital Earth that oddness was the rule among the various members of the galactic civilization. All sorts and varieties of life-forms had been discovered, described and studied, each with its singular differences, each with certain similarities, and each quite "odd" in reference to any of the others.

In Dal this awareness of the oddness and difference of other races was particularly acute. He knew that to Tiger and Jack he himself seemed odd, both anatomically and in other ways. His fine gray fur and his four-fingered hands set him apart from them—he would never be mistaken for an Earthman, even in the densest fog. But these were comprehensible differences. His close attachment to Fuzzy was something else, and still seemed beyond their ability to understand.

He had spent one whole evening patiently trying to make Jack understand just how his attachment to the little pink creature was more than just the fondness of a man for his dog.

"Well, what would you call it, then?"

"Symbiosis is probably the best word for it," Dal had replied. "Two life-forms live together, and each one helps the other—that's all symbiosis is. Together each one is better off than either one would be alone. We all of us live in symbiosis with the bacteria in our digestive tracts, don't we? We provide them with a place to live and grow, and they help us digest our food. It's a kind of a partnership—and Fuzzy and I are partners in the same sort of way."

Jack had argued, and then lost his temper, and finally grudgingly agreed that he supposed he would have to tolerate it even if it didn't make sense to him.

But the creatures on 31 Brucker VII were "odd" far beyond the reasonable limits of oddness—so far beyond it that the doctors could not believe the things that their eyes and their instruments were telling them.

When Tiger and Jack came back to the *Lancet* after their first trip to the planet's surface, they were visibly shaken. Geographically, they had found it just as it had been described in the exploratory reports—a barren, desert land with only a few large islands of vegetation in the equatorial regions.

"But the people!" Jack said. "They don't fit into *any* kind of pattern. They've got houses—at least I guess you'd call them houses—but every one of them is like every other one, and they're all crammed together in tight little bunches, with nothing for miles in between. They've got an advanced technology, a good communications system, manufacturing techniques and everything, but they just don't use them."

"It's more than that," Tiger said. "They don't seem to *want* to use them."

"Well, it doesn't add up, to me," Jack said. "There are thousands of towns and cities down there, all of them miles apart, and yet they had to go dig an old rusty jet scooter out of storage and get the motor rebuilt just specially to take us from one place to another. I know things can get disorganized with a plague in the land, but this plague just hasn't been going on that long."

"What about the sickness?" Dal asked. "Is it as bad as it sounded?"

"Worse, if anything," Tiger said gloomily. "They're dying by the thousands, and I hope we got those suits of ours decontaminated, because I don't want any part of this disease."

Graphically, he described the conditions they had found among the stricken people. There was no question that a plague was stalking the land. In the rutted mud roads of the villages and towns the dead were piled in gutters, and in all of the cities a deathly stillness hung over the streets. Those who had not yet succumbed to the illness were nursing and feeding the sick ones, but these unaffected ones were growing scarcer and scarcer. The whole living population seemed resigned to hopelessness, hardly noticing the strangers from the patrol ship.

But worst of all were those in the final stages of the disease, wandering vaguely about the street, their faces blank and their jaws slack as though they were living in a silent world of their own, cut off from contact with the rest. "One of them almost ran into me," Jack said. "I was right in front of him, and he didn't see me or hear me."

"But don't they have *any* knowledge of antisepsis or isolation?" Dal asked.

Tiger shook his head. "Not that we could see. They don't know what's causing this sickness. They think that it's some kind of curse, and they never dreamed that it might be kept from spreading."

Already Tiger and Jack had taken the first routine steps to deal with the sickness. They gave orders to move the unaffected people in every town and village into isolated barracks and stockades. For half a day Tiger tried to explain ways to prevent the spread of a bacteria or virus-borne disease. The people had stared at him as if he were talking gibberish; finally he gave up trying to explain, and just laid down rules which the people were instructed to follow. Together they had collected standard testing specimens of body fluids and tissue from both healthy and afflicted Bruckians, and come back to the *Lancet* for a breather.

Now all three doctors began work on the specimens. Cultures were inoculated with specimens from respiratory tract, blood and tissue taken from both sick and well. Half a dozen fatal cases were brought to the ship under specially controlled conditions for autopsy examination, to reveal both the normal anatomical characteristics of this strange race of people and the damage the disease was doing. Down on the surface Tiger had already inoculated a dozen of the healthy ones with various radioactive isotopes to help outline the normal metabolism and biochemistry of the people. After a short sleep period on the *Lancet*, he went back down alone to follow up on these, leaving Dal and Jack to carry on the survey work in the ship's lab.

It was a gargantuan task that faced them. They knew that in any race of creatures they could not hope to recognize the abnormal unless they knew what the normal was. That was the sole reason for the extensive biomedical surveys that were done on new contract planets. Under normal conditions, a survey crew with specialists in physiology, biochemistry, anatomy, radiology, pharmacology and pathology might spend months or even years on a new planet gathering base-line information. But here there was neither time nor facilities for such a study. Even in the twenty-four hours since the patrol ship arrived, the number of dead had increased alarmingly.

Alone on the ship, Dal and Jack found themselves working as a well organized team. There was no time here for argument or duplicated efforts; everything the two doctors did was closely co-ordinated. Jack seemed to have forgotten his previous antagonism completely. There was a crisis here, and more work than three men could possibly do in the time available. "You handle anatomy and pathology," Jack told Dal at the beginning. "You can get the picture five times as fast as I can, and your pathology slides are better than most commercial ones. I can do the best job on the cultures, once I get the growth media all set up."

Bit by bit they divided the labor, checking in with Tiger by radio on the results of the isotopes studies he was running on the planet's surface. Bit by bit the data was collected, and Earthman and Garvian worked more closely than ever before as the task that faced them appeared more and more formidable.

But the results of their tests made no sense whatever. Tiger returned to the ship after forty-eight hours with circles under his eyes, looking as though he had been trampled in a crowd. "No sleep, that's all," he said breathlessly as he crawled out of his decontaminated pressure suit. "No time for it. I swear I ran those tests a dozen times and I still didn't get any answers that made sense."

"The results you were sending up sounded plenty strange," Jack said. "What was the trouble?"

"I don't know," Tiger said, "but if we're looking for a biological pattern here, we haven't found it yet as far as I can see."

"No, we certainly haven't," Dal exploded. "I thought I was doing something wrong somehow, because these blood chemistries I've been doing have been ridiculous. I can't even find a normal level for blood sugar, and as for the enzyme systems…" He tossed a sheaf of notes down on the counter in disgust. "I don't see how these people could even be alive, with a botched-up metabolism like this! I've never heard of anything like it."

"What kind of pathology did you find?" Tiger wanted to know.

"Nothing," Dal said. "Nothing at all. I did autopsies on the six that you brought up here and made slides of every different kind of tissue I could find. The anatomy is perfectly clear cut, no objections there. These people are very similar to Earth-type monkeys in structure, with heart and lungs and vocal cords and all. But I can't find any reason why they should be dying. Any luck with the cultures?"

Jack shook his head glumly. "No growth on any of the plates. At first I thought I had something going, but if I did, it died, and I can't find any sign of it in the filtrates."

"But we've got to have *something* to work on," Tiger said desperately. "Look, there are some things that always measure out the same in *any* intelligent creature no matter where he comes from. That's the whole basis of galactic medicine. Creatures may develop and adapt in different ways, but the basic biochemical reactions are the same."

"Not here, they aren't," Dal said. "Take a look at these tests!"

They carried the heap of notes they had collected out into the control room and began sifting and organizing the data, just as a survey team would do, trying to match it with the pattern of a thousand other living creatures that had previously been studied. Hours passed, and they were farther from an answer than when they began.

Because this data did not fit a pattern. It was *different*. No two individuals showed the same reactions. In every test the results were either flatly impossible or completely the opposite of what was expected.

Carefully they retraced their steps, trying to pinpoint what could be going wrong.

"There's *got* to be a laboratory error," Dal said wearily. "We must have slipped up somewhere."

"But I don't see where," Jack said. "Let's see those culture tubes again. And put on a pot of coffee. I can't even think straight any more."

Of the three of them, Jack was beginning to show the strain the most. This was his special field, the place where he was supposed to excel, and nothing was happening. Reports coming up from the planet were discouraging; the isolation techniques they had tried to institute did not seem to be working, and the spread of the plague was accelerating. The communiqués from the Bruckians were taking on a note of desperation.

Jack watched each report with growing apprehension. He moved restlessly from lab to control room, checking and rechecking things, trying to find some sign of order in the chaos.

"Try to get some sleep," Dal urged him. "A couple of hours will freshen you up a hundred per cent."

"I can't, I've already tried it," Jack said.

"Go ahead. Tiger and I can keep working on these things for a while."

"No, no, it's not that," Jack said. "Without a diagnosis, we can't do a thing. Until we have that, our hands are tied, and we aren't even getting close to it. We don't even know whether this is a bacteria, or a virus, or what. Maybe the Bruckians are right. Maybe it's a curse."

"I don't think the Black Service of Pathology would buy that for a diagnosis," Tiger said sourly.

"The Black Service would choke on it—but what other answer do we have? You two have been doing all you can, but diagnosis is *my* job. I'm supposed to be good at it, but the more we dig into this, the farther away we seem to get."

"Do you want to call for help?" Tiger said.

Jack shook his head helplessly. "I'm beginning to think we should have called for help a long time ago," he said. "We're into this over our heads now and we're still going down. At the rate those people are dying down there, we don't have time to call for help now." He stared at the piles of notes on the desk and his face was very white. "I don't know, I just don't know," he said. "The diagnosis on this thing should have been duck soup. I thought it was going to be a real feather in my cap, just walking in and nailing it down in a few hours. Well, I'm whipped. I don't know what to do. If either of you can think of an answer, it's all yours, and I'll admit it to Black Doctor Tanner himself."

It was bitter medicine for Blue Doctor Jack Alvarez to swallow, but that fact gave no pleasure to Dal or Tiger now. They were as baffled as Jack was, and would have welcomed help from anyone who could offer it.

And, ironically, the first glimpse of the truth came from the direction they least expected.

From the very beginning Fuzzy had been watching the proceedings from his perch on the swinging platform in the control room. If he sensed that Dal Timgar was ignoring him and leaving him to his own devices much of the time, he showed no sign of resentment. The tiny creature seemed to realize that something important was consuming his master's energy and attention, and contented himself with an affectionate pat now and then as Dal went through the control room. Everyone assumed without much thought that Fuzzy was merely being tolerant of the situation. It was not until they had finally given up in desperation and Tiger was trying to contact a Hospital Ship for help, that Dal stared up at his little pink friend with a puzzled frown.

Tiger put the transmitter down for a moment. "What's wrong?" he said to Dal. "You look as though you just bit into a rotten apple."

"I just remembered that I haven't fed him for twenty-four hours," Dal said.

"Who? Fuzzy?" Tiger shrugged. "He could see you were busy."

Dal shook his head. "That wouldn't make any difference to Fuzzy. When he gets hungry, he gets hungry, and he's pretty self-centered. It wouldn't matter what I was doing, he should have been screaming for food hours ago."

Dal walked over to the platform and peered down at his pink friend in alarm. He took him up and rested him on his shoulder, a move that invariably sent Fuzzy into raptures of delight. Now the little creature just sat there, trembling and rubbing half-heartedly against Dal's neck.

Dal held him out at arm's length. "Fuzzy, *what's the matter with you?*"

"Do you think something's wrong with him?" Jack said, looking up suddenly. "Looks like he's having trouble keeping his eyes open."

"His color isn't right, either," Tiger said. "He looks kind of blue."

Quite suddenly the little black eyes closed and Fuzzy began to tremble violently. He drew himself up into a tight pink globule as the fuzz-like hair disappeared from view.

Something was unmistakably wrong. As he held the shivering creature, Dal was suddenly aware that something had been nibbling at the back of his mind for hours. Not a clear-cut thought, merely an impression of pain and anguish and sickness, and now as he looked at Fuzzy the impression grew so strong it almost made him cry out.

Abruptly, Dal knew what he had to do. Where the thought came from he didn't know, but it was crystal clear in his mind. "Jack, where is our biggest virus filter?" he asked quietly.

Jack stared at him. "Virus filter? I just took it out of the autoclave an hour ago."

"Get it," Dal said, "and the suction machine too. *Quickly!*"

Jack went down the corridor like a shot, and reappeared a moment later with the big porcelain virus filter and the suction tubing attached to it. Swiftly Dal dumped the limp little creature in his hand into the top of the filter jar, poured in some sterile saline, and started the suction.

Tiger and Jack watched him in amazement. "What are you doing?" Tiger said.

"Filtering him," Dal said. "He's infected. He must have been exposed to the plague somehow, maybe when our little Bruckian visitor came on board the other day. And if it's a virus that's causing this plague, the virus filter ought to hold it back and still let Fuzzy's molecular structure through."

They watched and sure enough a bluish-pink fluid began moving down through the porcelain filter, and dripping through the funnel into the beaker below. Each drop coalesced in the beaker as it fell until Fuzzy's whole body had been sucked through the filter and into the jar below. He was still not quite his normal pink color, but as the filter went dry, a pair of frightened shoe-button eyes appeared and he poked up a pair of ears. Presently the fuzz began appearing on his body again.

And on the top of the filter lay a faint gray film. "Don't touch it!" Dal said. "That's real poison." He slipped on a mask and gloves, and scraped a bit of the film from the filter with a spatula. "I think we have it," he said. "The virus that's causing the plague on this planet."

# CHAPTER TEN
## *The Boomerang Clue*

It was a virus, beyond doubt. The electron microscope told them that, now that they had the substance isolated and could examine it. In the culture tubes in the *Lancet*'s incubators, it would begin to grow nicely, and then falter and die, but when guinea pigs were inoculated in the ship's laboratory, the substance proved its virulence. The animals injected with tiny bits of the substance grew sick within hours and very quickly died.

The call to the Hospital Ship was canceled as the three doctors worked in feverish excitement. Here at last was something they could grapple with, something so common among the races of the galaxy that the doctors felt certain that they could cope with it. Very few, if any, higher life forms existed that did not have some sort of submicroscopic parasite afflicting them. Bacterial infection was a threat on every inhabited world, and the viruses—the tiniest of all submicroscopic organisms—were the most difficult and dangerous of them all.

And yet virus plagues had been stopped before, and they could be stopped again.

Jack radioed down to the planet's surface that the diagnosis had been made; as soon as the proper medications could be prepared, the doctors would land to begin treatment. There was a new flicker of hopefulness in the Bruckian's response, and an appeal to hurry. With renewed energy the doctors went back to the lab to start working on the new data.

But trouble continued to dog them. This was no ordinary virus. It proved resistant to every one of the antibiotics and antiviral agents in the *Lancet*'s stockroom. No drug seemed to affect it, and its molecular structure was different from any virus that had ever been recorded before.

"If one of the drugs would only just slow it up a little, we'd be ahead," Tiger said in perplexity. "We don't have anything that even touches it, not even the purified globulins."

"What about antibodies from the infected people?" Jack suggested. "In every virus disease I've ever heard of, the victim's own body starts making antibodies against the invading virus. If enough antibodies are made fast enough, the virus dies and the patient is immune from then on."

"Well, these people don't seem to be making any antibodies at all," Tiger said. "At least not as far as I can see. If they were, at least some of them would be recovering from the disease. So far not a single one has recovered once the thing started. They all just go ahead and die."

"I wonder," Dal said, "if Fuzzy had any defense."

Jack looked up. "How do you mean?"

"Well, Fuzzy was infected, we know that. He might have died too, if we hadn't caught it in time—but as it worked out, he didn't. In fact, he looks pretty healthy right now."

"That's fine for Fuzzy," Jack said impatiently, "but I don't see how we can push the whole population of 31 Brucker VII through a virus filter. They're flesh-and-blood creatures."

"That's not what I mean," Dal said. "Maybe Fuzzy's body developed antibodies against the virus while he was infected. Remember, he doesn't have a rigid body structure like we do. He's mostly just basic protein, and he can synthesize pretty much anything he wants to or needs to."

Jack blinked. "It's an idea, at least. Is there any way we can get some of his body fluid away from him? Without getting bit, I mean?"

"No problem there," Dal said. "He can regenerate pretty fast if he has enough of the right kind of food. He won't miss an ounce or two of excess tissue."

He took a beaker over to Fuzzy's platform and began squeezing off a little blob of pink material. Fuzzy seemed to sense what Dal wanted; obligingly he thrust out a little pseudopod which Dal pinched off into the beaker. With the addition of a small amount of saline solution, the tissue dissolved into thin, pink suspension.

In the laboratory they found two or three of the guinea pigs in the last stages of the infection, and injected them with a tiny bit of the pink solution. The effect was almost unbelievable. Within twenty minutes all of the injected animals began to perk up, their eyes brighter, nibbling at the food in their cages, while the ones that had not been injected got sicker and sicker.

"Well, there's our answer," Jack said eagerly. "If we can get some of this stuff injected into our friends down below, we may be able to protect the healthy ones from getting the plague, and cure the sick ones as well. If we still have enough time, that is."

They had landing permission from the Bruckian spokesman within minutes, and an hour later the *Lancet* made an orderly landing on a newly-repaved landing field near one of the central cities on the seventh planet of 31 Brucker.

Tiger and Jack had obviously not exaggerated the strange appearance of the towns and cities on this plague-ridden planet, and Dal was appalled at the ravages of the disease that they had come to fight. Only one out of ten of the Bruckians was still uninfected, and another three out of the ten were clearly in the late stages of the disease, walking about blankly and blindly, stumbling into things in their paths, falling to the ground and lying mute and helpless until death came to release them. Under the glaring red sun, weary parties of stretcher bearers went about the silent streets, moving their grim cargo out to the mass graves at the edge of the city.

The original spokesman who had come up to the *Lancet* was dead, but another had taken his place as negotiator with the doctors—an older, thinner Bruckian who looked as if he carried the total burden of his people on his shoulders. He greeted them eagerly at the landing field. "You have found a solution!" he cried. "You have found a way to turn the tide—but hurry! Every moment now is precious."

During the landing procedures, Dal had worked to prepare enough of the precious antibody suspension, with Fuzzy's co-operation, to handle a large number of inoculations. By the time the ship touched down he had a dozen flasks and several hundred syringes ready. Hundreds of the unafflicted people were crowding around the ship, staring in open wonder as Dal, Jack and Tiger came down the ladder and went into close conference with the spokesman.

It took some time to explain to the spokesman why they could not begin then and there with the mass inoculations against the plague. First, they needed test cases, in order to make certain that what they thought would work in theory actually produced the desired results. Controls were needed, to be certain that the antibody suspension alone was bringing about the changes seen and not something else. At last, orders went out from the spokesman. Two hundred uninfected Bruckians were admitted to a large roped-off area near the ship, and another two hundred in late stages of the disease were led stumbling into another closed area. Preliminary skin-tests of the antibody suspension showed no sign of untoward reaction. Dal began filling syringes while Tiger and Jack started inoculating the two groups.

"If it works with these cases, it will be simple to immunize the whole population," Tiger said. "From the amounts we used on the guinea pigs, it looks as if only tiny amounts are needed. We may even be able to train the Bruckians to give the injections themselves."

"And if it works we ought to have a brand new medical service contract ready for signature with Hospital Earth," Jack added eagerly. "It won't be long before we have those Stars, you wait and see! If we can only get this done fast enough."

They worked feverishly, particularly with the group of terminal cases. Many were dying even as the shots were being given, while the first symptoms of the disease were appearing in some of the unafflicted ones. Swiftly Tiger and Jack went from patient to patient while Dal kept check of the names, numbers and locations of those that were inoculated.

And even before they were finished with the inoculations, it was apparent that they were taking effect. Not one of the infected patients died after inoculation was completed. The series took three hours, and by the time the four hundred doses were administered, one thing seemed certain: that the antibody was checking the deadly march of the disease in some way.

The Bruckian spokesman was so excited he could hardly contain himself; he wanted to start bringing in the rest of the population at once. "We've almost exhausted this first batch of the material," Dal told him. "We will have to prepare more—but we will waste time trying to move a whole planet's population here. Get a dozen aircraft ready, and a dozen healthy, intelligent workers to help us. We can show them how to use the material, and let them go out to the other population centers all at once."

Back aboard the ship they started preparing a larger quantity of the antibody suspension. Fuzzy had regenerated back to normal weight again, and much to Dal's delight had been splitting off small segments of pink protoplasm in a circle all around him, as though anticipating further demands on his resources. A quick test-run showed that the antibody was also being regenerated. Fuzzy was voraciously hungry, but the material in the second batch was still as powerful as in the first.

The doctors were almost ready to go back down, loaded with enough inoculum and syringes to equip themselves and a dozen field workers when Jack suddenly stopped what he was doing and cocked an ear toward the entrance lock.

"What's wrong?" Dal said.

"Listen a minute."

They stopped to listen. "I don't hear anything," Tiger said.

Jack nodded. "I know. That's what I mean. They were hollering their heads off when we came back aboard. Why so quiet now?"

He crossed over to the viewscreen scanning the field below, and flipped on the switch. For a moment he just stared. Then he said: "Come here a minute. I don't like the looks of this at all."

Dal and Tiger crowded up to the screen. "What's the matter?" Tiger said. "I don't see...*wait a minute!*"

"Yes, you'd better look again," Jack said. "What do you think, Dal?"

"We'd better get down there fast," Dal said, "and see what's going on. It looks to me like we've got a tiger by the tail..."

They climbed down the ladder once again, with the antibody flasks and sterile syringes strapped to their backs. But this time the greeting was different from before.

The Bruckian spokesman and the others who had not yet been inoculated drew back from them in terror as they stepped to the ground. Before, the people on the field had crowded in eagerly around the ship; now they were standing in silent groups staring at the doctors fearfully and muttering among themselves.

But the doctors could see only the inoculated people in the two roped-off areas. Off to the right among the infected Bruckians who had received the antibody there were no new dead—but there was no change for the better, either. The sick creatures drifted about aimlessly, milling like animals in a cage, their faces blank, their jaws slack, hands wandering foolishly. Not one of them had begun reacting normally, not one showed any sign of recognition or recovery.

But the real horror was on the other side of the field. Here were the healthy ones, the uninfected ones who had received preventative inoculations. A few hours before they had been left standing in quiet, happy groups, talking among themselves, laughing and joking…

But now they weren't talking any more. They stared across at the doctors with slack faces and dazed eyes, their feet shuffling aimlessly in the dust. All were alive, but only half-alive. The intelligence and alertness were gone from their faces; they were like the empty shells of the creatures they had been a few hours before, indistinguishable from the infected creatures in the other compound.

Jack turned to the Bruckian spokesman in alarm. "What's happened here?" he asked. "What's become of the ones we inoculated? Where have you taken them?"

The spokesman shrank back as though afraid Jack might reach out to touch him. "Taken them!" he cried. "We have moved none of them! Those are the ones you poisoned with your needles. What have you done to make them like this?"

"It—it must be some sort of temporary reaction to the injection," Jack faltered. "There was nothing that we used that could possibly have given them the disease, we only used a substance to help them fight it off."

The Bruckian was shaking his fist angrily. "It's no reaction, it is the plague itself! What kind of evil are you doing? You came here to help us, and instead you bring us more misery. Do we not have enough of that to please you?"

Swiftly the doctors began examining the patients in both enclosures, and on each side they found the same picture. One by one they checked the ones that had previously been untouched by the plague, and found only the sagging jaws and idiot stares.

"There's no sense examining every one," Tiger said finally. "They're all the same, every one."

"But this is impossible," Jack said, glancing apprehensively at the growing mob of angry Bruckians outside the stockades. "What could have happened? What have we done?"

"I don't know," Tiger said. "But whatever we've done has turned into a boomerang. We knew that the antibody might not work, and the disease might just go right ahead, but we didn't anticipate anything like this."

"Maybe some foreign protein got into the batch," Dal said.

Tiger shook his head. "It wouldn't behave like *this*. And we were careful getting it ready. All we've done was inject an antibody against a specific virus. All it could have done was to kill the virus, but these people act as though they're infected now."

"But they're not dying," Dal said. "And the sick ones we injected stopped dying, too."

"So what do we do now?" Jack said.

"Get one of these that changed like this aboard ship and go over him with a fine-toothed comb. We've got to find out what's happened."

He led one of the stricken Bruckians by the hand like a mindless dummy across the field toward the little group where the spokesman and his party stood. The crowd on the field were moving in closer; an angry cry went up when Dal touched the sick creature.

"You'll have to keep this crowd under control," Dal said to the spokesman. "We're going to take this one aboard the ship and examine him to see what this reaction could be, but this mob is beginning to sound dangerous."

"They're afraid," the spokesman said. "They want to know what you've done to them, what this new curse is that you bring in your syringes."

"It's not a curse, but something has gone wrong. We need to learn what, in order to deal with it."

"The people are afraid and angry," the spokesman said. "I don't know how long I can control them."

And indeed, the attitude of the crowd around the ship was very strange. They were not just fearful; they were terrified. As the doctors walked back to the ship leading the stricken Bruckian behind them, the people shrank back with dreadful cries, holding up their hands as if to ward off some monstrous evil. Before, in the worst throes of the plague, there had been no sign of this kind of reaction. The people had seemed apathetic and miserable, resigned hopelessly to their fate, but now they were reacting in abject terror. It almost seemed that they were more afraid of these walking shells of their former selves than they were of the disease itself.

But as the doctors started up the ladder toward the entrance lock the crowd surged in toward them with fists raised in anger. "We'd better get help, and fast," Jack said as he slammed the entrance lock closed behind them. "I don't like the looks of this a bit. Dal, we'd better see what we can learn from this poor creature here."

As Tiger headed for the earphones, Dal and Jack went to work once again, checking the blood and other body fluids from the stricken Bruckian. But now, incredibly, the results of their tests were quite different from those they had obtained before. The blood sugar and protein determinations fell into the pattern they had originally expected for a creature of this type. Even more surprising, the level of the antibody against the plague virus was high—far higher than it could have been from the tiny amount that was injected into the creature.

"They must have been making it themselves," Dal said, "and our inoculation was just the straw that broke the camel's back. All of those people must have been on the brink of symptoms of the infection, and all we did was add to the natural defenses they were already making."

"Then why did the symptoms appear?" Jack said. "If that's true, we should have been *helping* them, and look at them now!"

Tiger appeared at the door, scowling. "We've got real trouble, now," he said. "I can't get through to a hospital ship. In fact, I can't get a message out at all. These people are jamming our radios."

"But why?" Dal said.

"I don't know, but take a look outside there."

Through the viewscreen it seemed as though the whole field around the ship had filled up with the crowd. The first reaction of terror now seemed to have given way to blind fury; the people were shouting angrily, waving their clenched fists at the ship as the spokesman tried to hold them back.

Then there was a resounding crash from somewhere below, and the ship lurched, throwing the doctors to the floor. They staggered to their feet as another blow jolted the ship, and another.

"Let's get a screen up," Tiger shouted. "Jack, get the engines going. They're trying to board us, and I don't think it'll be much fun if they ever break in."

In the control room they threw the switches that activated a powerful protective energy screen around the ship. It was a device that was carried by all GPP Ships as a means of protection against physical attack. When activated, an energy screen was virtually impregnable, but it could only be used briefly; the power it required placed an enormous drain on a ship's energy resources, and a year's nuclear fuel could be consumed in a few hours.

Now the screen served its purpose. The ship steadied, still vibrating from the last assault, and the noise from below ceased abruptly. But when Jack threw the switches to start the engines, nothing happened at all.

"Look at that!" he cried, staring at the motionless dials. "They're jamming our electrical system somehow. I can't get any turn-over."

"Try it again," Tiger said. "We've got to get out of here. If they break in, we're done for."

"They can't break through the screen," Dal said.

"Not as long as it lasts. But we can't keep it up indefinitely."

Once again they tried the radio equipment. There was no response but the harsh static of the jamming signal from the ground below. "It's no good," Tiger said finally. "We're stuck here, and we can't even call for help. You'd think if they were so scared of us they'd be glad to see us go."

"I think there's more to it than that," Dal said thoughtfully. "This whole business has been crazy from the start. This just fits in with all the rest." He picked Fuzzy off his perch and set him on his shoulder as if to protect him from some unsuspected threat. "Maybe they're afraid of us, I don't know. But I think they're afraid of something else a whole lot worse."

There was nothing to be done but wait and stare hopelessly at the mass of notes and records that they had collected on the people of 31 Brucker VII and the plague that afflicted them.

Until now, the *Lancet*'s crew had been too busy to stop and piece the data together, to try to see the picture as a whole. But now there was ample time, and the realization of what had been happening here began to dawn on them.

They had followed the well-established principles step by step in studying these incredible people, and nothing had come out as it should. In theory, the steps they had taken should have yielded the answer. They had come to a planet where an entire population was threatened with a dreadful disease. They had identified the disease, found and isolated the virus that caused it, and then developed an antibody that effectively destroyed the virus—in the laboratory. But when they had tried to apply the antibody in the afflicted patients, the response had been totally unexpected. They had stopped the march of death among those they had inoculated, and had produced instead a condition that the people seemed to dread far more than death.

"Let's face it," Dal said, "we bungled it somehow. We should have had help here right from the start. I don't know where we went wrong, but we've done something."

"Well, it wasn't your fault," Jack said gloomily. "If we had the right diagnosis, this wouldn't have happened. And I *still* can't see the diagnosis. All I've been able to come up with is a nice mess."

"We're missing something, that's all," Dal said. "The information is all here. We just aren't reading it right, somehow. Somewhere in here is a key to the whole thing, and we just can't see it."

They went back to the data again, going through it step by step. This was Jack Alvarez's specialty—the technique of diagnosis, the ability to take all the available information about a race and about its illness and piece it together into a pattern that made sense. Dal could see that Jack was now bitterly angry with himself, yet at every turn he seemed to strike another obstacle—some fact that didn't jibe, a missing fragment here, a wrong answer there. With Dal and Tiger helping he started back over the sequence of events, tryingto make sense out of them, and came up squarely against a blank wall.

The things they had done should have worked; instead, they had failed. A specific antibody used against a specific virus should have destroyed the virus or slowed its progress, and there seemed to be no rational explanation for the dreadful response of the uninfected ones who had been inoculated for protection.

And as the doctors sifted through the data, the Bruckian they had brought up from the enclosure sat staring off into space, making small noises with his mouth and moving his arms aimlessly. After a while they led him back to a bunk, gave him a medicine for sleep and left him snoring gently. Another hour passed as they pored over their notes, with Tiger stopping from time to time to mop perspiration from his forehead. All three were aware of the moving clock hands, marking off the minutes that the force screen could hold out.

And then Dal Timgar was digging into the pile of papers, searching frantically for something he could not find. "That first report we got," he said hoarsely. "There was something in the very first information we ever saw on this planet..."

"You mean the Confederation's data? It's in the radio log." Tiger pulled open the thick log book. "But what..."

"It's there, plain as day, I'm sure of it," Dal said. He read through the report swiftly, until he came to the last paragraph—a two-line description of the largest creatures the original Exploration Ship had found on the planet, described by them as totally unintelligent and only observed on a few occasions in the course of the exploration. Dal read it, and his hands were trembling as he handed the report to Jack. "I knew the answer was there!" he said. "Take a look at that again and think about it for a minute."

Jack read it through. "I don't see what you mean," he said.

"I mean that I think we've made a horrible mistake," Dal said, "and I think I see now what it was. We've had this whole thing exactly 100 per cent backward from the start, and that explains everything that's happened here!"

Tiger peered over Jack's shoulder at the report. "Backward?"

"As backward as we could get it," Dal said. "We've assumed all along that these flesh-and-blood creatures down there were the ones that were calling us for help because of a virus plague that was attacking and killing them. All right, look at it the other way. Just suppose that the intelligent creature that called us for help was the *virus*, and that those flesh-and-blood creatures down there with the blank, stupid faces are the *real* plague we ought to have been fighting all along!"

## CHAPTER ELEVEN
### Dal Breaks a Promise

For a moment the others just stared at their Garvian crewmate. Then Jack Alvarez snorted. "You'd better go back and get some rest," he said. "This has been a tougher grind than I thought. You're beginning to show the strain."

"No, I mean it," Dal said earnestly. "I think that is exactly what's been happening."

Tiger looked at him with concern. "Dal, this is no time for double talk and nonsense."

"It's not nonsense," Dal said. "It's the answer, if you'll only stop and think."

"An intelligent *virus*?" Jack said. "Who ever heard of such a thing? There's never been a life-form like that reported since the beginning of the galactic exploration."

"But that doesn't mean there couldn't be one," Dal said. "And how would an exploratory crew ever identify it, if it existed? How would they ever even suspect it? They'd miss it completely—unless it happened to get into trouble itself and try to call for help!" Dal jumped up in excitement.

"Look, I've seen a dozen articles showing how such a thing was theoretically possible...a virus life-form with billions of submicroscopic parts acting together to form an intelligent colony. The only thing a virus-creature would need that other intelligent creatures don't need would be some kind of a host, some sort of animal body to live in so that it could use its intelligence."

"It's impossible," Jack said scornfully. "Why don't you give it up and get some rest? Here we sit with our feet in the fire, and all you can do is dream up foolishness like this."

"I'm not so sure it's foolishness," Tiger Martin said slowly. "Jack, maybe he's got something. A couple of things would fit that don't make sense at all."

"All sorts of things would fit," Dal said. "The viruses we know have to have a host—some other life-form to live in. Usually they are parasites, damaging or destroying their hosts and giving nothing in return, but some set up real partnership housekeeping with their hosts so that both are better off."

"You mean a symbiotic relationship," Jack said.

"Of course," Dal said. "Now suppose these virus-creatures were intelligent, and came from some other place looking for a new host they could live with. They wouldn't look for an intelligent creature, they would look for some *unintelligent* creature with a good strong body that would be capable of doing all sorts of things if it only had an intelligence to guide it. Suppose these virus-creatures found a simple-minded, unintelligent race on this planet and tried to set up a symbiotic relationship with it. The virus-creatures would need a host to provide a home and a food supply. Maybe they in turn could supply the intelligence to raise the host to a civilized level of life and performance. Wouldn't that be a fair basis for a sound partnership?"

Jack scratched his head doubtfully. "And you're saying that these virus-creatures came here after the exploratory ship had come and gone?"

"They must have! Maybe they only came a few years ago, maybe only months ago. But when they tried to invade the unintelligent creatures the exploratory ship found here, they discovered that the new host's body couldn't tolerate them. His body reacted as if they were parasitic invaders, and built up antibodies against them. And those body defenses were more than the virus could cope with."

Dal pointed to the piles of notes on the desk. "Don't you see how it adds up? Right from the beginning we've been assuming that these monkey-like creatures here on this planet were the dominant, intelligent life-forms. Anatomically they were ordinary cellular creatures like you and me, and when we examined them we expected to find the same sort of biochemical reactions we'd find with any such creatures. And all our results came out wrong, because we were dealing with a combination of two creatures—the host and a virus. Maybe the creatures on 31 Brucker VII were naturally blank-faced idiots before the virus came, or maybe the virus was forced to damage some vital part just in order to fight back—but it was the *virus* that was being killed by its own host, not the other way around."

Jack studied the idea, no longer scornful. "So you think the virus-creatures called for help, hoping we could find some way to free them from the hosts that were killing them. And when Fuzzy developed a powerful antibody against them, and we started using the stuff—" Jack broke off, shaking his head in horror. "Dal, if you're right, we were literally *slaughtering our own patients* when we gave those injections down there!"

"Exactly," Dal said. "Is it any wonder they're so scared of us now? It must have looked like a deliberate attempt to wipe them out, and now they're afraid that we'll go get help and *really* move in against them."

Tiger nodded. "Which was precisely what we were planning, if you stop to think about it. Maybe that was why they were so reluctant to tell us anything about themselves. Maybe they've already been mistaken for parasitic invaders before, wherever in the universe they came from."

"But if this is true, then we're really in a jam," Jack said. "What can we possibly do for them? We can't even repair the damage that we've already done. What sort of treatment can we use?"

Dal shook his head. "I don't know the answer to that one, but I do know we've got to find out if we're right. An intelligent virus-creature has as much right to life as any other intelligent life-form. If we've guessed right, then there's a lot that our intelligent friends down there haven't told us. Maybe there'll be some clue there. We've just got to face them with it, and see what they say."

Jack looked at the viewscreen, at the angry mob milling around on the ground, held back from the ship by the energy screen. "You mean just go out there and say, 'Look fellows, it was all a mistake, we didn't really mean to do it?' " He shook his head. "Maybe you want to tell them. Not me!"

"Dal's right, though," Tiger said. "We've got to contact them somehow. They aren't even responding to radio communication, and they've scrambled our outside radio and fouled our drive mechanism somehow. We've got to settle this while we still have an energy screen."

There was a long silence as the three doctors looked at each other. Then Dal stood up and walked over to the swinging platform. He lifted Fuzzy down onto his shoulder. "It'll be all right," he said to Jack and Tiger. "I'll go out."

"They'll tear you to ribbons!" Tiger protested.

Dal shook his head. "I don't think so," he said quietly. "I don't think they'll touch me. They'll greet me with open arms when I go down there, and they'll be eager to talk to me."

"Are you crazy?" Jack cried, leaping to his feet. "We can't let you go out there."

"Don't worry," Dal said. "I know exactly what I'm doing. I'll be able to handle the situation, believe me."

He hesitated a moment, and gave Fuzzy a last nervous pat, settling him more firmly on his shoulder. Then he started down the corridor for the entrance lock.

He had promised himself long before…many years before…that he would never do what he planned to do now, but now he knew that there was no alternative. The only other choice was to wait helplessly until the power failed and the protective screen vanished and the creatures on the ground outside tore the ship to pieces.

As he stood in the airlock waiting for the pressure to shift to outside normal, he lifted Fuzzy down into the crook of his arm and rubbed the little creature between the shoe-button eyes. "You've got to back me up now," he whispered softly. "It's been a long time, I know that, but I need help now. It's going to be up to you."

Dal knew the subtle strength of his people's peculiar talent. From the moment he had stepped down to the ground the second time with Tiger and Jack, even with Fuzzy waiting back on the ship, he had felt the powerful wave of horror and fear and anger rising up from the Bruckians, and he had glimpsed the awful idiot vacancy of the minds of the creatures in the enclosure, in whom the intelligent virus was already dead. This had required no effort; it just came naturally into his mind, and he had known instantly that something terrible had gone wrong.

In the years on Hospital Earth, he had carefully forced himself never to think in terms of his special talent. He had diligently screened off the impressions and emotions that struck at him constantly from his classmates and from others that he came in contact with. Above all, he had fought down the temptation to turn his power the other way, to use it to his own advantage.

But now, as the lock opened and he started down the ladder, he closed his mind to everything else. Hugging Fuzzy close to his side, he turned his mind into a single tight channel. He drove the thought out at the Bruckians with all the power he could muster: *I come in peace. I mean you no harm. I have good news, joyful news. You must be happy to see me, eager to welcome me...*

He could feel the wave of anger and fear strike him like a physical blow as soon as he appeared in the entrance lock. The cries rose up in a wave, and the crowd surged in toward the ship. With the energy field released, there was nothing to stop them; they were tripping over each other to reach the bottom of the ladder first, shouting threats and waving angry fists, reaching up to grab at Dal's ankles as he came down...

And then as if by magic the cries died in the throats of the ones closest to the ladder. The angry fists unclenched, and extended into outstretched hands to help him down to the ground. As though an ever-widening wave was spreading out around him, the aura of peace and good will struck the people in the crowd. And as it spread, the anger faded from the faces; the hard lines gave way to puzzled frowns, then to smiles. Dal channeled his thoughts more rigidly, and watched the effect spread out from him like ripples in a pond, as anger and suspicion and fear melted away to be replaced by confidence and trust.

Dal had seen it occur a thousand times before. He could remember his trips on Garvian trading ships with his father, when the traders with their fuzzy pink friends on their shoulders faced cold, hostile, suspicious buyers. It had seemed almost miraculous the way the suspicions melted away and the hostile faces became friendly as the buyers' minds became receptive to bargaining and trading. He had even seen it happen on the *Teegar* with Tiger and Jack, and it was no coincidence that throughout the galaxy the Garvians—always accompanied by their fuzzy friends—had assumed the position of power and wealth and leadership that they had.

And now once again the pattern was being repeated. The Bruckians who surrounded Dal were smiling and talking eagerly; they made no move to touch him or harm him.

The spokesman they had talked to before was there at his elbow, and Dal heard himself saying, "We have found the answer to your problem. We know now the true nature of your race, and the nature of your intelligence. You were afraid that we would find out, but your fears were groundless. We will not turn our knowledge against you. We only want to help you."

An expression almost like despair had crossed the spokesman's face as Dal spoke. Now he said, "It would be good—if we could believe you. But how can we? We have been driven for so long and come so far, and now you would seek to wipe us out as parasites and disease-carriers."

Dal saw the Bruckian creature's eyes upon him, saw the frail body tremble and the lips move, but he knew now that the intelligence that formed the words and the thoughts behind them, the intelligence that made the lips speak the words, was the intelligence of a creature far different from the one he was looking at—a creature formed of billions of submicroscopic units, imbedded in every one of the Bruckian's body cells, trapped there now and helpless against the antibody reaction that sought to destroy them. This was the intelligence that had called for help in its desperate plight, but had not quite dared to trust its rescuers with the whole truth.

But was this strange virus-creature good or evil, hostile or friendly? Dal's hand lay on Fuzzy's tiny body, but he felt no quiver, no vibration of fear. He looked across the face of the crowd, trying with all his strength to open his mind to the feelings and emotions of these people. Often enough, with Fuzzy nearby, he had felt the harsh impact of hostile, cruel, brutal minds, even when the owners of those minds had tried to conceal their feelings behind smiles and pleasant words. But here there was no sign of the sickening feeling that kind of mind produced, no hint of hostility or evil.

He shook his head. "Why should we want to destroy you?" he said. "You are good, and peaceful. We know that; why should we harm you? All you want is a place to live, and a host to join with you in a mutually valuable partnership. But you did not tell us everything you could about yourselves, and as a result we have destroyed some of you in our clumsy attempts to learn your true nature."

They talked then, and bit by bit the story came out. The life-form was indeed a virus, unimaginably ancient, and intelligent throughout millions of years of its history. Driven by over-population, a pure culture of the virus-creatures had long ago departed from their original native hosts, and traveled like encapsulated spores across space from a distant galaxy. The trip had been long and exhausting; the virus-creatures had retained only the minimum strength necessary to establish themselves in a new host, some unintelligent creature living on an uninhabited planet, a creature that could benefit by the great intelligence of the virus-creatures, and provide food and shelter for both. Finally, after thousands of years of searching, they had found this planet with its dull-minded, fruit-gathering inhabitants. These creatures had seemed perfect as hosts, and the virus-creatures had thought their long search for a perfect partner was finally at an end.

It was not until they had expended the last dregs of their energy in anchoring themselves into the cells and tissues of their new hosts that they discovered to their horror that the host-creatures could not tolerate them. Unlike their original hosts, the bodies of these creatures began developing deadly antibodies that attacked the virus invaders. In their desperate attempts to hold on and fight back, the virus-creatures had destroyed vital centers in the new hosts, and one by one they had begun to die. There was not enough energy left for the virus-creatures to detach themselves and move on; without some way to stem the onslaught of the antibodies, they were doomed to total destruction.

"We were afraid to tell you doctors the truth," the spokesman said. "As we wandered and searched we discovered that creatures like ourselves were extreme rarities in the universe, that most creatures similar to us were mindless, unintelligent parasites that struck down their hosts and destroyed them. Wherever we went, life-forms of your kind regarded us as disease-bearers, and their doctors taught them ways to destroy us. We had hoped that from you we might find a way to save ourselves—then you unleashed on us the one weapon we could not fight."

"But not maliciously," Dal said. "Only because we did not understand. And now that we do, there may be a way to help. A difficult way, but at least a way. The antibodies themselves can be neutralized, but it may take our biochemists and virologists and all their equipment months or even years to develop and synthesize the proper antidote."

The spokesman looked at Dal, and turned away with a hopeless gesture. "Then it is too late, after all," he said. "We are dying too fast. Even those of us who have not been affected so far are beginning to feel the early symptoms of the antibody attack." He smiled sadly and reached out to stroke the small pink creature on Dal's arm. "Your people too have a partner, I see. We envy you."

Dal felt a movement on his arm and looked down at Fuzzy. He had always taken his little friend for granted, but now he thought of the feeling of emptiness and loss that had come across him when Fuzzy had been almost killed. He had often wondered just what Fuzzy might be like if his almost-fluid, infinitely adaptable physical body had only been endowed with intelligence. He had wondered what kind of a creature Fuzzy might be if he were able to use his remarkable structure with the guidance of an intelligent mind behind it...

He felt another movement on his arm, and his eyes widened as he stared down at his little friend.

A moment before, there had been a single three-inch pink creature on his elbow. But now there were two, each just one-half the size of the original. As Dal watched, one of the two drew away from the other, creeping in to snuggle closer to Dal's side, and a pair of shoe-button eyes appeared and blinked up at him trustingly. But the other creature was moving down his arm, straining out toward the Bruckian spokesman...

Dal realized instantly what was happening. He started to draw back, but something stopped him. Deep in his mind he could sense a gentle voice reassuring him, saying, *It's all right, there is nothing to fear, no harm will come to me. These creatures need help, and this is the way to help them.*

He saw the Bruckian reach out a trembling hand. The tiny pink creature that had separated from Fuzzy seemed almost to leap across to the outstretched hand. And then the spokesman held him close, and the new Fuzzy shivered happily.

The virus-creatures had found a host. Here was the ideal kind of body for their intelligence to work with and mold, a host where antibody-formation could be perfectly controlled. Dal knew now that the problem had almost been solved once before, when the virus-creature had reached Fuzzy on the ship; if they had only waited a little longer they would have seen Fuzzy recover from his illness a different creature entirely than before.

Already the new creature was dividing again, with half going on to the next of the Bruckians. To a submicroscopic virus, the body of the host would not have to be large; soon there would be a sufficient number of hosts to serve the virus-creatures' needs forever. As he started back up the ladder to the ship, Dal knew that the problem on 31 Brucker VII had found a happy and permanent solution.

Back in the control room Dal related what had happened from beginning to end. There was only one detail that he concealed. He could not bring himself to tell Tiger and Jack of the true nature of his relationship with Fuzzy, of the odd power over the emotions of others that Fuzzy's presence gave him. He could tell by their faces that they realized that he was leaving something out; they had watched him go down to face a blood-thirsty mob, and had seen that mob become docile as lambs as though by magic. Clearly they could not understand what had happened, yet they did not ask him.

"So it was Fuzzy's idea to volunteer as a new host for the creatures," Jack said.

Dal nodded. "I knew that he could reproduce, of course," he said. "Every Garvian has a Fuzzy, and whenever a new Garvian is born, the father's Fuzzy always splits so that half can join the new-born child. It's like the division of a cell; within hours the Fuzzy that stayed down there will have divided to provide enough protoplasm for every one of the surviving intelligent Bruckians."

"And your diagnosis was the right one," Jack said.

"We'll see," Dal said. "Tomorrow we'll know better."

But clearly the problem had been solved. The next day there was an excited conference between the spokesman and the doctors on the *Lancet*. The Bruckians had elected to maintain the same host body as before. They had gotten used to it; with the small pink creatures serving as a shelter to protect them against the deadly antibodies, they could live in peace and security. But they were eager, before the *Lancet* disembarked, to sign a full medical service contract with the doctors from Hospital Earth. A contract was signed, subject only to final acceptance and ratification by the Hospital Earth officials.

Now that their radio was free again, the three doctors jubilantly prepared a full account of the problem of 31 Brucker and its solution, and dispatched the news of the new contract to the first relay station on its way back to Hospital Earth. Then, weary to the point of collapse, they retired for the first good sleep in days, eagerly awaiting an official response from Hospital Earth on the completed case and the contract.

"It ought to wipe out any black mark Dr. Tanner has against any of us," Jack said happily. "And especially in Dal's case." He grinned at the Red Doctor. "This one has been yours, all the way. You pulled it out of the fire after I flubbed it completely, and you're going to get the credit, if I have anything to say about it."

"We should all get credit," Dal said. "A new contract isn't signed every day of the year. But the way we all fumbled our way into it, Hospital Earth shouldn't pay much attention to it anyway."

But Dal knew that he was only throwing up his habitual shield to guard against disappointment. Traditionally, a new contract meant a Star rating for each of the crew that brought it in. All through medical school Dal had read the reports of other patrol ships that had secured new contracts with uncontacted planets, and he had seen the fanfare and honor that were heaped on the doctors from those ships. And for the first time since he had entered medical school years before, Dal now allowed himself to hope that his goal was in sight.

He wanted to be a Star Surgeon more than anything else. It was the one thing that he had wanted and worked for since the cruel days when the plague had swept his homeland, destroying his mother and leaving his father an ailing cripple. And since his assignment aboard the *Lancet*, one thought had filled his mind: to turn in the scarlet collar and cuff in return for the cape and silver star of the full-fledged physician in the Red Service of Surgery.

Always before there had been the half-conscious dread that something would happen, that in the end, after all the work, the silver star would still remain just out of reach, that somehow he would never quite get it.

But now there could be no question. Even Black Doctor Tanner could not deny a new contract. The crew of the *Lancet* would be called back to Hospital Earth for a full report on the newly contacted race, and their days as probationary doctors in the General Practice patrol would be over.

After they had slept themselves out, the doctors prepared the ship for launching, and made their farewells to the Bruckian spokesman.

"When the contract is ratified," Jack said, "a survey ship will come here. They will have all of the information that we have gathered, and they will spend many months gathering more. Tell them everything they want to know. Don't conceal anything, because once they have completed their survey, any General Practice Patrol ship in the galaxy will be able to answer a call for help and have the information they need to serve you."

They delayed launching hour by hour waiting for a response from Hospital Earth, but the radio was silent. They thought of a dozen reasons why the message might have been delayed, but the radio silence continued. Finally they strapped down and lifted the ship from the planet, still waiting for a response.

When it finally came, there was no message of congratulations, nor even any acknowledgment of the new contract. Instead, there was only a terse message:

PROCEED TO REFERENCE POINT 43621 SECTION XIX AND STAND BY FOR INSPECTION PARTY

Tiger took the message and read it in silence, then handed it to Dal.

"What do they say?" Jack said.

"Read it," Dal said. "They don't mention the contract, just an inspection party."

"Inspection party! Is that the best they can do for us?"

"They don't sound too enthusiastic," Tiger said. "At least you'd think they could acknowledge receipt of our report."

"It's probably just part of the routine," Dal said. "Maybe they want to confirm our reports from our own records before they commit themselves."

But he knew that he was only whistling in the dark. The moment he saw the terse message, he knew something had gone wrong with the contract. There would be no notes of congratulation, no returning in triumph and honor to Hospital Earth.

Whatever the reason for the inspection party, Dal felt certain who the inspector was going to be.

It had been exciting to dream, but the scarlet cape and the silver star were still a long way out of reach.

## CHAPTER TWELVE
*The Showdown*

It was hours later when their ship reached the contact point co-ordinates. There had been little talk during the transit; each of them knew already what the other was thinking, and there wasn't much to be said. The message had said it for them.

Dal's worst fears were realized when the inspection ship appeared, converting from Koenig drive within a few miles of the *Lancet*. He had seen the ship before—a sleek, handsomely outfitted patrol class ship with the insignia of the Black Service of

Pathology emblazoned on its hull, the private ship of a Four-star Black Doctor.

But none of them anticipated the action taken by the inspection ship as it drew within lifeboat range of the *Lancet*.

A scooter shot away from its storage rack on the black ship, and a crew of black-garbed technicians piled into the *Lancet*'s entrance lock, dressed in the special decontamination suits worn when a ship was returning from a plague spot into uninfected territory.

"What is this?" Tiger demanded as the technicians started unloading decontamination gear into the lock. "What are you doing with that stuff?"

The squad leader looked at him sourly. "You're in quarantine, Doc," he said. "Class I, all precautions, contact with unidentified pestilence. If you don't like it, argue with the Black Doctor, I've just got a job to do."

He started shouting orders to his men, and they scattered throughout the ship, with blowers and disinfectants, driving antiseptic sprays into every crack and cranny of the ship's interior, scouring the hull outside in the rigid pattern prescribed for plague ships. They herded the doctors into the decontamination lock, stripped them of their clothes, scrubbed them down and tossed them special sterilized fatigues to wear with masks and gloves.

"This is idiotic," Jack protested. "We aren't carrying any dangerous organisms!"

The squad leader shrugged indifferently. "Tell it to the Black Doctor, not me. All I know is that this ship is under quarantine until it's officially released, and from what I hear, it's not going to be released for quite some time."

At last the job was done, and the scooter departed back to the inspection ship. A few moments later they saw it returning, this time carrying just three men. In addition to the pilot and one technician, there was a single passenger: a portly figure dressed in a black robe, horn-rimmed glasses and cowl.

The scooter grappled the *Lancet*'s side, and Black Doctor Hugo Tanner climbed wheezing into the entrance lock, followed by the technician. He stopped halfway into the lock to get his breath, and paused again as the lock swung closed behind him. Dal was shocked at the physical change in the man in the few short weeks since he had seen him last. The Black Doctor's face was gray; every effort of movement brought on paroxysms of coughing. He looked sick, and he looked tired, yet his jaw was still set in angry determination.

The doctors stood at attention as he stepped into the control room, hardly able to conceal their surprise at seeing him. "Well?" the Black Doctor snapped at them. "What's the trouble with you? You act like you've seen a ghost or something."

"We—we'd heard that you were in the hospital, sir."

"Did you, now!" the Black Doctor snorted. "Hospital! Bah! I had to tell the press something to get the hounds off me for a while. These young puppies seem to think that a Black Doctor can just walk away from his duties any time he chooses to undergo their fancy surgical procedures. And you know who's been screaming the loudest to get their hands on me. The Red Service of Surgery, that's who!"

The Black Doctor glared at Dal Timgar. "Well, I dare say the Red Doctors will have their chance at me, all in good time. But first there are certain things which must be taken care of." He looked up at the attendant. "You're quite certain that the ship has been decontaminated?"

The attendant nodded. "Yes, sir."

"And the crewmen?"

"It's safe to talk to them, sir, as long as you avoid physical contact."

The Black Doctor grunted and wheezed and settled himself down in a seat. "All right now, gentlemen," he said to the three, "let's have your story of this affair in the Brucker system, right from the start."

"But we sent in a full report," Tiger said.

"I'm aware of that, you idiot. I have waded through your report, all thirty-five pages of it, and I only wish you hadn't been so long-winded. Now I want to hear what happened directly from you. Well?"

The three doctors looked at each other. Then Jack began the story, starting with the first hesitant "greeting" that had come through to them. He told everything that had happened without embellishments: their first analysis of the nature of the problem, the biochemical and medical survey that they ran on the afflicted people, his own failure to make the diagnosis, the incident of Fuzzy's sudden affliction, and the strange solution that had finally come from it. As he talked the Black Doctor sat back with his eyes half closed, his face blank, listening and nodding from time to time as the story proceeded.

And Jack was carefully honest and fair in his account. "We were all of us lost, until Dal Timgar saw the significance of what had happened to Fuzzy," he said. "His idea of putting the creature through the filter gave us our first specimen of the isolated virus, and showed us how to obtain the antibody. Then after we saw what happened with our initial series of injections, we were really at sea, and by then we couldn't reach a hospital ship for help of any kind." He went on to relate Dal's idea that the virus itself might be the intelligent creature, and recounted the things that happened after Dal went down to talk to the spokesman again with Fuzzy on his shoulder.

Through it all the Black Doctor listened sourly, glancing occasionally at Dal and saying nothing. "So is that all?" he said when Jack had finished.

"Not quite," Jack said. "I want it to be on the record that it was my failure in diagnosis that got us into trouble. I don't want any misunderstanding about that. If I'd had the wit to think beyond the end of my nose, there wouldn't have been any problem."

"I see," the Black Doctor said. He pointed to Dal. "So it was this one who really came up with the answers and directed the whole program on this problem, is that right?"

"That's right," Jack said firmly. "He should get all the credit."

Something stirred in Dal's mind and he felt Fuzzy snuggling in tightly to his side. He could feel the cold hostility in the Black Doctor's mind, and he started to say something, but the Black Doctor cut him off. "Do you agree to that also, Dr. Martin?" he asked Tiger.

"I certainly do," Tiger said. "I'll back up the Blue Doctor right down the line."

The Black Doctor smiled unpleasantly and nodded. "Well, I'm certainly happy to hear you say that, gentlemen. I might say that it is a very great relief to me to hear it from your own testimony.

Because this time there shouldn't be any argument from either of you as to just where the responsibility lies, and I'm relieved to know that I can completely exonerate you two, at any rate."

Jack Alvarez's jaw went slack and he stared at the Black Doctor as though he hadn't heard him properly. "Exonerate us?" he said. "Exonerate us from what?"

"From the charges of incompetence, malpractice and conduct unbecoming to a physician which I am lodging against your colleague in the Red Service here," the Black Doctor said angrily. "Of course, I was confident that neither of you two could have contributed very much to this bungling mess, but it is reassuring to have your own statements of that fact on the record. They should carry more weight in a Council hearing than any plea I might make in your behalf."

"But—but what do you mean by a Council hearing?" Tiger stammered. "I don't understand you! This—this problem is *solved.* We solved it as a patrol team, all of us. We sent in a brand new medical service contract from those people..."

"Oh, yes. *That!*" The Black Doctor drew a long pink dispatch sheet from an inner pocket and opened it out. The doctors could see the photo reproductions of their signatures at the bottom. "Fortunately—for you two—this bit of nonsense was brought to my attention at the first relay station that received it. I personally accepted it and withdrew it from the circuit before it could reach Hospital Earth for filing."

Slowly, as they watched him, he ripped the pink dispatch sheet into a dozen pieces and tossed it into the disposal vent. "So much for that," he said slowly. "I can choose to overlook your foolishness in trying to cloud the important issues with a so-called 'contract' to divert attention, but I'm afraid I can't pay much attention to it, nor allow it to appear in the general report. And of course I am forced to classify the *Lancet* as a plague ship until a bacteriological and virological examination has been completed on both ship and crew. The planet itself will be considered a galactic plague spot until proper measures have been taken to insure its decontamination."

The Black Doctor drew some papers from another pocket and turned to Dal Timgar. "As for you, the charges are clear enough.

You have broken the most fundamental rules of good judgment and good medicine in handling the 31 Brucker affair. You have permitted a General Practice Patrol ship to approach a potentially dangerous plague spot without any notification of higher authorities. You have undertaken a biochemical and medical survey for which you had neither the proper equipment nor the training qualifications, and you exposed your ship and your crewmates to an incredible risk in landing on such a planet. You are responsible for untold—possibly fatal—damage to over two hundredindividuals of the race that called on you for help. You have even subjected the creature that depends upon your own race for its life and support to virtual slavery and possible destruction; and finally, you had the audacity to try to cover up your bungling with claims of arranging a medical service contract with an uninvestigated race."

The Black Doctor broke off as an attendant came in the door and whispered something in his ear. Doctor Tanner shook his head angrily, "I can't be bothered now!"

"They say it's urgent, sir."

"Yes, it's always urgent." The Black Doctor heaved to his feet. "If it weren't for this miserable incompetent here, I wouldn't have to be taking precious time away from my more important duties." He scowled at the *Lancet* crewmen. "You will excuse me for a moment," he said, and disappeared into the communications room.

The moment he was gone from the room, Jack and Tiger were talking at once. "He couldn't really be serious," Tiger said. "It's impossible! Not one of those charges would hold up under investigation."

"Well, I think it's a frame-up," Jack said, his voice tight with anger. "I knew that some people on Hospital Earth were out to get you, but I don't see how a Four-star Black Doctor could be a party to such a thing. Either someone has been misinforming him, or he just doesn't understand what happened."

Dal shook his head. "He understands, all right, and he's the one who's determined to get me out of medicine. This is a flimsy excuse, but he has to use it, because it's now or never. He knows that if we bring in a contract with a new planet, and it's formally ratified, we'll all get our Stars and he'd never be able to block me again. And Black DoctorTanner is going to be certain that I don't get that Star, or die trying."

"But this is completely unfair," Jack protested. "He's turning our own words against you! You can bet that he'll have a survey crew down on that planet in no time, bringing home a contract just the same as the one we wrote, and there won't be any questions asked about it."

"Except that I'll be out of the service," Dal said. "Don't worry. You'll get the credit in the long run. When all the dust settles, he'll be sure that you two are named as agents for the contract. He doesn't want to hurt you, it's me that he's out to get."

"Well, he won't get away with it," Tiger said. "We can see to that. It's not too late to retract our stories. If he thinks he can get rid of you with something that wasn't your fault, he's going to find out that he has to get rid of a lot more than just you."

But Dal was shaking his head. "Not this time, Tiger. This time you keep out of it."

"What do you mean, keep out of it?" Tiger cried. "Do you think I'm going to stand by quietly and watch him cut you down?"

"That's exactly what you're going to do," Dal said sharply. "I meant what I said. I want you to keep your mouth shut. Don't say anything more at all, just let it be."

"But I can't stand by and do nothing! When a friend of mine needs help—"

"Can't you get it through your thick skull that this time I don't want your help?" Dal said. "Do me a favor this time. *Leave me alone.* Don't stick your thumb in the pie."

Tiger just stared at the little Garvian. "Look, Dal, all I'm trying to do—"

"I know what you're trying to do," Dal snapped, "and I don't want any part of it. I don't need your help, I don't *want* it. Why do you have to force it down my throat?"

There was a long silence. Then Tiger spread his hands helplessly. "Okay," he said, "if that's the way you want it." He turned away from Dal, his big shoulders slumping. "I've only been trying to make up for some of the dirty breaks you've been handed since you came to Hospital Earth."

"I know that," Dal said, "and I've appreciated it. Sometimes it's been the only thing that's kept me going. But that doesn't mean that you own me. Friendship is one thing; proprietorship is something else. I'm not your private property."

He saw the look on Tiger's face, as though he had suddenly turned and slapped him viciously across the face. "Look, I know it sounds awful, but I can't help it. I don't want to hurt you, and I don't want to change things with us, but *I'm a person just like you are.* I can't go on leaning on you any longer. Everybody has to stand on his own somewhere along the line. You do, and I do, too. And that goes for Jack, too."

They heard the door to the communications shack open, and the Black Doctor was back in the room. "Well?" he said. "Am I interrupting something?" He glanced sharply at the tight-lipped doctors. "The call was from the survey section," he went on blandly. "A survey crew is on its way to 31 Brucker to start gathering some useful information on the situation. But that is neither here nor there. You have heard the charges against the Red Doctor here. Is there anything any of you want to say?"

Tiger and Jack looked at each other. The silence in the room was profound.

The Black Doctor turned to Dal. "And what about you?"

"I have something to say, but I'd like to talk to you alone."

"As you wish. You two will return to your quarters and stay there."

"The attendant, too," Dal said.

The Black Doctor's eyes glinted and met Dal's for a moment. Then he shrugged and nodded to his attendant. "Step outside, please. We have a private matter to discuss."

The Black Doctor turned his attention to the papers on the desk as Dal stood before him with Fuzzy sitting in the crook of his arm. From the moment that the notice of the inspection ship's approach had come to the *Lancet*, Dal had known what was coming. He had been certain what the purpose of the detainment was, and who the inspector would be, yet he had not really been worried. In the back of his mind, a small, comfortable thought had been sustaining him.

It didn't really matter how hostile or angry Black Doctor Tanner might be; he knew that in a last-ditch stand there was one way the Black Doctor could be handled.

He remembered the dramatic shift from hostility to friendliness among the Bruckians when he had come down from the ship with Fuzzy on his shoulder. Before then, he had never considered using his curious power to protect himself and gain an end; but since then, without even consciously bringing it to mind, he had known that the next time would be easier. If it ever came to a showdown with Black Doctor Tanner, a trap from which he couldn't free himself, there was still this way. *The Black Doctor would never know what happened*, he thought. *It would just seem to him, suddenly, that he had been looking at things the wrong way. No one would ever know.*

But he knew, even as the thought came to mind, that this was not so. Now, face to face with the showdown, he knew that it was no good. One person would know what had happened: himself. On 31 Brucker, he had convinced himself that the end justified the means; here it was different.

For a moment, as Black Doctor Tanner stared up at him through the horn-rimmed glasses, Dal wavered. Why should he hesitate to protect himself? he thought angrily. This attack against him was false and unfair, trumped up for the sole purpose of destroying his hopes and driving him out of the Service. Why shouldn't he grasp at any means, fair or unfair, to fight it?

But he could hear the echo of Black Doctor Arnquist's words in his mind: *I beg of you not to use it. No matter what happens, don't use it.* Of course, Doctor Arnquist would never know, for sure, that he had broken faith…but *he* would know…

"Well," Black Doctor Tanner was saying, "speak up. I can't waste much more time dealing with you. If you have something to say, say it."

Dal sighed. He lifted Fuzzy down and slipped him gently into his jacket pocket. "These charges against me are not true," he said.

The Black Doctor shrugged. "Your own crewmates support them with their statements."

"That's not the point. They're not true, and you know it as well as I do. You've deliberately rigged them up to build a case against me."

The Black Doctor's face turned dark and his hands clenched on the papers on the desk. "Are you suggesting that I have nothing better to do than to rig false charges against one probationer out of seventy-five thousand traveling the galaxy?"

"I'm suggesting that we are alone here," Dal said. "Nobody else is listening. Just for once, right now, we can be honest. We both know what you're trying to do to me. I'd just like to hear you admit it once."

The Black Doctor slammed his fist down on the table. "I don't have to listen to insolence like this," he roared.

"Yes, you do," Dal said. "Just this once. Then I'll be through." Suddenly Dal's words were tumbling out of control, and his whole body was trembling with anger. "You have been determined from the very beginning that I should never finish the medical training that I started. You've tried to block me time after time, in every way you could think of. You've almost succeeded, but never quite made it until this time. But now you *have* to make it. If that contract were to go through I'd get my Star, and you'd never again be able to do anything about it. So it's now or never if you're going to break me."

"Nonsense!" the Black Doctor stormed. "I wouldn't lower myself to meddle with your kind. The charges speak for themselves."

"Not if you look at them carefully. You claim I failed to notify Hospital Earth that we had entered a plague area—but our records of our contact with the planet prove that we did only what any patrol ship would have done when the call came in. We didn't have enough information to know that there was a plague there, and when we finally did know the truth we could no longer make contact with Hospital Earth. You claim that I brought harm to two hundred of the natives there, yet if you study our notes and records, you will see that our errors there were unavoidable. We couldn't have done anything else under the circumstances, and if we hadn't done what we did, we would have been ignoring the basic principles of diagnosis and treatment which we've been taught. And your charges don't mention that by possibly harming two hundred of the Bruckians, we found a way to save two million of them from absolute destruction."

The Black Doctor glared at him. "The charges will stand up, I'll see to that."

"Oh, I'm sure you will! You can ram them through and make them stick before anybody ever has a chance to examine them carefully. You have the power to do it. And by the time an impartial judge could review all the records, your survey ship will have been there and gathered so much more data and muddied up the field so thoroughly that no one will ever be certain that the charges aren't true. But you and I know that they wouldn't really hold up under inspection. We know that they're false right down the line and that you're the one who is responsible for them."

The Black Doctor grew darker, and he trembled with rage as he drew himself to his feet. Dal could feel his hatred almost like a physical blow and his voice was almost a shriek.

"All right," he said, "if you insist, then the charges are lies, made up specifically to break you, and I'm going to push them through if I have to jeopardize my reputation to do it. You could have bowed out gracefully at any time along the way and saved yourself dishonor and disgrace, but you wouldn't do it. Now, I'm going to force you to. I've worked my lifetime long to build the reputation of Hospital Earth and of the Earthmen that go out to all the planets as representatives. I've worked to make the Confederation respect Hospital Earth and the Earthmen who are her doctors. You don't belong here with us. You forced yourself in, you aren't an Earthman and you don't have the means or resources to be a doctor from Hospital Earth. If you succeed, a thousand others will follow in your footsteps, chipping away at the reputation that we have worked to build, and I'm not going to allow one incompetent alien bungler pretending to be a surgeon to walk in and destroy the thing I've fought to build—"

The Black Doctor's voice had grown shrill, almost out of control. But now suddenly he broke off, his mouth still working, and his face went deathly white. The finger he was pointing at Dal wavered and fell. He clutched at his chest, his breath coming in great gasps and staggered back into the chair. "Something's happened," his voice croaked. "I can't breathe."

Dal stared at him in horror for a moment, then leaped across the room and jammed his thumb against the alarm bell.

Red Doctor Dal Timgar knew at once that there would be no problem in diagnosis here. The Black Doctor slumped back in his seat, gasping for air, his face twisted in pain as he labored just to keep on breathing. Tiger and Jack burst into the room, and Dal could tell that they knew instantly what had happened.

"Coronary," Jack said grimly.

Dal nodded. "The question is, just how bad."

"Get the cardiograph in here. We'll soon see."

But the electrocardiograph was not needed to diagnose the nature of the trouble. All three doctors had seen the picture often enough—the sudden, massive blockage of circulation to the heart that was so common to creatures with central circulatory pumps, the sort of catastrophic accident which could cause irreparable crippling or sudden death within a matter of minutes.

Tiger injected some medicine to ease the pain, and started oxygen to help the labored breathing, but the old man's color did not improve. He was too weak to talk; he just lay helplessly gasping for air as they lifted him up onto a bed. Then Jack took an electrocardiograph tracing and shook his head.

"We'd better get word back to Hospital Earth, and fast," he said quietly. "He just waited a little too long for that cardiac transplant, that's all. This is a bad one. Tell them we need a surgeon out here just as fast as they can move, or the Black Service is going to have a dead physician on its hands."

There was a sound across the room, and the Black Doctor motioned feebly to Tiger. "The cardiogram," he gasped. "Let me see it."

"There's nothing for you to see," Tiger said. "You mustn't do anything to excite yourself."

"Let me see it." Dr. Tanner took the thin strip of paper and ran it quickly through his fingers. Then he dropped it on the bed and lay his head back hopelessly. "Too late," he said, so softly they could hardly hear him. "Too late for help now."

Tiger checked his blood pressure and listened to his heart. "It will only take a few hours to get help," he said. "You rest and sleep now. There's plenty of time."

He joined Dal and Jack in the corridor. "I'm afraid he's right, this time," he said. "The damage is severe, and he hasn't the strength to hold out very long. He might last long enough for a surgeon and operating team to get here, but I doubt it. We'd better get the word off."

A few moments later he put the earphones aside. "It'll take six hours for the nearest help to get here," he said. "Maybe five and a half if they really crowd it. But when they get a look at that cardiogram on the screen they'll just throw up their hands. He's got to have a transplant, nothing less, and even if we can keep him alive until a surgical team gets here the odds are a thousand to one against his surviving the surgery."

"Well, he's been asking for it," Jack said. "They've been trying to get him into the hospital for a cardiac transplant for years. Everybody's known that one of those towering rages would get him sooner or later."

"Maybe he'll hold on better than we think," Dal said. "Let's watch and wait."

But the Black Doctor was not doing well. Moment by moment he grew weaker, laboring harder for air as his blood pressure crept slowly down. Half an hour later the pain returned; Tiger took another tracing while Dal checked his venous pressure and shock level.

As he finished, Dal felt the Black Doctor's eyes on him. "It's going to be all right," he said. "There'll be time for help to come."

Feebly the Black Doctor shook his head. "No time," he said. "Can't wait that long." Dal could see the fear in the old man's eyes. His lips began to move again as though there were something more he wanted to say; but then his face hardened, and he turned his head away helplessly.

Dal walked around the bed and looked down at the tracing, comparing it with the first one that was taken. "What do you think, Tiger?"

"It's no good. He'll never make it for five more hours."

"What about right now?"

Tiger shook his head. "It's a terrible surgical risk."

"But every minute of waiting makes it worse, right?"

"That's right."

"Then I think we'll stop waiting," Dal said. "We have a prosthetic heart in condition for use, don't we?"

"Of course."

"Good. Get it ready now." It seemed as though someone else were talking. "You'll have to be first assistant, Tiger. We'll get him onto the heart-lung machine, and if we don't have help available by then, we'll have to try to complete the transplant. Jack, you'll give anaesthesia, and it will be a tricky job. Try to use local blocks as much as you can, and have the heart-lung machine ready well in advance. We'll only have a few seconds to make the shift. Now let's get moving."

Tiger stared at him. "Are you sure that you want to do this?"

"I never wanted anything less in my life," Dal said fervently. "But do you think he can survive until a Hospital Ship arrives?"

"No."

"Then it seems to me that I don't have any choice. You two don't need to worry. This is a surgical problem now, and I'll take full responsibility."

The Black Doctor was watching him, and Dal knew he had heard the conversation. Now the old man lay helplessly as they moved about getting the surgical room into preparation. Jack prepared the anaesthetics, checked and rechecked the complex heart-lung machine which could artificially support circulation and respiration at the time that the damaged heart was separated from its great vessels. The transplant prosthetic heart had been grown in the laboratories on Hospital Earth from embryonic tissue; Tiger removed it from the frozen specimen locker and brought it to normal body temperature in the special warm saline bath designed for the purpose.

Throughout the preparations the Black Doctor lay watching, still conscious enough to recognize what was going on, attempting from time to time to shake his head in protest but not quite succeeding. Finally Dal came to the bedside. "Don't be afraid," he said gently to the old man. "It isn't safe to try to delay until the ship from Hospital Earth can get here. Every minute we wait is counting against you. I think I can manage the transplant if I start now. I know you don't like it, but I am the Red Doctor in authority on this ship. If I have to order you, I will."

The Black Doctor lay silent for a moment, staring at Dal. Then the fear seemed to fade from his face, and the anger disappeared. With a great effort he moved his head to nod. "All right, son," he said softly. "Do the best you know how."

Dal knew from the moment he made the decision to go ahead that the thing he was undertaking was all but hopeless.

There was little or no talk as the three doctors worked at the operating table. The overhead light in the ship's tiny surgery glowed brightly; the only sound in the room was the wheeze of the anaesthesia apparatus, the snap of clamps and the doctors' own quiet breathing as they worked desperately against time.

Dal felt as if he were in a dream, working like an automaton, going through mechanical motions that seemed completely unrelated to the living patient that lay on the operating table. In his training he had assisted at hundreds of organ transplant operations; he himself had done dozens of cardiac transplants, with experienced surgeons assisting and guiding him until the steps of the procedure had become almost second nature. On Hospital Earth, with the unparalleled medical facilities available there, and with well-trained teams of doctors, anaesthetists and nurses the technique of replacing an old worn-out damaged heart with a new and healthy one had become commonplace. It posed no more threat to a patient than a simple appendectomy had posed three centuries before.

But here in the patrol ship's operating room under emergency conditions there seemed little hope of success. Already the Black Doctor had suffered violent shock from the damage that had occurred in his heart. Already he was clinging to life by a fragile thread; the additional shock of the surgery, of the anaesthesia and the necessary conversion to the heart-lung machine while the delicate tissues of the new heart were fitted and sutured into place vessel by vessel was more than any patient could be expected to survive.

Yet Dal had known when he saw the second cardiogram that the attempt would have to be made. Now he worked swiftly, his frail body engulfed in the voluminous surgical gown, his thin fingers working carefully with the polished instruments. Speed and skill were all that could save the Black Doctor now, to offer him the one chance in a thousand that he had for survival.

But the speed and skill had to be Dal's. Dal knew that, and the knowledge was like a lead weight strapped to his shoulders. If Black Doctor Hugo Tanner was fighting for his life now, Dal knew that he too was fighting for his life—the only kind of life that he wanted, the life of a physician.

Black Doctor Tanner's antagonism to him as an alien, as an incompetent, as one who was unworthy to wear the collar and cuff of a physician from Hospital Earth, was common knowledge. Dal realized with perfect clarity that if he failed now, his career as a physician would be over; no one, not even himself, would ever be entirely certain that he had not somehow, in some dim corner of his mind, allowed himself to fail.

Yet if he had not made the attempt and the Black Doctor had died before help had come, there would always be those who would accuse him of delaying on purpose.

His mouth was dry; he longed for a drink of water, even though he knew that no water could quench this kind of thirst. His fingers grew numb as he worked, and moment by moment the sense of utter hopelessness grew stronger in his mind. Tiger worked stolidly across the table from him, inexpert help at best because of the sketchy surgical training he had had. Even his solid presence in support here did not lighten the burden for Dal. There was nothing that Tiger could do or say that would help things or change things now. Even Fuzzy, waiting alone on his perch in the control room, could not help him now. Nothing could help now but his own individual skill as a surgeon, and his bitter determination that he must not and would not fail.

But his fingers faltered as a thousand questions welled up in his mind. Was he doing this right? This vessel here...clamp it and tie it? Or dissect it out and try to preserve it? This nerve plexus...which one was it? How important? How were the blood pressure and respirations doing? Was the Black Doctor holding his own under the assault of the surgery?

The more Dal tried to hurry the more he seemed to be wading through waist-deep mud, unable to make his fingers do what he wanted them to do. How could he save ten seconds, twenty seconds, a half a minute? That half a minute might make the difference between success or failure, yet the seconds ticked by swiftly and the procedure was going slowly.

Too slowly. He reached a point where he thought he could not go on. His mind was searching desperately for help—any kind of help, something to lean on, something to brace him and give him support. And then quite suddenly he understood something clearly that had been nibbling at the corners of his mind for a long time. It was as if someone had snapped on a floodlight in a darkened room, and he saw something he had never seen before.

He saw that from the first day he had stepped down from the Garvian ship that had brought him to Hospital Earth to begin his medical training, he had been relying upon crutches to help him.

Black Doctor Arnquist had been a crutch upon whom he could lean. Tiger, for all his clumsy good-heartedness and for all the help and protection he had offered, had been a crutch. Fuzzy, who had been by his side since the day he was born, was still another kind of crutch to fall back on, a way out, a port of haven in the storm. They were crutches, every one, and he had leaned on them heavily.

But now there was no crutch to lean on. He had a quick mind with good training. He had two nimble hands that knew their job, and two legs that were capable of supporting his weight, frail as they were. He knew now that he had to stand on them squarely, for the first time in his life.

And suddenly he realized that this was as it should be. It seemed so clear, so obvious and unmistakable that he wondered how he could have failed to recognize it for so long. If he could not depend on himself, then Black Doctor Hugo Tanner would have been right all along. If he could not do this job that was before him on his own strength, standing on his own two legs without crutches to lean on, how could he claim to be a competent physician? What right did he have to the goal he sought if he had to earn it on the strength of the help of others? It was *he* who wanted to be a Star Surgeon—not Fuzzy, not Tiger, nor anyone else.

He felt his heart thudding in his chest, and he saw the operation before him as if he were standing in an amphitheater peering down over some other surgeon's shoulder. Suddenly everything else was gone from his mind but the immediate task at hand. His fingers began to move more swiftly, with a confidence he had never felt before. The decisions to be made arose, and he made them without hesitation, and knew as he made them that they were right.

And for the first time the procedure began to move. He murmured instructions to Jack from time to time, and placed Tiger's clumsy hands in the places he wanted them for retraction. "Not there, back a little," he said. "That's right. Now hold this clamp and release it slowly while I tie, then reclamp it. Slowly now…that's the way! Jack, check that pressure again."

It seemed as though someone else were doing the surgery, directing his hands step by step in the critical work that had to be done. Dal placed the connections to the heart-lung machine perfectly, and moved with new swiftness and confidence as the great blood vessels were clamped off and the damaged heart removed. A quick check of vital signs, chemistries, oxygenation, a sharp instruction to Jack, a caution to Tiger, and the new prosthetic heart was in place. He worked now with painstaking care, manipulating the micro-sutures that would secure the new vessels to the old so firmly that they were almost indistinguishable from a healed wound, and he knew that it was going *right* now, that whether the patient ultimately survived or not, he had made the right decision and had carried it through with all the skill at his command.

And then the heart-lung machine fell silent again, and the carefully applied nodal stimulator flicked on and off, and slowly, at first hesitantly, then firmly and vigorously, the new heart began its endless pumping chore. The Black Doctor's blood pressure moved up to a healthy level and stabilized; the gray flesh of his face slowly became suffused with healthy pink. It was over, and Dal was walking out of the surgery, his hands trembling so violently that he could hardly get his gown off. He wanted to laugh and cry at the same time, and he could see the silent pride in the others' faces as they joined him in the dressing room to change clothes.

He knew then that no matter what happened he had vindicated himself. Half an hour later, back in the sickbay, the Black Doctor was awake, breathing slowly and easily without need of supplemental oxygen. Only the fine sweat standing out on his forehead gave indication of the ordeal he had been through.

Swiftly and clinically Dal checked the vital signs as the old man watched him. He was about to turn the pressure cuff over to Jack and leave when the Black Doctor said, "Wait."

Dal turned to him. "Yes, sir?"

"You did it?" the Black Doctor said softly.

"Yes, sir."

"It's finished? The transplant is done?"

"Yes," Dal said. "It went well, and you can rest now. You were a good patient."

For the first time Dal saw a smile cross the old man's face. "A foolish patient, perhaps," he said, so softly that no one but Dal could hear, "but not so foolish now, not so foolish that I cannot recognize a good doctor when I see one."

And with a smile he closed his eyes and went to sleep.

## CHAPTER FOURTEEN
### Star Surgeon

It was amazing to Dal Timgar just how good it seemed to be back on Hospital Earth again.

In the time he had been away as a crewman of the *Lancet*, the seasons had changed, and the port of Philadelphia lay under the steaming summer sun. As Dal stepped off the shuttle ship to join the hurrying crowds in the great space-port, it seemed almost as though he were coming home.

He thought for a moment of the night not so long before when he had waited here for the shuttle to Hospital Seattle, to attend the meeting of the medical training council. He had worn no uniform then, not even the collar and cuff of the probationary physician, and he remembered his despair that night when he had thought that his career as a physician from Hospital Earth was at an end.

Now he was returning by shuttle from Hospital Seattle to the port of Philadelphia again, completing the cycle that had been started many months before. But things were different now. The scarlet cape of the Red Service of Surgery hung from his slender shoulders now, and the light of the station room caught the polished silver emblem on his collar. It was a tiny bit of metal, but its significance was enormous. It announced to the world Dal Timgar's final and permanent acceptance as a physician; but more, it symbolized the far-reaching distances he had already traveled, and would travel again, in the service of Hospital Earth.

It was the silver star of the Star Surgeon.

The week just past had been both exciting and confusing. The hospital ship had arrived five hours after Black Doctor Hugo Tanner had recovered from his anaesthesia, moving in on the *Lancet* in frantic haste and starting the shipment of special surgical supplies, anaesthetics and maintenance equipment across in lifeboats almost before contact had been stabilized. A large passenger boat hurtled away from the hospital ship's side, carrying a pair of Four-star surgeons, half a dozen Three-star Surgeons, two Radiologists, two Internists, a dozen nurses and another Four-star Black Doctor across to the *Lancet*; and when they arrived at the patrol ship's entrance lock, they discovered that their haste had been in vain.

It was like Grand Rounds in the general wards of Hospital Philadelphia, with the Four-star Surgeons in the lead as they tramped aboard the patrol ship. They found Black Doctor Tanner sitting quietly at his bedside reading a journal of pathology and taking notes. He glared up at them when they burst in the door without even knocking.

"But are you feeling well, sir?" the chief surgeon asked him for the third time.

"Of course I'm feeling well. Do you think I'd be sitting here if I weren't?" the Black Doctor growled. "Dr. Timgar is my surgeon and the physician in charge of this case. Talk to him. He can give you all the details of the matter."

"You mean you permitted a probationary physician to perform this kind of surgery?" The Four-star Surgeon cried incredulously.

"I did not!" the Black Doctor snapped. "He had to drag me kicking and screaming into the operating room. But fortunately for me, this particular probationary physician had the courage of his convictions, as well as wit enough to realize that I would not survive if he waited for you to gather your army together. But I think you will find the surgery was handled with excellent skill. Again, I must refer you to Dr. Timgar for the details. I was not paying attention to the technique of the surgery, I assure you."

"But sir," the chief surgeon broke in, "how could there have been surgery of any sort here? The dispatch that came to us listed the *Lancet* as a plague ship—"

"*Plague ship!*" the Black Doctor exploded. "Oh, yes. Egad! I—hum!—imagine that the dispatcher must have gotten his signals mixed somehow. Well, I suppose you want to examine me. Let's have it over with."

The doctors examined him within an inch of his life. They exhausted every means of physical, laboratory and radiological examination short of re-opening his chest and looking in, and at last the chief surgeon was forced reluctantly to admit that there was nothing left for him to do but provide post-operative follow-up care for the irascible old man.

And by the time the examination was over and the Black Doctor was moved aboard the hospital ship, word had come through official channels to the *Lancet* announcing that the quarantine order had been a dispatcher's unfortunate error, and directing the ship to return at once to Hospital Earth with the new contract that had been signed on 31 Brucker VII. The crewmen of the *Lancet* had special orders to report immediately to the medical training council at Hospital Seattle upon arrival, in order to give their formal General Practice Patrol reports and to receive their appointments respectively as Star Physician, Star Diagnostician and Star Surgeon. The orders were signed with the personal mark of Hugo Tanner, Physician of the Black Service of Pathology.

Now the ceremony and celebration in Hospital Seattle were over, and Dal had another appointment to keep. He lifted Fuzzy from his elbow and tucked him safely into an inner jacket pocket to protect him from the crowd in the station, and moved swiftly through to the subway tubes.

He had expected to see Black Doctor Arnquist at the investment ceremonies, but there had been neither sign nor word from him. Dal tried to reach him after the ceremonies were over; all he could learn was that the Black Doctor was unavailable. And then a message had come through to Dal under the official Hospital Earth headquarters priority, requesting him to present himself at once at the grand council building at Hospital Philadelphia for an interview of the utmost importance.

He followed the directions on the dispatch now, and reached the grand council building well ahead of the appointed time. He followed corridors and rode elevators until he reached the twenty-second story office suite where he had been directed to report. The whole building seemed alive with bustle, as though something of enormous importance was going on; high-ranking physicians of all the services were hurrying about, gathering in little groups at the elevators and talking among themselves in hushed voices. Even more strange, Dal saw delegation after delegation of alien creatures moving through the building, some in the special atmosphere-maintaining devices necessary for their survival on Earth, some characteristically alone and unaccompanied, others in the company of great retinues of underlings. Dal paused in the main concourse of the building as he saw two such delegations arrive by special car from the port of Philadelphia.

"Odd," he said quietly, reaching in to stroke Fuzzy's head. "Quite a gathering of the clans, eh? What do you think? Last time I saw a gathering like this was back at home during one of the centennial conclaves of the Galactic Confederation."

On the twenty-second floor, a secretary ushered him into an inner office. There he found Black Doctor Thorvold Arnquist, in busy conference with a Blue Doctor, a Green Doctor and a surgeon. The Black Doctor looked up, and beamed. "That will be all right now, gentlemen," he said. "I'll be in touch with you directly."

He waited until the others had departed. Then he crossed the room and practically hugged Dal in delight. "It's good to see you, boy," he said, "and above all, it's good to see that silver star at last. You and your little pink friend have done a good job, a far better job than I thought you would do, I must admit."

Dal perched Fuzzy on his shoulder. "But what is this about an interview? Why did you want to see me, and what are all these people doing here?"

Dr. Arnquist laughed. "Don't worry," he said. "You won't have to stay for the council meeting. It will be a long boring session, I fear. Doubtless every single one of these delegates at some time in the next few days will be standing up to give us a three hour oration, and it is my ill fortune as a Four-star Black Doctor to have to sit and listen and smile through it all. But in the end, it will be worth it, and I thought that you should at least know that your name will be mentioned many times during these sessions."

"My name?"

"You didn't know that you were a guinea pig, did you?" the Black Doctor said.

"I…I'm afraid I didn't."

"An unwitting tool, so to speak," the Black Doctor chuckled. "You know, of course, that the Galactic Confederation has been delaying and stalling any action on Hospital Earth's application for full status as one of the Confederation powers and for a seat on the council. We had fulfilled two criteria for admission without difficulty—we had resolved our problems at home so that we were free from war on our own planet, and we had a talent that is much needed and badly in demand in the galaxy, a job to do that would fit into the Confederation's organization. But the Confederation has always had a third criterion for its membership, a criterion that Hospital Earth could not so easily prove or demonstrate."

The Black Doctor smiled. "After all, there could be no place in a true Confederation of worlds for any one race of people that considered itself superior to all the rest. No race can be admitted to the Confederation until its members have demonstrated that they are capable of tolerance, willing to accept the members of other races on an equal footing. And it has always been the nature of Earthmen to be intolerant, to assume that one who looks strange and behaves differently must somehow be inferior."

The Black Doctor crossed the room and opened a folder on the desk. "You can read the details some other time, if you like. You were selected by the Galactic Confederation from a thousand possible applicants, to serve as a test case, to see if a place could be made for you on Hospital Earth. No one here was told of your position—not even you—although certain of us suspected the truth. The Confederation wanted to see if a well-qualified, likeable and intelligent creature from another world would be accepted and elevated to equal rank as a physician with Earthmen."

Dal stared at him. "And I was the one?"

"You were the one. It was a struggle, all right, but Hospital Earth has finally satisfied the Confederation. At the end of this conclave we will be admitted to full membership and given a permanent seat and vote in the galactic council. Our probationary period will be over. But enough of that. What about you? What are your plans? What do you propose to do now that you have that star on your collar?"

They talked then about the future. Tiger Martin had been appointed to the survey crew returning to 31 Brucker VII, at his own request, while Jack was accepting a temporary teaching post in the great diagnostic clinic at Hospital Philadelphia. There were a dozen things that Dal had considered, but for the moment he wanted only to travel from medical center to medical center on Hospital Earth, observing and studying in order to decide how he would best like to use his abilities and his position as a Physician from Hospital Earth. "It will be in surgery, of course," he said. "Just where in surgery, or what kind, I don't know just yet. But there will be time enough to decide that."

"Then go along," Dr. Arnquist said, "with my congratulations and blessing. You have taught us a great deal, and perhaps you have learned some things at the same time."

Dal hesitated for a moment. Then he nodded. "I've learned some things," he said, "but there's still one thing that I want to do before I go."

He lifted his little pink friend gently down from his shoulder and rested him in the crook of his arm. Fuzzy looked up at him, blinking his shoe-button eyes happily. "You asked me once to leave Fuzzy with you, and I refused. I couldn't see then how I could possibly do without him; even the thought was frightening. But now I think I've changed my mind."

He reached out and placed Fuzzy gently in the Black Doctor's hand. "I want you to keep him," he said. "I don't think I'll need him any more. I'll miss him, but I think it would be better if I don't have him now. Be good to him, and let me visit him once in a while."

The Black Doctor looked at Dal, and then lifted Fuzzy up to his own shoulder. For a moment the little creature shivered as if afraid. Then he blinked twice at Dal, trustingly, and snuggled in comfortably against the Black Doctor's neck.

Without a word Dal turned and walked out of the office. As he stepped down the corridor, he waited fearfully for the wave of desolation and loneliness he had felt before when Fuzzy was away from him.

But there was no hint of those desolate feelings in his mind now. And after all, he thought, why should there be? He was not a Garvian any longer. He was a Star Surgeon from Hospital Earth.

He smiled as he stepped from the elevator into the main lobby and crossed through the crowd to the street doors. He pulled his scarlet cape tightly around his throat. Drawing himself up to the full height of which he was capable, he walked out of the building and strode down onto the street.

## THE END